Praise for *USA TODAY* bestselling author Merline Lovelace

"Merline Lovelace rocks! Like Nora Roberts, she delivers top-rate suspense with great characters, rich atmosphere and a crackling plot!"
—*New York Times* and *USA TODAY* bestselling author Mary Jo Putney

"Lovelace's many fans have come to expect her signature strong, brave, resourceful heroines and she doesn't disappoint."
—*Booklist*

"Spicy, smart and very entertaining."
—*RT Book Reviews* on *Baby, It's Cold Outside*

"Ms. Lovelace wins our hearts with a tender love story featuring a fine hero who will make every woman's heart beat faster."
—*RT Book Reviews* on *Wrong Bride, Right Groom*

MERLINE LOVELACE

A retired Air Force officer, Merline Lovelace served at bases all over the world, including tours in Taiwan, Vietnam and at the Pentagon. When she hung up her uniform for the last time, she decided to combine her love of adventure with a flair for storytelling, basing many of her tales on her experiences in the service.

Since then, she's produced more than eighty action-packed novels, many of which have made *USA TODAY* and Waldenbooks bestseller lists. More than ten million copies of her works are in print in thirty countries. Named an Oklahoma's Writer of the Year and an Oklahoma Female Veteran of the Year, Merline is also a recipient of Romance Writers of America's prestigious RITA® Award.

USA TODAY Bestselling Author

Merline Lovelace

Full Throttle

Wrong Bride, Right Groom

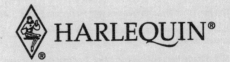

HARLEQUIN®

TORONTO • NEW YORK • LONDON
AMSTERDAM • PARIS • SYDNEY • HAMBURG
STOCKHOLM • ATHENS • TOKYO • MILAN • MADRID
PRAGUE • WARSAW • BUDAPEST • AUCKLAND

Recycling programs
for this product may
not exist in your area.

ISBN-13: 978-0-373-68810-4

FULL THROTTLE & WRONG BRIDE, RIGHT GROOM

Copyright © 2010 by Harlequin Books S.A.

The publisher acknowledges the copyright holder of the individual works as follows:

FULL THROTTLE
Copyright © 2004 by Merline Lovelace

WRONG BRIDE, RIGHT GROOM
Copyright © 1996 by Merline Lovelace

This edition published by arrangement with Harlequin Books S.A.

For questions and comments about the quality of this book please contact us at Customer_eCare@Harlequin.ca.

® and TM are trademarks of the publisher. Trademarks indicated with ® are registered in the United States Patent and Trademark Office, the Canadian Trade Marks Office and in other countries.

www.eHarlequin.com

Printed in U.S.A.

CONTENTS

To my buds on the RomVets loop—
women who all served their country and are
now turning out great novels! Thanks for
sharing your expertise on aircraft malfunctions,
explosive devices and general all-around fun stuff.

FULL THROTTLE

Chapter 1

Kate Hargrave was a good five miles into her morning jog when she spotted a plume of dust rising from the desert floor. Swiping at the sweat she'd worked up despite the nip September had brought to the high desert, she squinted through the shimmering New Mexico dawn at the vehicle churning up that long brown rooster tail.

A senior weather researcher with the National Oceanographic and Atmospheric Agency, Kate had logged hundreds of hours of flight time as one of NOAA's famed Hurricane Hunters. The pilots she flew with all possessed a steady hand on the controls, nerves of steel and an unshakable belief in their ability to look death in the eye and stare it down. So when she gauged the speed of the pickup hurtling straight toward her, she had no doubt who was at its wheel.

USAF Captain Dave Scott—a seasoned test pilot with hundreds of hours in both rotary and fixed-wing aircraft. Scott had been yanked off an assignment with Special Operations to become the newest addition to the supersecret test cadre tucked away in this remote corner of southeastern New Mexico.

He was supposed to have arrived last night but had phoned Captain Westfall from somewhere along the road and indicated he'd check in first thing this morning. No explanations for the delay, or none the navy captain in charge of the supersecret Pegasus project had relayed to his crew, anyway.

That alone was enough to put a dent in Kate's characteristically sunny good nature. She and the rest of the small, handpicked cadre had been here for weeks now. They'd been working almost around the clock to conduct final operational testing on the new all-weather, all-terrain attack-assault vehicle code-named Pegasus. The urgency of their mission had been burned into their brains from day one. That Captain Scott would delay his arrival—even by as little as eight hours of admittedly dead time—didn't particularly sit well with Kate.

Then there was the fact that the air force had pegged Scott to replace Lieutenant Colonel Bill Thompson, the original air force representative to the project. Everyone on the team had liked and respected the easygoing and highly experienced test pilot. Unfortunately, Bill had suffered a heart attack after being infected by the vicious virus that attacked him and a number of other members of the test cadre some days ago.

Now Bill was off the Pegasus project and probably off flying status for the rest of his life. His abrupt departure had ripped a gaping hole in the tight, close team of officers and civilians plucked from all branches of the military to work on the project. Dave Scott would have to scramble to catch up with the rest of the test cadre *and* prove himself worthy to fill Bill Thompson's boots.

"Sure hope you're up to it, fella."

With that fervent wish, Kate lengthened her stride. She'd just as soon not come face-to-face with her new associate out here in the desert. Her hair was a tangled mess and her turquoise spandex running suit sported damp patches of sweat. With luck and a little more oomph to her pace, she could veer off onto the dirt track that ringed the perimeter of the site before Scott hit the first checkpoint.

She should have known she couldn't outrun a sky jock. The speeding pickup skidded to a stop at the checkpoint while Kate was still some distance from the perimeter trail.

The dazzling light shooting through the peaks of the Guadalupe Mountains off to the east illuminated the vehicle. The truck was battered. Dust streaked. An indeterminate color between blue and gray. She couldn't see the driver, though. He was still too far away and the bright rays glinting off the windshield formed an impenetrable shield.

She'd get a glimpse of him soon enough, Kate guessed wryly. From the bits and pieces of background information she'd gathered about Captain Dave Scott, she knew he wasn't the type to cruise by a female in a tight jogging suit. Or one in support hose and black oxfords, for that matter. Rumor had it Scott was the love-'em-and-leave-'em type, with a string of satisfied lovers stretching from coast to coast.

Kate knew the breed.

All too well.

So she wasn't surprised when the pickup cleared the checkpoint, roared into gear and kicked up dust for another quarter mile or so. Scant yards from Kate, it fishtailed to a halt once more.

Dust swirled. The truck's engine idled with a low, throaty growl. The driver's-side window whirred down. A well-muscled forearm appeared, followed by a rugged profile. With his creased straw cowboy hat and sun-weathered features, Scott might have been one of the locals who'd adapted so well to life here in the high desert. The hat shaded the upper portion of his face. The lower portion consisted of the tip of a nose, a mouth bracketed by laugh lines and a blunt, square chin. The rolled sleeve of his white cotton shirt showed a sprinkling of hair bleached to gold by the sun. Mirrored aviator sunglasses shielded his eyes, but the grin he flashed Kate was pure sex.

"Well, well." The drawl was deep and rich and carried clearly on the morning air. "This assignment is looking better by the moment."

Kate had heard variations of the same line a hundred or more times in her career. Her ready smile, flaming auburn hair and generous curves had attracted the attention of every male she'd ever worked with. She'd long ago learned to separate the merely goggling from the seriously annoying and handle both with breezy competence. Edging to the side of the dirt road, she jogged toward the idling vehicle. Her voice held only dry amusement as she offered a word of advice.

"Pull in your tongue and hit the gas pedal, flyboy. Captain Westfall's expecting you."

His chin dipped. Eyes a clear, startling blue peered over the rim of the sunglasses and locked with hers.

"The captain can wait," he replied. "You, on the other hand…"

He didn't finish. Or if he did, Kate didn't hear him.

She'd kept her gaze engaged with his a half second too long and run right off the edge of the road.

Her well-worn Nikes came down not on hard-packed dirt, but empty air. With a smothered oath, she plunged into the shallow ditch beside the road. Her right leg hit with a jar that rattled every bone in her body before going out from under her. A moment later she landed smack on her rear atop a fat, prickly tumbleweed.

So much for breezy competence!

Scott was out of the pickup almost before Kate and the tumbleweed connected. His low-heeled boots scattered rock and dirt as he scrambled into the shallow depression. When he hunkered down beside her, she expected at least a minimal expression of concern. What she got was a swift, assessing glance followed by a waggle of his sun-streaked eyebrows.

"And here I woke up this morning thinking the next few weeks were going to be all work and no play."

Kate cocked an eyebrow. Best to set him straight right here, right now. "You thought right, Captain."

"I don't know about that." Dipping his chin, he gave her another once-over. "Things are lookin' good from where I'm squatting. *Very* good."

Kate sucked in a swift breath. Behind their screen of sun-bleached lashes, his eyes were electric blue. The little white lines at their corners disappeared when he smiled, which he did with devastating effect.

Thank heavens she'd been inoculated against Scott's brand of lazy charm and cocky self-assurance. The inoculation had been painful, sure, but once administered was supposed to last a lifetime.

Unfortunately, she hadn't been inoculated against the effects of sharp, stinging barbs to the backside. The prickly weed had penetrated right through her spandex running tights. Now that Kate had recovered from the initial shock of her fall, she felt its sharp, stinging bite.

"How about unsquatting," she suggested dryly, "and helping me up?"

"My pleasure."

Rising with the careless grace of an athlete, he reached for her hand. His palm felt tough and callused against her skin, his skin warm to the touch.

Of course Kate's blasted ankle had to give out the moment she gained her feet. With a grunt, she fell right into his conveniently waiting arms. This time he had the decency to show some concern. At least that was the excuse he gave for swooping her up.

"You must have come down hard on that ankle."

Hefting her not-inconsiderable weight, he cradled her against his chest. His very solid, very muscled chest, Kate couldn't help noticing.

"I'd better get you to the base."

He was already out of the ditch and striding around the back of the pickup before she could tell him she had a more pressing problem to worry about than her ankle. She tried to think of a subtle way to inform him of her dilemma. None came immediately to mind. Sighing, she stopped him just as he opened the passenger door and prepared to deposit her inside.

"Before you plop me down on that seat, I think you should know I'm sporting a collection of needle-sharp stickers. I landed on a tumbleweed," she added when he flashed her a startled look. "I need to remove a few unwanted thistles from my posterior."

"Damn!" His mouth took a wicked curve. "And I was just thinking my day couldn't get any better."

His leer was so exaggerated, she didn't even try to hold back her sputter of laughter. "Let's not make this any more embarrassing than it already is. Just put me down and I'll, er, perform an emergency extraction."

He set her on her feet and gave her a hopeful look. "I'll be glad to assist in the operation."

"I can manage."

Making no effort to hide his disappointment, he watched with unabashed interest while Kate grabbed the door handle to steady herself and twisted around. It took some contorting to reach all the thorny stickers. One by one, she flicked them off into the ditch.

"You missed one," Scott advised as she dusted the back of her thigh. "A little lower."

Removing the last twig, she leaned her weight on her ankle to test it. The pain was already subsiding, thank goodness. Pasting a smile on her face, she turned to her would-be rescuer.

"I'm Lieutenant Commander Kate Hargrave, by the way. I'm with the National Oceanographic and Atmospheric Agency."

As a lieutenant commander in NOAA's commissioned-officer corps, Kate outranked an air force captain. The fact that Scott had just watched a senior officer pluck thorns out of her bottom appeared to afford him no end of amusement. His eyes glinting between those ridiculously thick gold-tipped lashes, he introduced himself.

"Dave Scott. Airplane driver."

To her profound disgust, Kate discovered her inoculation against handsome devils like this one wasn't quite as effective as she'd thought. Or as permanent. Shivers danced along her skin as she gazed up at him. He was so close she could see the beginnings of a bristly gold beard. The way his cheeks creased when he smiled. The reflection of her sweat-sheened face in his mirrored glasses.

She got an up close whiff of him, too. Unlike Kate, he still carried a morning-shower scent, clean and shampooy, coated with only a faint tang of dust. No woodsy aftershave for Captain Dave Scott, she noted, then wondered why the heck she'd bothered to take such a detailed inventory.

This wasn't smart, Kate thought as her heart thumped painfully against her ribs. Not smart at all. She'd learned the hard way not to trust too-handsome charmers like this one. If nothing else, her brief, disastrous marriage had taught her to go with her head and not her hormones where men were concerned.

Added to that was the fact that she and Scott would be working together for the next few weeks. In extremely close proximity. Despite her flamboyant looks and sensual figure, Kate was a professional to her toes. A woman didn't acquire a long string of initials after her name and the title of senior weather research scientist at the National Oceanographic and Atmospheric Agency without playing the game by the rules.

"Do Not Fool Around With the Hired Help" ranked right up there as rule number two. Or maybe it was three. Within the top five, anyway.

Not that Kate was thinking about fooling around with Captain Dave Scott. Just the opposite! Still, goose bumps danced along her spine as he took her elbow to assist her into the pickup's passenger seat. Once she was comfortably ensconced, he rounded the front end of the truck and climbed behind the wheel.

"So how long have you been on-site?" he asked, putting the vehicle into gear.

"From day one."

When his boot hit the gas pedal, Kate braced herself for the thrust. Instead of jerking forward, however, the pickup seemed to coil its legs like some powerful, predatory beast and launched into a silent run. Obviously, Scott had installed one heck of an engine inside the truck's less-than-impressive frame.

Interesting, she thought. The captain was a whole lot like his vehicle. All coiled muscle and heart-stopping blue eyes under a battered straw cowboy hat and rumpled white shirt.

"So what's the skinny?" he asked. "Is Pegasus ready to fly?"

Instantly, Kate's thoughts shifted from the man beside her to the machine housed in a special hangar constructed of materials designed to resist penetration by even the most sophisticated spy satellites.

"Almost," she replied. "Bill Thompson had his heart attack just as we were finishing ground tests."

"I never met Thompson, but I've heard of him. The AF lost a damned good pilot."

"Yes, it did. So did Pegasus. You've got a lot of catching up to do," she warned him, "and not much time to do it."

"No problem."

The careless reply set Kate's jaw. She and the rest of the cadre had been hard at it for weeks now. If Scott thought he was going to waltz in and get up to speed on the top secret project in a few hours, he had one heck of a surprise waiting for him.

Unaware that he'd just scratched her exactly the wrong way, the captain seemed more interested in Kate than the project that would soon consume him.

"I saw your career brief in the package headquarters sent as part of my orientation package. Over a thousand hours in the P-3. That's pretty impressive."

It was, by Kate's standards as well as Scott's. Only the best of the best got to fly aboard NOAA's specially configured fleet of aircraft, including the P-3 Orion. Flying into the eye of a howling hurricane took guts, determination and a cast-iron stomach. Honesty forced Kate to add a qualifier, though.

"Not all those hours were hurricane time. Occasionally we saw blue sky."

"I went up once with the air force's Hurricane Hunters based at Keesler."

Kate stiffened. Her ex-husband was assigned to the Air Force Reserve unit at Keesler Air Force Base, on Mississippi's Gulf Coast. That's where she'd met John, during a conference that included all agencies involved in tracking and predicting the fury unleashed all too often on the Gulf by Ma Nature.

That's also where she'd found the jerk with his tongue down the mouth of a nineteen-year-old bimbette. Kate had few fond memories of Keesler.

"So how was your flight?" she asked, shoving aside the reminder of her most serious lapse in judgment.

"Let's just say once was enough."

"Flying into a maelstrom of wind and rain isn't for the faint of heart," she agreed solemnly.

He cracked a grin at that. When he pulled his gaze from the road ahead, laughter shimmered in his blue eyes.

"No, ma'am. It surely isn't."

Kate didn't reply, but she knew darn well Scott was anything *but* faint of heart. When the air force had identified him as Bill Thompson's replacement, she'd activated her extensive network of friends and information sources to find out everything she could about the man. Her sources confirmed he'd packed a whole bunch of flying time into his ten years in the military.

Flying that included several hundred combat hours in both the Blackhawk helicopter and the AC-130H gunship. A highly modified version of the air force's four-engine turboprop workhorse, the gunship provided surgically accurate firepower in support of both conventional and unconventional forces, day or night.

Kate didn't doubt Scott had provided just that surgically accurate support during recent tours in both Afghanistan and Iraq. After Iraq, he'd been sent to the 919th Special Operations Wing at Hurlburt Field, Florida, to fly the latest addition to the air force inventory—the tilt-wing CV-22 Osprey.

Since the Osprey combined the lift characteristics of a helicopter and the long-distance flight capability of a fixed-wing aircraft, Scott's background made him a natural choice as short-notice replacement for Bill Thompson. If—*when!*—Pegasus completed its operational tests, it might well replace both the C-130 and the CV-122 as the workhorse of the battlefield.

Thinking of the tense weeks ahead, Kate chewed on her lower lip and said little until they'd passed through the second checkpoint and entered the compound housing the Pegasus test complex.

The entire complex had been sited and constructed

in less than two months. Unfortunately, the builders had sacrificed aesthetics to exigency. The site had all the appeal of a prison camp. Rolls of concertina wire surrounded the clump of prefabricated modular buildings and trailers, all painted a uniformly dull tan to blend in with the desert landscape. White-painted rocks marked the roads and walkways between the buildings. Aside from a few picnic tables scattered among the trailers, everything was starkly functional.

Separate modular units housed test operations, the computer-communications center and a dispensary. The security center, nicknamed Rattlesnake Ops after the leather-tough, take-no-prisoners military police guarding the site, occupied another unit. A larger unit contained a fitness center and the dining hall, which also served as movie theater and briefing room when the site's commanding officer wanted to address the entire cadre. The hangar that housed Pegasus loomed over the rest of the structures like a big, brooding mammoth.

Personnel were assigned to the trailers, two or three to a unit. Kate and the other two women officers on-site shared one unit. Scott would bunk down with Major Russ McIver, the senior Marine Corps rep. Kate directed him to the line of modular units unofficially dubbed Officers Row.

"You probably want to change into your uniform before checking in with Captain Westfall. Your trailer is the second one on the left. Westfall's is the unit standing by itself at the end of the row."

"First things first," Scott countered, pulling up at the small dispensary. "Let's get your ankle looked at."

"I'll take care of that. You'd best get changed and report in."

"Special Ops would drum me out of the brotherhood if I left a lady to hobble around on a sore ankle."

He meant it as a joke, but his careless attitude toward his new assignment was starting to seriously annoy Kate. Her mouth thinned as he came around the front of the pickup. Sliding out of the passenger seat, she stood firmly on both feet to address him.

"I don't think you've grasped the urgency of our mission. I'll manage here, Captain. You report in to the C.O."

Her tone left no doubt. It was an order from a superior officer to a subordinate.

Scott cocked an eyebrow. For a moment, his eyes held something altogether different from the teasing laughter he'd treated her to up to this point.

The dangerous glint was gone almost as quickly as it had come. Tipping her a two-fingered salute, he replied in an easy, if somewhat exaggerated, drawl.

"Yes, ma'am."

Dave took care not to spin out and leave Lieutenant Commander Hargrave in a swirl of dust. His eyes on the rearview mirror, he followed her careful progress up the clinic steps.

The woman was stubborn as well as gorgeous. And not above pulling rank on him. Well, that pretty well fit with what he'd heard about her.

The sexy Hurricane Hunter couldn't know it but her ex-husband had piloted the mission Dave had flown with the reserve unit out of Keesler. The man had had a few things to say about the wife who'd just dumped him, none of them particularly flattering. She was, according to the still-bitter aviator, ambitious as hell, fearless in the air, a tiger in bed and a real ball-breaker out of it.

Dave figured three out of four was good enough for him.

Yes, sir, he thought as he caught a last glimpse of turquoise spandex in the mirror. This assignment was looking better and better by the minute.

Chapter 2

Showered, shaved and wrapped in the familiar comfort of his green Nomex flight suit, Dave tracked down the officer in command of the Pegasus project. He found Captain Westfall at the Test Operations Building.

"Captain Scott reporting for duty, sir."

The tall, lean naval officer in khakis creased to blade-edged precision returned Dave's salute, then offered his hand.

"Welcome aboard, Captain Scott."

The man's gravelly voice and iron grip matched his salt-and-pepper buzz cut. His skin was tanned to near leather, no doubt the result of years spent pacing a deck in sun, wind and salt spray. His piercing gray eyes took deliberate measure of the latest addition to his team. Dave didn't exactly square his shoulders, but he found himself standing a little taller under Westfall's intense scrutiny.

"Did you take care of that bit of personal business you mentioned when you called last night?"

"Yes, sir."

Dave most certainly had. Fighting a grin, he thought of the waitress who'd all but wrapped herself around him when he'd stopped for a cheeseburger in Chorro. The cluster of sunbaked adobe buildings was the closest thing that passed for a town around these parts. The town might appear tired and dusty, but its residents were anything but. One particular resident, anyway.

Dave would carry fond memories of that particular stop for a long time.

Although…

All the while he'd soaped and scraped away the bristles and road dust, his thoughts had centered more on a certain redhead than on the waitress who'd delayed his arrival at the Pegasus site by a few hours. Kate Hargrave was still there, inside his head, teasing him with her fiery hair, her luscious curves and those green cat's eyes.

As if reading his mind, Westfall folded his arms. "I understand you brought Lieutenant Commander Hargrave in this morning."

Word sure got around fast. Dave had dropped off

the gorgeous weather officer at the dispensary less than twenty minutes ago.

"Yes, sir. We bumped into each other on the road into the site. Have you had a report on her condition? How's her ankle?"

"Doc Richardson says she'll be fine. Only a slight muscle strain." A flinty smile creased Westfall's cheeks. "Knowing Commander Hargrave, she'll work out the kinks and be back in fighting form within a few hours."

"That's good to hear."

The smile disappeared. Westfall's gray eyes drilled into his new subordinate. "Yes, it is. I can't afford to lose another key member of my test cadre. You've got some catching up to do, Captain."

"Yes, sir."

"I've set up a series of briefings for you, starting at oh-nine-hundred. First, though, I want you to meet the rest of the team. And get a look at the craft you'll be piloting." He flicked a glance at his watch. "I've asked the senior officers and engineers to assemble in the hangar. They should be in place by now."

The hangar was the cleanest Dave had ever seen. No oil spills smudged the gleaming, white-painted floor. No greasy equipment was shoved up against the wall. Just rack after rack of black boxes and the sleek white capsule that was Pegasus. It took everything Dave had to tear his gaze from the delta-winged craft and acknowledge the introductions Captain Westfall performed.

"Since Pegasus is intended for use by all branches of the military, we've pulled together representatives from each of the uniformed services. I understand you've already met Major Russ McIver."

"Right."

The square-jawed marine had just been exiting his trailer when Dave pulled up. They'd exchanged little more than a quick handshake before Dave hurried in to hit the showers and pull on his uniform. From the package headquarters had sent him, though, he knew McIver had proven himself in both Kosovo and Kabul. The marine's function was to test Pegasus's capability as a vehicle for inserting a fully armed strike team deep into enemy territory.

"This is Major Jill Bradshaw," Westfall announced, "chief of security for the site."

A brown-eyed blonde in desert fatigues and an armband with MP stenciled in big white letters, the major held out her hand. "Good to have you on board, Captain. Come by Rattlesnake Ops after the briefing and we'll get you officially cleared in."

"Will do."

The petite brunette next to Bradshaw smiled a welcome. "Lieutenant Caroline Dunn, Coast Guard. Welcome to Project Pegasus, Captain Scott."

"Thanks."

Dave liked her on the spot. From what he'd read of the woman's résumé, she'd racked up an impressive number of hours in command of a Coast Guard cutter. He appreciated both her experience and her warm smile.

"Dr. Cody Richardson," Westfall said next, indicating a tall, black-haired officer in khakis. The silver oak leaf on Richardson's left collar tab designated his rank. On the right tab was the insignia of the Public Health Service—an anchor with a chain fouling it.

A world-renowned expert in biological agents, Richardson held both an M.D. and a Ph.D. His mission was to test the nuclear, biological and chemical defense suite installed in Pegasus. He also served as on-site physician.

"Heard you provided ambulance service this morning," the doc commented, taking Dave's hand in a firm, no-nonsense grip.

"I did. How's your patient?"

His patient answered for herself. Stepping forward, Lieutenant Commander Hargrave gave Dave a cool smile.

"Fit for duty and ready to get to work."

He sure couldn't argue with the "fit" part. Damned if he'd ever seen anyone fill out a flight suit the way Kate Hargrave did. She, too, wore fire-retardant Nomex, but hers was the NOAA version—sky blue instead of the military's pea green. The zippered, one-piece bag sported an American flag on the left shoulder, a leather name patch above her left breast and NOAA's patch above her right. A distinctive unit emblem was Velcroed to her right shoulder.

It featured a winged stallion on a classic shield-shaped device. The bottom two-thirds of the shield was red. The top third showed a blue field studded with seven silver stars. Captain Westfall saw Dave eyeing the patch and reached into his pocket.

"This is for you. I issued one to the entire test cadre when we first assembled. The winged steed speaks for itself. The stars represent each of the seven uniformed services."

Dave's glance swept the assembled group once more. They were all there, all seven. Army. Navy. Marine Corps. Air Force. Coast Guard. Public Health Service. And NOAA, as represented by the delectable Kate Hargrave. The four military branches. Three predominately civilian agencies with small cadres of uniformed officers.

Dave had been assigned to some joint and unified commands before, but never one with this diversity. Despite their variations in mission and uniform, though, each of these officers had sworn the same oath when they were commissioned. To protect and defend the Constitution of the United States against all enemies.

Dave might possess a laid-back attitude toward life in general, but he took that oath very seriously. No one who'd served in combat could do otherwise.

Captain Westfall took a few moments more to introduce the project's senior civilian scientists and engineers. That done, he and the entire group walked Dave over to the vehicle they'd gathered to test and—hopefully!—clear for operational use.

Pegasus was as sweet up close as it had looked from across the hangar. Long, cigar-shaped, with a bubble canopy, a side hatch and fat, wide-tracked wheels. Designed to operate on land, in the air and in water. The gray-haired Captain Westfall stroked the gleaming white fuselage with the same air of proud propriety a horse breeder might give the winner of the Triple Crown.

"You're seeing the craft in its swept-wing mode," he intoned in his deep voice.

Dave nodded, noting the propellers were folded flat, the engines tilted to horizontal, and the wings tucked almost all the way into the belly of the craft.

"The wide-track wheels allow Pegasus to operate on land in this mode."

"And damned well, too," Dr. Richardson put in with a quick glance at the trim blond Major Bradshaw.

"We encountered some unexpected difficulties during the mountain phase of land operations," she told Dave. "You know about the virus that hit the site and affected Bill Thompson's heart. It hit me, too, while I was up in the mountains conducting a prerun check. Cody... Dr. Richardson and Major McIver rode Pegasus to the rescue."

She'd corrected her slip into informality quickly,

but not before Dave caught the glance she and the doc exchanged. Well, well. So it wasn't all work and no play on the site after all.

"Glad to hear Pegasus can run," Dave commented. "The real test will be to see if he can fly."

He saw at once he'd put his foot in it. Backs stiffened. Eyes went cool. Even Caroline Dunn, the friendly Coast Guard officer, arched an eyebrow.

"Pegasus is designed as a multiservice, all-weather, all-terrain assault vehicle," Captain Westfall reminded him. "Our job is to make sure it operates equally well on land, on water *and* in the air."

There was only one answer to that. Dave gave it. "Yes, sir."

He recovered a little as the walk-around continued and the talk turned to the specifics of the craft's power, torque, engine thrust and instrumentation. Dave had done his homework, knew exactly what was required to launch Pegasus into the air. By the end of the briefing, his hands were itching to wrap around the throttles.

The rest of the day was taken up with the administrivia necessary in any new assignment. Major Bradshaw gave Dave a security briefing and issued a high-tech ID that not only cleared him into the site but also tracked his every movement. Doc Richardson conducted an intake interview and medical assessment. The senior test engineers presented detailed briefings of Pegasus's performance during the land tests.

By the time 7:00 p.m. rolled around, Dave's stomach was issuing noisy feed-me demands. The sandwich he and the briefers had grabbed for lunch had long since ceased to satisfy the needs of his six-two frame. He caught the tail end of the line at the dining hall and joined a table of troops in desert fatigues.

Like the officer cadre, enlisted personnel at the site came from every branch of the service. Army MPs provided security. Navy personnel operated most of the support facilities. Air force troops maintained the site's extensive communications and computer networks. The marine contingent was small, Dave learned, only about ten noncoms whose expertise was essential in testing Pegasus's performance as a troop transport and forward-insertion vehicle.

He scarfed down a surprisingly delicious concoction of steak and enchiladas, then returned to the unit he shared with Russ McIver to unpack and stow his gear. McIver wasn't in residence and the unpacking didn't take long. All Dave had brought with him was an extra flight suit, a set of blues on the off chance he'd have to attend some official function away from the site, workout sweats, jeans, some comfortable shirts and one pair of dress slacks. His golf shoes and clubs he left in the truck. With any luck, he'd get Pegasus soaring the first time up and have time to hit some of New Mexico's golf courses before heading back to his home base in Florida.

Changing out of his uniform into jeans and a gray USAF sweatshirt with the arms ripped out, he stashed his carryall under his bed and explored the rest of the two-bedroom unit. It was similar to a dozen others he'd occupied at forward bases and a whole lot more comfortable than his quarters in Afghanistan.

A passing glance showed Russ McIver's room was spartan in its neat orderliness. As was the front room. Carpeted in an uninspiring green, the area served as a combination eating, dining and living room. The furniture was new and looked comfortable, if not particularly elegant. The fridge was stocked with two boxes of high-nutrition health bars and four six-packs of Coors Light.

"That's what I admire most about marines," Dave announced to the empty trailer. "They take only the absolute necessities into the field with them."

Helping himself, he popped a top and prepared to attack the stack of briefing books and technical manuals he'd plopped down on the kitchenette counter. The rise and fall of voices just outside the unit drew him to the door.

When he stepped out into the early-evening dusk, the first thing that hit him was the explosion of color to the west. Like a smack to the face, it grabbed his instant attention. Reds, golds, blacks, pinks, oranges and blues, all swirling together in a deep purple sky. The gaudy combination reminded Dave of the paintings he'd seen in every truck stop and roadside gift shop on the drive out. Black velvet and bright slashes of color. But this painting was for real, and it was awesome.

The second thing that hit him was the silence his appearance had generated among the officers clustered around a metal picnic table. It was as if an outsider had crashed an exclusive, members-only party. Which he had, Dave thought wryly.

His new roommate broke the small silence. Lifting an arm, McIver waved him over. "Hey, Scott. Bring your beer and join us."

"Thanks." Puffs of sand swirled under Dave's feet as he crossed to the table. "It's your beer, by the way. I'll contribute to the fund or restock the refrigerator as necessary."

"No problem."

The others shifted to make room for him. Like Dave, they'd shed their uniforms. Most wore cutoffs or jeans. Kate Hargrave, he noted with a suddenly dry throat, was in spandex again. Biker shorts this time. Black. Showing lots of slim, tanned thigh.

Damn!

"We were just talking about you," she said as he claimed a corner of the metal bench.

No kidding. He hadn't been hit with a silence like that since the last time he'd walked in on his brother and sister-in-law in the middle of one of the fierce arguments they pretended never happened. As always, Jacqueline had clammed up tight in the presence of a third party. Ryan had just looked angry and miserable. As always.

Jaci was a lot like Kate Hargrave, Dave decided. Not as beautiful. Certainly not as well educated. But just as tough and *very* good at putting a man in his place. Or trying to.

"Must have been a boring conversation," he returned, stretching his legs out under the table. "I'm not much to talk about."

"We were speculating how long it's going to take you to get up to speed."

"I'll be ready to fly when Pegasus is."

Kate arched a delicately penciled auburn eyebrow. "The first flight was originally scheduled for next week. After Bill's heart attack, Captain Westfall put it on hold."

"I talked to him late this afternoon. He's going to put the flight back on as scheduled."

The nonchalant announcement produced another startled silence. Cody Richardson broke it this time.

"Are you sure you can complete your simulator training and conduct the necessary preflight test runs by next week, Scott?"

Dave started to reply that he intended to give it the ole college try. Just in time, he bit back the laconic quip. It didn't take a genius to see that this gathering under the stars was some kind of nightly ritual. And that Dave was still the odd man out. He'd remain out until he proved himself. Problem was, he'd long ago passed the point of either wanting or needing to prove anything. His record spoke for him.

"Yeah," he answered the doc instead. "I'm sure."

The talk turned to the machine then, the one that had brought them all to this corner of the desert. Dave said little, preferring to listen and add to his first impressions of the group.

There were definitely some personalities at work here, he decided after a few moments of lively discussion. Caroline Dunn, the Coast Guard officer, looked as if a stiff wind could blow her away, but her small form housed a sharp mind and an iron will. That became evident when Russ McIver made the mistake of suggesting some modifications to the sea trials. Dunn cut his feet right out from under him.

Then there was the site's top cop, Army Major Jill Bradshaw. Out of uniform, she lost some of her cool, don't-mess-with-me aura. Particularly around the doc, Dave noted with interest. Yep, those two most certainly had something cooking.

Which left Kissable Kate. Dave would be a long time getting to sleep tonight. The weather scientist did things to spandex that made a man ache to peel off every inch of the slick, rubbery fabric. Slowly. Inch by delicious inch.

So he didn't exactly rush off when the small gathering broke up and the others drifted away, leaving him and Kate and a sky full of stars. Dave retained his comfortable slouch while she played with her diet-drink can and eyed him thoughtfully across the dented metal tabletop.

Light from the high-intensity spots mounted around the compound gave her hair a dark copper tint. She'd caught it back with a plastic clip, but enough loose tendrils escaped for Dave to weave an erotic fantasy or two before she shoved her drink can aside.

"Look, we may have gotten off to a wrong start this morning."

"Can't agree with you on that one," he countered. "Scooping a beautiful woman into my arms ten seconds after laying eyes on her constitutes one heck of a good start in my mind."

"That's exactly what I mean. I don't want you to make the mistake of thinking you'll be scooping me up again."

"Why not?"

The lazy amusement in his voice put an edge in hers.

"I made a few calls. Talked to some people who know you. Does the name Denise Hazleton strike a bell?"

"Should it?"

"No, I guess not. Denise said you never quite got around to last names and probably wouldn't remember her first. She's a lieutenant stationed at Luke Air Force Base, in Arizona. You were hitting on her girlfriend the night the two of you hooked up."

"Hmm. Hooking up with one woman while hitting on another. Not good, huh?"

"Not in my book."

Kate hadn't really expected him to show remorse or guilt. She wouldn't have believed him if he had. But neither was she prepared for the hopeful gleam that sprang into his eyes.

"Did I get lucky with either?"

Well, at least he was honest. The man didn't make any attempt to disguise his nature. He was what he was.

"Yes, you did," she answered. "Which is why..."

"What else did she say?"

"I beg your pardon?"

"Denise. What else did she tell you?"

A bunch! Interspersed with long, breathy sighs and a fervent hope that Captain Dave Scott would find his way back to Luke soon.

"Let's just say you left her with a smile on her face."

"We aim to please," Scott said solemnly, even as the glint in his blue eyes deepened. Too late, Kate realized he'd been stringing her along.

"The point is," she said firmly, "I was married to a man a lot like you. A helluva pilot, but too handsome for his own—or anyone else's—good. It didn't work for us and I want you to know right up-front I've sworn off the type."

One sun-bleached eyebrow hooked. He studied Kate for long moments. "That flight I told you about?

The one I took a year or so ago with the air force Hurricane Hunters out of Keesler?"

"Yes?"

"Your ex-husband was the pilot."

Kate's mouth twisted. Obviously she wasn't the only one who got an earful. "You don't have to tell me. I'll just assume John implied I didn't leave *him* with a smile on his face."

"Something along those lines."

She cocked her head, curious now about the workings of this man's mind. "And that didn't scare you off?"

His grin came back, swift and slashing and all male. "No, ma'am."

"It should have. As I said, it didn't work out between John and me. Just as it wouldn't work between the two of us."

"Well, I'm not looking for a deep, meaningful relationship, you understand…."

"Somehow I didn't think you were," Kate drawled.

"But that's not to say we couldn't test the waters."

"No, thanks."

She scooted off the end of the bench and rose. She'd said what needed saying. The conversation was finished.

Evidently Scott didn't agree. Uncoiling his long frame from the opposite bench, he came around to her side of the table.

"You're a scientist. You tote a Ph.D. after your name. I would think you'd want to conduct a series of empirical tests and collect some irrefutable data before you write us off."

"I've collected all the data I need."

"Denise might not agree."

There it was again. That glint of wicked laughter.

"I'm sure she wouldn't," Kate agreed.

"Then I'd say you owe it to yourself to perform at least one definitive test."

His hand came up, curled under her chin, tipped her face. Kate knew she could stop this with a single word. She hadn't reached the rank of lieutenant commander in NOAA's small commissioned-officer corps without learning how to handle herself in just about any situation.

She could only blame curiosity—and the determination to show Dave Scott she meant business—for the way she stood passive and allowed him to conduct the experiment.

Chapter 3

He knew how to kiss. Kate would give him that.

He didn't swoop. Didn't zero in hard and fast. He took things slow, easy, his mouth playing with hers, his breath a warm wash against her lips. Just tantalizing enough to stir small flickers of pleasure under her skin. Just teasing enough to make her want more.

Sternly, Kate resisted the urge to tilt her head and make her mouth more accessible. Not that Scott required her assistance. His thumb traced a slow circle on the underside of her chin and gently nudged it to a more convenient angle for his greater height. By the time the experiment ended, Kate was forced to admit the truth.

"That was nice."

"Nice, huh?"

"Very nice," she conceded. "But it didn't light any fires."

Not major ones, anyway. Just those irritating little flickers still zapping along her nerve endings.

"That was only an engine check." His thumb made another lazy circle on the underside of her chin. "Next time, we'll rev up to full throttle."

It wouldn't do any good to state bluntly there wouldn't be a next time. Dave Scott would only take that as another personal challenge.

"Tell you what." Deliberately, she eased away from his touch. "I'll let you know when I'm ready to rev my engines. Until then, we focus only on our mission while on-site. Agreed?"

"If that's what you want."

She leveled a steady look at him. Ignored the little crinkle of laugh lines at the corners of his eyes. Disregarded the way the deepening shadows cast his face into intriguing planes and angles.

"That's what I want."

Kate had almost as much trouble convincing her roommates she wanted to stick strictly to business as she had convincing Dave Scott.

Cari and Jill were both waiting when she returned to the modular unit that served as their quarters. The unit was functional at best—three cracker box-size bedrooms, an even smaller kitchen and a living area equipped with furniture more designed for utility than for comfort. The three women had added a few personal touches. Kate had tacked up some posters showing the earth's weather in all its infinite variety. Cloudbursts over the Grand Canyon. Snow dusting the peaks of the Andes. The sun blazing down on a Swiss alpine meadow. Cari had added a shelf crammed with the whodunits and thrillers she devoured like candy. Jill stuck to her army roots and had draped a green flag depicting the crossed dueling pistols of the Military Police over one bare wall. The result wouldn't win any house-beautiful awards, but the three officers had grown used to it.

They'd also grown used to each other's idiosyncrasies. No small feat for women accustomed to being on their own and in charge. Still, their close quarters made for few secrets—as Cari proceeded to demonstrate. Curled in her favorite chair, the Coast Guard officer propped the thick technical manual she'd been studying on her chest and demanded an account.

"Okay, Hargrave, *re-port*. What's with you and the latest addition to our merry band?"

"Other than the fact he drove me into the compound after my tumble this morning, nothing."

Polite disbelief skipped across Cari's heart-shaped face. Jill Bradshaw was more direct.

"Ha! Some weather officer you are. *We* all heard the thunder rumbling around you and Scott. You sure lightning isn't about to strike?"

"I should be so lucky."

Kate plopped down beside her on the sofa and yanked the clip out of her hair. Raking her fingers through the heavy mass, she gave the cop a rueful smile.

"I'll tell you this much. Dave isn't like Cody, Jill. You struck gold there."

"Yeah, right," the blonde snorted. "I had to put him on his face in the dirt before either of us got around to recognizing that fact. Not to mention almost arresting him for suspected sabotage."

Kate's smile dimmed at the memory of those tense days when a mysterious virus had attacked one team member after another. As chief of security, Jill's investigation had centered on the Public Service officer—who just happened to be one of the country's foremost experts in biological agents.

"Besides which," Jill continued with a shrug, "Cody and I are doing our best to play things cool until we wind up the Pegasus project."

It was Kate's turn to snort. "The temperature goes up a good twenty degrees Celsius whenever you two are in the same vicinity."

Loftily, her roommate ignored the interruption. "From where we sit," Jill said, including Cari in the general assessment, "your Captain Scott doesn't look like he knows how to cool his jets."

"First, he's not *my* Captain Scott. Second, we conducted a little experiment a few moments ago, the nature of which is highly classified," she added firmly when both women flashed interested looks. "Bottom line, the captain and I agreed to focus solely on Pegasus while on-site. As the three of us should be doing right now."

Jill took the hint and stopped probing. An intensely private person herself, she hadn't looked forward to sharing cramped quarters with two other women. After weeks with the gregarious Kate and friendly Caroline, she'd learned to open up a bit. Falling head over heels for the handsome doc assigned to the project had certainly aided in her metamorphosis.

"Speaking of Pegasus," Cari said, patting the thick three-ring binder propped on her stomach. "Captain Westfall sent over a revised test plan while you were out, uh, experimenting with Dave Scott. Our air force flyboy starts simulator training tomorrow morning."

"Yikes!" Kate's feet hit the floor with a thud. "I'd better get to work. I want to input a different weather-sequence pattern into the simulator program. Talk to you guys later."

Heading for her bedroom, she settled at the small desk wedged in a corner and flipped up the lid of a slim, titanium-cased notebook computer. The communications wizards assigned to the Pegasus project had rigged wireless high-speed satellite links for the PCs on-site. Kate could access the National Oceanographic and Atmospheric Agency databases from just about anywhere in the compound.

The databases were treasure troves containing

information collected over several centuries. Kate took pride in the fact that NOAA could trace its roots back to 1807, when President Thomas Jefferson created the U.S. Coast and Geodetic Survey, the oldest scientific agency in the federal government. Congress got involved in 1890 when it created a Weather Bureau, the forerunner of the current National Weather Service. In 1970 President Nixon combined weather and coastal surveys, along with many other departments to create NOAA.

The major component of the Department of Commerce, NOAA had responsibilities that now included all U.S. weather and climate forecasting, monitoring ocean and atmospheric data, managing marine fisheries and mammals, mapping and charting all U.S. waters and managing coastal zones. Counted among its vast resources were U.S. weather and environmental satellites, a fleet of ships and aircraft, twelve research laboratories and several supercomputers.

Civilians constituted most of NOAA's personnel, but a small cadre of uniformed officers served within all components of the agency, as well as with the military services, NASA, the Department of State and the new Department of Homeland Security. A privileged few like Kate got to fly with the Hurricane Hunters based out of the Aviations Operations Center in Tampa.

Kate hadn't intended to join NOAA or its officer corps, had never *heard* of the agency when she started working part-time in a TV station while still in high school. Before long, she was helping analyze data and put together weather reports. She didn't seriously consider a career in weather, though, until Hurricane Andrew devastated her grandparents' retirement community just outside Miami. She spent weeks helping the heartbroken couple sort through the soggy remains of fifty-two years of marriage. The experience gave her keen insight into the way natural disasters impacted people's lives.

After that wrenching experience, weather became not just a part-time job, but a passion. Kate majored in meteorology in college, served an internship with the National Weather Service's Tornado Center in Oklahoma, went on to earn a master's and then a doctorate in environmental sciences. Now one of the senior scientists assigned to NOAA's Air Operations Center, Kate regularly devoured materials on everything from tidal waves to meteor showers.

Captain Westfall had handpicked Kate for the Pegasus project based on her expertise and her reputation within the agency for always producing results. Pegasus wasn't designed to fly or swim through hurricanes, but it was expected to operate on land, in the air and at sea. Kate had drawn on NOAA's extensive databases to design tests that would stress the vehicle's instrumentation and its crew to the max in each environment.

For the land runs, she'd simulated sandstorms, raging blizzards, flood conditions and blistering heat.

For the airborne phase of the tests, she planned to subject the craft to an even more drastic assortment of natural phenomena.

Her fingers flew over the keyboard, reviewing the test parameters, adjusting weather-severity levels, adding electronic notes to herself and the senior test engineer who'd have to approve any modifications to the plan.

A final click of the mouse saved the changes. Kate sat back, a small smile on her face.

"Okay, Captain Dave Scott. This little package ought to put you through your paces. You and Pegasus both."

Still smiling, she changed into a well-washed, comfortable sleep shirt. It was early, not quite ten, but she'd have to be up by six to squeeze in her morning run.

Usually Kate zonked out within moments of hitting the sack. Tonight she couldn't seem to erase the image of a certain pilot. Or the memory of his mouth brushing hers. Damn, the man was good! Despite her every intention to the contrary, he'd certainly left her wanting more.

Okay, and what woman wouldn't? Kate rationalized. With his muscled shoulders, gleaming blue eyes and come-and-get-me grin, the man was sex on the hoof. Then there was his attitude. So damned cocky and confident. She had to admire his seemingly unshakable belief in his own abilities, even as she felt a growing urge to take him down a peg or two.

Well, he'd get a chance to show what he was made of tomorrow.

Rolling over, Kate punched her pillow.

Her inner alarm woke her well before six. The clock radio beside her bed went off just as she was lacing her running shoes. Killing the alarm, Kate put on a pot of coffee for her roommates and slipped outside to conduct her warm-up exercises. The muscles she'd pulled yesterday morning issued a sharp protest, but the ache eased within moments. Properly stretched and loose, she set out at an easy lope for the gate guarding the compound.

The MP on duty tipped her a salute. Kate returned it with a smile and lengthened her stride. The dirt road that formed the only access to the site arrowed straight ahead, a pale track in the light filtering through the peaks to the east. The steady plop of her sneakers against the dirt and the rhythm of her own breathing soon took Kate to her special, private world.

Her morning run was a sacred ritual, one she conducted whenever she didn't have a flight scheduled or a hurricane to track. The stillness of early morning cleared her head of yesterday's issues and centered her on the ones ahead. Given her penchant for pizza and greasy cheeseburgers, the long, punishing runs also kept her naturally lush curves from becoming downright generous.

After her divorce, these moments alone in the dawn had helped her regain her perspective. It had taken her a while to get past the hurt. Even longer to recognize that John's angry accusation that Kate was too driven, too ambitious, masked his own unwillingness to abandon the niche he'd carved for himself in his world. He didn't want change—or a wife who thrived on challenges.

With an impatient shake of her head, Kate put the past out of her mind. This was her quiet time, her small slice where she should be thinking about the day ahead.

So she wasn't particularly thrilled when she caught the echo of a loping tread behind her. Most of the other personnel at the test cadre fulfilled their mandatory physical fitness requirements at the site's small but well-equipped gym. Once a week Russ McIver rousted the marine contingent on station for a ten-mile run. With full backpacks, no less. Aside from that grunting, huffing squad, Kate usually had the dawn to herself.

When thuds drew closer, she threw a look over her shoulder. Dave Scott caught her glance and jerked his chin in acknowledgment.

Well, hell!

An irritated frown creased Kate's forehead. She thought she'd made herself clear last night. Apparently Captain Scott hadn't been listening. Her mouth set, she brought her head back around and kept to her pace.

He came up alongside her a few moments later. "Mornin', Commander. You sure you should be running on that ankle?"

She ignored the question and the easy smile he aimed her way. "I thought we reached an agreement last night."

"We did."

"And this is how you intend to stick to your end of the bargain?"

"Maybe I misunderstood things." He sounded genuinely puzzled as he matched his longer stride to hers. "I thought we agreed to focus on business while on-site."

"Exactly."

"So I'm focusing. Captain Westfall made it clear he expected all military to maintain a vigorous physical-conditioning program."

"And you just happened to choose an early-morning run for your PE program?"

The sarcasm went right past the captain.

"I figured the rest of the day was going to be pretty busy," he replied. "I also figured you might want some company. Just in case you went into a ditch and made contact with another tumbleweed."

"Sorry, cowboy, you figured wrong. Company is the last thing I want on my morning run. I use the time to clear my head and raise a little sweat."

"Not a problem," he said easily. "I like a little more

kick in my stride anyway. I wouldn't want to push you."

She shook her head. As challenges went, that one was about as subtle as a bull moose pawing the ground.

"If you want a race…"

She skimmed her glance over the desert landscape now bathed in the reds and golds of morning. A half mile or so ahead, a solitary cactus raised its arms as if to welcome the new day.

"See that cactus? If I reach it first, you pick another time to run. Agreed?"

"Agr— Hey!"

She shot forward, feeding off a rush of pure adrenaline. Kate loved pushing herself to the max. In the air, surrounded by a riot of black, angry clouds and howling winds. On the playing field, whether participating or watching. In her personal life, which she had to admit had taken on an unexpected edge since Dave Scott appeared on the scene all of twenty-four hours ago.

Unfortunately, most men didn't appreciate being left in the dust. Kate had learned that lesson the hard way from her ex. She figured now was as good a time as any to administer the same lesson to Dave Scott.

She almost succeeded. The cool desert air was stabbing into her lungs as she drew level with the cactus. At that moment, Scott drew level with her. They whizzed past the plant side by side, matching stride for stride.

Panting, Kate slowed her breakneck pace. Scott did the same, his breath coming a whole lot easier than hers.

"What do you know?" he said, that damned glint in his eye. "A tie."

"Did you hold back?" she asked sharply.

"What do you think?"

"Dammit, Scott!"

"Hey, you set the ground rules. You win, I run another time. I win, I run when and where I please. A tie…"

"A tie means we do it again," Kate snapped. She didn't like losing *or* ending matters in a draw.

"Okay by me. So how far do you plan to run this morning?"

"Another mile or so," she bit out.

"That works. I need to hit the showers and make a pass through the dining hall before I show up at test ops for my first simulator run."

Kate chewed on her lower lip. A few strides later, she offered a grudging bit of advice.

"You might want to skip the dining hall. You're going to hit some rough weather this morning. You won't impress your fellow cadre members if you upchuck the first time you're at the controls."

He gave her a quick glance. "Taking me on a wild ride, are you?"

"Like you wouldn't believe, cowboy."

As soon as the words were out, Kate wished them back. She couldn't believe she'd let herself walk into that bit of double entendre. To her surprise, Scott didn't jump on it with wolfish glee. He looked thoughtful for a moment before nodding his thanks.

"I appreciate the warning. I'll go light on the grits and gravy."

"Good idea."

The warning surprised Dave. Given what he'd heard about Kate Hargrave's competitive personality, he would have guessed she'd take secret delight in knocking him down a peg or two. She'd certainly pulled out all the stops in their little footrace a moment ago. Dave had burned more energy than he wanted to admit trying to catch her. Once she got back up to full power she was going to give him one helluva run for his money.

A smile of pure anticipation tugged at his lips. Behind his laid-back exterior, Dave was every bit as competitive as Commander Hargrave. He suspected all fliers had that edge, that instinctive need to beat the odds every time they climbed into the cockpit. But it had been a while since he'd felt the thrill of the chase this keenly. Even longer since he'd been shot down in flames.

Kate had all but waved a red flag in front of his face last night by insisting on their so-called agreement. Dave wouldn't break his word. He'd stick to the terms—as he interpreted them. He'd also do his damnedest to convince her to renegotiate their contract.

Dave wasn't quite sure how it had happened, but the challenge represented by Kate Hargrave was starting to rank right up there with that of Pegasus.

Chapter 4

The simulator crouched like a giant blue beetle on long, pneumatic legs. The capsule's front faced huge trifold screens. Once the ride began, the screens would show vivid, dizzying projections of earth and sky. Off to one side a control booth housed the simulator's team of operators, evaluators and observers.

Anticipation simmered in Dave's veins as he climbed the metal stairs to the capsule's entrance. This was his first time at the controls of a brand-new flying, fighting vehicle. He couldn't wait to see how it handled in this simulated environment.

A technician in white overalls with the cadre's distinctive red-and-blue patch prominently displayed waited for him on the platform.

"Ready to fly, Captain?"

"Ready as I'll ever be."

The technician grinned. "I've got a six-pack riding on you. Try not to crash and burn first time up."

"I'll do my best."

Ducking through the side hatch, Dave strapped himself into the operator's seat. Pegasus had been designed for one pilot. Driver. Captain. Whatever they called the individual in the front seat, he or she had to know how to switch from land to airborne to sea mode and operate safely in all three environments. No small feat for anyone, even the highly experienced crew assembled here in the desert.

The tech checked the parachute pack built into the seat, adjusted the shoulder straps on Dave's harness and conducted a final communications check. Just before he closed the door, he offered a final bit of advice.

"Your puke 'n' go bag is right next to your left knee. In case you need it."

"Got it."

The door clanged shut, leaving Dave alone in the simulator. He'd spent most of yesterday and a good portion of last night poring over a fat technical manual, reacquainting himself with instrumentation that was familiar, studying the dials and digital displays that weren't.

He dragged out the black notebook containing the various operational checklists, propped it in the slot designed to hold it and studied the layout of the instruments. The simulator cockpit replicated the actual vehicle exactly. The same defense contractor who'd designed and built the three Pegasus prototypes had constructed the simulator.

Unfortunately, two of the three prototypes had crashed and burned during the developmental phase. Only one had survived and been delivered to the military for operational testing. The contractor was scrambling to produce additional test vehicles, but until they were delivered Dave sure as hell had better not crash the one remaining.

For that reason, these hours in the simulator were absolutely vital. Dave had to get a feel for the craft, had to learn to handle it in all possible situations, before he actually took it into the air. He took a last look around and flipped open the black notebook to the sheet containing the start-up checklist.

"Okay, team. Let's roll."

Captain Westfall's voice came through the headset. "Good luck, Scott."

"Thanks, sir."

Suddenly, the tall screens surrounding the front of the capsule came to life. Instead of dull white, they showed a desert landscape of silver greens and browns. Jagged mountains dominated the horizon. A brilliant blue sky beckoned.

Dave's gloved hand hovered over the red power switch. He dragged in a deep breath, let it out.

"Pegasus One, initiating power."

"Roger, Pegasus One."

Flicking the switch to on, Dave listened to the familiar hum of auxiliary power units feeding juice to the on-board systems. Screens lit up. Switches glowed red and green and yellow.

His gaze went to the digital display showing an outline of Pegasus. The craft was in land mode, its wings back and turboprop engines tucked away. In this mode the vehicle could race across the desert and climb mountains. Much as Dave would love to take this baby out for a run, his job was to test its wings.

"Pegasus One switching to airborne mode."

"Roger, One."

His thumb hit the center button beside the display. Right before his eyes, the shape of the vehicle outlined on the screen altered. Wings fanned out. Propeller blades were released from their tucked position. Rear stabilizers unfolded.

"Hot damn!"

"Come again, Captain?" The simulator operator's voice floated through his headset. "We didn't copy that."

"Sorry. That wasn't meant for public consumption. Pegasus One, locking into hover position."

Like the tilt-wing Osprey currently in use by the military, Pegasus incorporated Very Short Takeoff and Landing technology. With the engines in a vertical position, the craft could lift and hover like a chopper. Dave had logged several hundred hours in the Osprey and was feeling more confident by the moment.

"Pegasus One, powering up."

The familiar whine of engines revving filled his ears. The pedals shuddered under his boots. He took the craft to simulated full power and lifted off. Once airborne, he tilted the engines to horizontal. Pegasus seemed to leap to life.

They gave him a good hour to get a feel for the controls and build his confidence before the first system malfunction occurred. It was minor, a glitch in the navigational transponder. Dave corrected by switching from direct-satellite signal to relay-station signal.

A few moments later, his Doppler radar picked up some weather. A thunderstorm, racing right toward him from the west. That was Kate Hargrave's doing, Dave thought with a smile. Unless he missed his guess, he was in for a rough ride.

Sure enough, the turbulence proved too big to go around and too high to get above. Within moments, thunder crashed in his headset and lightning forked across the wide screens surrounding the capsule. Violent winds set Pegasus bucking and kicking like a wild mustang. Dave needed both hands and feet to maintain control. The wild jolting caused another malfunction. A blinking red light signaled an oil leak in engine one.

His pucker factor rising, Dave shut down the engine and fought to keep the craft in the air while diagnosing the source of the leak. He'd just narrowed it down, when a bolt of lightning slashed across the screen. Bright blue light filled the cockpit. A loud alarm sounded at the same instant another red warning light began to flash.

Hell! Number two engine took a hit. The damned thing was on fire.

Gritting his teeth, Dave flipped to the engine fire checklist. He had to restart engine one before shutting down two, though, or he'd fall right out of the sky. He got the starboard engine powered back up again, killed the other and activated the fire-suppression system.

At that point, the situation went from bad to downright ugly. The damned fire-suppression system didn't work. If anything, the fire appeared to be burning hotter, and electrical systems were shutting down faster than small-town storefronts on a Saturday night.

Too late, Dave remembered the pylons securing the engines to the wing were made of a magnesium alloy. The alloy was strong, light and flexible—all highly desirable qualities in an aircraft. But when magnesium burned, it produced its own oxygen and thus created a fire that was totally self-sustaining. Chances were this one would eat right through the wing and hit the fuel lines.

In any other aircraft, the pilot would bail out at this point. Dave was damned if he'd punch and lose the only Pegasus prototype left, even in a simulated situation. Sweating inside his flight suit, he tried every trick in the book and a few that had never been written down to save his craft. He was still fighting when his instrument panel went dead.

"Pegasus One, your flight is terminated."

Cursing under his breath, Dave slumped back in the seat and waited for his heart to stop jackhammering against his ribs. He glanced to his right, saw a grim-faced Captain Westfall standing behind the controller in the operator's booth. Kate was next to him, her hair a bright flame in the dimly lit booth. The other officers ringed her.

His mouth set into a hard, tight line, Dave keyed his mike. "Let's conduct the postflight critique. Then we'll try this little exercise again."

In the next two days Dave battled everything from wind shears and microbursts to turbulence that almost flipped over his craft and maintenance-generated crossed wires that caused his instruments to produce faulty readings.

On one flight, he lost cabin pressurization and discovered his oxygen mask wouldn't filter the carbon monoxide he exhaled. On another, an engine stuck halfway between the vertical and horizontal position. He almost crawled out of the simulator after that particular exercise. Both arms and legs ached from using brute physical strength to wrestle with the controls of the wildly gyrating vehicle.

As a result, he wasn't in the mood for another

critique of his flying skills when he joined Kate for a run the morning after that particular experience.

She'd come to accept his company with resignation if not an abundance of enthusiasm. Impatient, she paced the dirt just outside his trailer. Her hair was caught up in a ponytail, her body encased in slick-looking hot pink. Dave's stiff movements as he exited his quarters had her quirking an auburn eyebrow.

"Sure you want to run this morning?"

"Yeah."

"Better not overdo it. That last ride was a bitch."

"I was there, remember?"

His curt tone arched her eyebrow another notch. "Suit yourself."

Propping her foot on a rock, she stretched her calf muscles. The sight of all that hot pink bending and curving didn't help Dave's mood. He'd spent the past couple of nights mentally reviewing each phase of every simulated flight. When his mind wasn't churning over the effects of wing icing and emergency high-altitude landings, his thoughts had a distinct tendency to veer off in a direction that left him in even more of a sweat.

He'd replayed the kiss he and Kate had shared a dozen or more times in his mind, kicking himself each time for wimping it. He'd promised her the next one would *not* be slow and easy, and he was ready to deliver on his promise. More than ready.

Cursing himself for agreeing to her hands-off on-site policy, Dave cut his stretching exercise short.

"You ready?"

"Ready."

Kate set off at an easy pace. She'd spent enough time in this man's company by now to gauge his temper. For three days he'd been battling a machine and everything the test cadre had thrown at him. He'd won most of the battles, more than anyone had expected him to. But the ones he'd lost stuck in his craw like a fish bone.

He needed an outlet for his frustration and Kate intended to give him one. Not the one he'd no doubt prefer, she thought with a twinge of real regret. No hard, fast tussle between the sheets, muscles straining, bodies writhing, skin damp with sweat. Gulping at the image that leaped into her head, she kicked up the pace.

Dave lengthened his stride and kept up with her. He didn't indulge in his usual teasing banter. To Kate's surprise, she found she missed the give-and-take. They jogged in silence a while longer before she dropped the casual challenge.

"There's the cactus we used as a finish line the other day," she said. "We talked about a rematch. You up for it?"

He shot her a quick, hard glance. "Are you?"

In answer she merely smiled and took off in a burst of speed.

"Dammit!"

His curse was followed by the sound of his pounding footsteps. Kate didn't hold back. Fists clenched, feet pumping, heart galloping, she poured everything she had into the all-for-nothing sprint.

Mere yards from the cactus she glanced over her shoulder and debated whether to slow her pace. Her goal was to make Dave work off some of his pent-up frustration, not add to it with another defeat. The issue became moot, though, when he laid on a final burst of speed. It was all Kate could do to stay elbow-to-elbow with him as they sailed past the spiky cactus.

Grinning, she slowed her pace. "Well, what do you know," she panted. "Another tie."

"Only because you cheated. Again."

His scowl was gone, replaced by an answering grin that snatched what little air Kate had managed to draw into her already stressed lungs.

"You won't get the drop on me again," he warned.

"Think so, huh? Wait till you climb back in the simulator this morning. You're not going to know what hit you."

His groan was loud and long, but minus the surly edge. "I've already been hit with lightning, hail, ice and sandstorms. What the heck have you got left in your bag of tricks to throw at me?"

She tossed her head, laughing. "Oh, cowboy, I'm just warming up."

"I'll remember this. Trust me, I'm going to remember every jolt and lurch and sickening, thousand-foot drop."

"Ha! Threats don't scare me."

"They should." His voice dropped to a mock growl. "You're gonna pay, babe."

The promise hovered between them for an endless moment before being lost to the steady plop of their running shoes against the dirt road.

Their race might have relieved some of Dave's frustration, but it didn't help the tension that crawled up Kate's neck as the rest of the day turned into a replay of the ones that had gone before.

They put the sky jock through hell. Time and time again. Using a dial-a-disaster approach, they'd start with a minor problem like an electrical failure, then pile on problem after problem until Dave reached the point of what was politely referred to as task saturation. With six or seven major malfunctions occurring at once, he had to scramble to keep the issues sorted out and Pegasus in the air.

By the third simulated run, Kate was sweating under her flight suit and strung tight with nerves. This run would be the worst, she knew. It was an overland flight in winter weather conditions. Partway into the flight, Dave would encounter a phenomenon few pilots had ever dealt with. Swallowing, Kate glanced at the digital clock on the controller's console. Seven minutes until all hell broke loose.

Fists balled, she kept her eyes glued to the wide screens surrounding the capsule. The Alps rose in majestic splendor. Their snowcapped peaks speared into a dazzlingly blue sky. Dave was piloting his craft through a narrow valley. All systems were fully functioning.

Kate tore her gaze from the screens and watched the clock. Three minutes. Two.

She closed her eyes. Envisioned the cold, dense air mass sliding down the mountain. Picking up speed as gravity took over. Sweeping up snow. Gathering force and fury.

"What the…!"

Suddenly Dave was fighting for control in total whiteout conditions. The katabatic wind—the strongest on the planet save for tornadoes—had hit his craft with the force of a free-falling bulldozer. In the Antarctic, these dense, cold down drafts had been clocked at speeds in excess of two hundred miles per hour. In the Alps they came with the mistral, which tore down the Rhone valley through southern France and out into the Mediterranean.

Kate had intensified this particular mistral beyond what might reasonably be expected, given the simulated time of year and temperature. Now she watched with her heart in her throat as the display screens in the control booth showed a snow-blinded, out-of-control Pegasus flying straight at a towering peak.

Pull up! The silent prayer intensified to a near shriek inside her head. *Pull up!*

For a heart-stopping moment, she thought he'd make it. He yanked on the stick, got the craft's nose up, almost—*almost!*—maneuvered around the towering wall of snow and rock.

A second later, the displays went flat. The controller blew out a long, ragged breath and keyed his mike.

"Pegasus One, your flight is terminated."

A stark silence descended over the control booth. Russ McIver finally broke it. "That's twice Scott has augered in now."

His eyes flinty, Captain Westfall nodded. "I'm aware of that, Major."

"I don't think we can blame this one on pilot error or unfamiliarity with the systems," Kate said carefully. "I may have made the weather conditions too extreme for this scenario."

Russ set his jaw. "Extreme or not, if this had been a real mission we'd be calling for body bags right now."

As frustrated as everyone else in the booth, Cari Dunn dragged off her ball cap and raked a hand through her hair. "Why don't you wait for the debrief before you start burying the dead, McIver."

The marine stiffened up. "Are you addressing me, *Lieutenant?*"

"Yes, *Major,*" she snapped. "I am."

Dave's voice came over the intercom, cutting through the tension with the precision of a blade.

"Russ is right. I blew it. Let's run this one again."

Captain Westfall leaned into the mike. "You've

been at this twelve solid hours. Why don't you take a break and we'll run it tomorrow."

"I'm okay, sir. I'll take another stab at it. What the hell hit me, anyway?"

All eyes in the booth turned to Kate. She stepped up to the mike.

"It's called a katabatic wind, after the Greek word *kata,* meaning downward. It forms when a cold, dense mass of air slides down a mountainside, picks up speed and plunges to the valley below. This type of wind occurs everywhere on the planet but, uh, not usually with this much force."

She half expected him to mutter an angry curse. Kate knew she wouldn't be feeling too friendly if someone had just put her through that particular experience. To her surprise, a chuckle floated across the speakers.

"Don't forget, Hargrave. I'm keeping score. Every lurch. Every jolt. Every damned kata-whatever. Okay, team, let's power this baby up and see if I can get Pegasus to ride on the wind this time."

Chapter 5

The officers didn't gather at the picnic tables that night. Or the next. Dave kept them at the simulator, conducting run after run, analyzing the system failures, admitting his own with brutal honesty.

By Friday the entire test cadre was worn to the bone, but both Dave and Pegasus had proved their stuff. In simulated environments, anyway. The real test would come with the first actual flight on Monday morning.

Dave had planned to spend the weekend prepping for the flight, but Captain Westfall gathered his officers and senior civilians early Saturday to declare a stand-down.

"I received a request from the Joint Chiefs for

a briefing on our progress to date. I'm flying to Washington this morning and will return Sunday evening. We'll resume test operations on Monday."

His glance roamed from one to another of his senior officers and civilians. The strain of the past weeks showed clearly in their faces.

"Use this downtime to give your troops a break. You folks take one, too. I want everyone rested, relaxed and ready to launch Pegasus into the sky by oh-seven-hundred Monday morning."

He didn't get any arguments. Dave noted how Doc Richardson's glance skipped immediately to Jill Bradshaw. The blonde kept her expression deliberately neutral, but a slight flush rose in her cheeks. Dave would bet his last buck those two would have headed for the nearest motel as soon as this meeting broke up if not for the fact that Richardson stood next in order of rank.

"Commander Richardson has the stick until I return," Westfall said, confirming the doc's seniority. "He'll have to remain on-site during my absence, but the rest of you are free to take off."

"I haven't been off-site since I arrived," Russ McIver commented as the small group walked out into the bright morning sunlight. "I'll have to figure out what to do with myself."

"How about we hit the links?" Dave suggested. "I've got my golf clubs stashed in my truck. I hear Fort Bliss has a great course."

"Sorry, never had time to learn the game."

Cari couldn't resist. "Too busy polishing your combat boots?"

Mac's eyes narrowed. "My boots aren't the only articles that need polishing around here, Lieutenant. Your attitude could use a little work."

"Is that right?" The Coast Guard officer smiled politely. "Are you going to put me in a brace and work on my military manners?"

The marine gave her a long, considering look. "If I put you in a brace," he said finally, "your manners wouldn't be all we worked on."

Cari's smile slipped. Before she could decide just how to respond, Mac tipped two fingers in a casual salute and strode off. Frowning, the brunette watched him disappear around a corner before she spun on her heel and headed in the opposite direction.

"Well," Kate murmured when the dust settled. "That was interesting."

"Very," Jill Bradshaw agreed. The cop slanted a glance at Cody Richardson, and Dave guessed it wouldn't be long before the two of them disappeared as well. The doc couldn't leave the site, but this was a *big* site, with lots of long, empty stretches of road.

Dave guessed right. Not ten seconds later Jill said she needed to run a perimeter check and Cody volunteered to run it with her. That left Kate, who surprised Dave by falling in with his original suggestion.

"I've knocked around a few white balls in my

time. I wouldn't mind getting off-site for a few hours to find out if I've still got my swing."

She still had it. It was right there, in every long-legged stride. Dave could vouch for that.

"What kind of handicap do you carry?" he asked, wondering if she was as good at golf as she seemed to be at everything else.

"Seven."

Well, that answered that.

"What's yours?"

"Twelve."

Her mouth curved in a smug smile. "Looks like I'll have to give you some strokes, cowboy."

With a silent groan, Dave passed on that one.

"Of course," she continued, her competitive batteries already charging, "we'll have to adjust for the fact that you'll be using your own clubs and I'll have to make do with rentals."

"Of course."

"And I'll be in sneakers instead of golf shoes."

"Mine are soft spiked," Dave protested.

"Doesn't matter. They still give you a better grip on the turf."

"All right, already. We'll negotiate the handicaps when we get there. I'll pick you up in twenty minutes."

Thinking that this week from hell just might end a whole lot more enjoyably than he would have imagined a few hours ago, Dave peeled off and headed for his trailer to change out of his uniform and into civvies.

Kate couldn't believe the weight that rolled off her shoulders as Dave's battered pickup passed through the perimeter checkpoint. She loved working on the Pegasus project, was thrilled to have been chosen as the NOAA rep. Still, she hadn't realized how the weeks of excitement and pressure had accumulated until the pickup hit the county road. With that transition from packed dirt to pavement, she felt as though she was reentering the world.

Sighing, Kate slouched down in her seat. Desert landscape rolled by outside the pickup. Inside, the lively strains of Trisha Yearwood's latest hit rolled from the radio.

"Captain Westfall was right," she commented as the song ended. "We needed to stand down and give folks a break. I can't believe how good it feels to get off-site for a few hours."

Dave nodded, but didn't comment. As the newest member of the group, Kate supposed he could hardly complain about the stress. Not that the entire cadre hadn't done their best to pile it on him this week.

If all those hours in the simulator had gotten to him, it didn't show in his face or lazy slouch. Like Kate, he'd changed into comfortable slacks and a knit shirt. The short-sleeved shirt was collared, as required by many golf courses, and looked as though Ralph Lauren had designed it with him in mind.

The cobalt color deepened the blue of his eyes and contrasted vividly with his tanned skin and tawny hair. Kate was still secretly admiring the way the knit stretched across his muscled shoulders when they passed through the small town of Chorro.

A few miles beyond the town, Dave pulled up at an intersection. The two-lane county road they were traveling wound through the desert. To the west, it led to Las Cruces. To the east, to El Paso and the army post at Fort Bliss. The road intersecting it ran north toward Alamogordo and south to God knew where in Mexico.

Dave hooked his wrists over the steering wheel and angled Kate a considering glance. She couldn't tell what he was thinking, but it was clear he had some change of plan in mind.

"Why the stop?" she asked.

"I'm thinking we might extend this excursion for more than a few hours."

"Extend it how?"

"I hear there's a great course up by Ruidoso, at the Inn of the Mountain Gods. The fairways wind through the mountains and the tee boxes are at some of the highest elevation in the country. You hit a golf ball at seven thousand feet," he offered as added inducement, "and it'll fly almost to the next county."

"You take a swing at seven thousand feet," Kate retorted, "and it's all you can do to suck in enough air for another."

Rueful laughter filled his eyes. "I've been sucking in a whole *bunch* of air this week. I can manage more than one swing if you can."

It was the laughter that snagged her, not the challenge. Kate had had a front-row seat this past week. She'd witnessed Dave's frustration, watched him push himself twice as hard as the team had pushed him. The fact that he could laugh at his failures—and had yet to brag about his successes—went a long way to altering her initial perception of him as just another hotshot sky jock.

She glanced at the narrow road winding toward the distant mountains. "Isn't Ruidoso a good hundred miles from here?"

"More or less."

"It'll take us all day to drive up there and squeeze in eighteen holes. We'll be driving back through the mountains at night."

"Unless we decide to stay over."

"Stay over? I didn't bring so much as a toothbrush with me. I don't usually need one to play golf," she tacked on with a touch of sarcasm.

"Ever hear of drugstores?"

Kate started to enumerate all the reasons why spinning a simple round of golf into a weekend expedition wasn't a good idea. Number one on her list was the fact that their agreement to focus strictly on Pegasus applied while on-site. How they handled matters off-site had yet to be negotiated.

To her disgust, Kate found that also topped her list

of reasons to head for Ruidoso. She wasn't stupid or into self-denial. This man turned her on. She thought she'd been inoculated against handsome charmers like Dave Scott. Obviously, the inoculation had worn off.

He'd shown what he was made of this week. Maybe she should see what he was like away from their work environment. Discover if there was more to the man than that sexy body and his awesome skills as an aviator.

"Why don't we play this by ear?" she suggested. "See how long it takes to get there. And how we feel after eighteen holes."

"Sounds like a plan to me. Let me call and make sure we can get on the course this afternoon."

A quick call to information on his cell phone produced the number for the Inn of the Mountain Gods. The gods must have been smiling, because Dave managed to snag a 1:20 tee time that someone had just canceled. With a satisfied smile, he pocketed his cell phone, hooked an elbow on the window frame and aimed his pickup north.

Kate fell instantly in love with Ruidoso.

A onetime hideout of Billy the Kid, the old mining town was nestled high in the Sierra Blanca Mountains and surrounded by the Lincoln National Forest. Ski resorts, casinos, a racetrack, art galleries, boutiques and the many nearby lakes gave evidence that Ruidoso offered year-round fun for all ages and tastes.

Kate could envision the town blanketed in fresh white powder. Imagine it in summer, swarming with tourists eager to escape the blistering heat at lower elevations. Almost see the profusion of wildflowers that must carpet the high meadows in spring.

But she was sure fall *had* to be the most perfect time to visit. Tall green pines and blue spruce spilled down the slopes surrounding the town, interspersed with stands of oak, maple and aspen that added breathtaking splashes of color. Kate's delighted gaze drank in flaming reds, shimmering golds, impossibly bright oranges.

"Oh, boy. I hope this golf course of yours has scenery like this!"

It did. Owned and operated by the Mescalero Apaches, the resort was located on their reservation some miles out of Ruidoso. Mountains blazing with color surrounded the brand-new hotel and casino. Shimmering lake waters lapped at pebbled shores and reflected both the resort and the mountain peaks. The golf course, Kate saw as Dave parked in the lot behind a clubhouse constructed of pine and soaring glass, wasn't for the faint of heart.

The first hole—the very first!—required a clean shot over a stretch of clear blue lake to a small island. The second shot had to carry over water again to a raised green. Low bridges constructed of pine linked the island to shore and allowed access by cart.

"Forget handicaps!" Kate exclaimed. "We'll be lucky if we don't lose all our balls on the first hole."

Grinning, Dave hefted his bag. "Oh, no! You're not going to wiggle out of giving me strokes. I'm not handing you any advantage this time, Commander."

With another look at that killer first hole, Kate headed for the pro shop. Dave propped his bag on the rack by the door and followed her inside. His clubs, Kate noted, were well used and the finest that money could buy. Evidently the man took his golf as seriously as he did his flying.

The pro fixed her up with a decent rental set and they just had time to grab a lunch of Indian tacos washed down with ice-cold beer. Then Kate dragged a visor down low on her forehead to block the glare off the lake and teed up. After a few practice swings with a four iron, she sent her ball sailing across the water. It landed smack in the center of the small green island.

Dave gave a low whistle. "Nice shot."

"Thanks."

She couldn't help sashaying a bit as she strolled to the back of the tee box to help track his ball in flight. Not that it needed tracking. The little white sphere soared in a high, sweet arc and plopped down not two feet from hers.

When he turned to her with a smug grin, Kate knew the battle was on.

* * *

The war raged for seventeen holes.

Grudgingly, Kate gave him the strokes he demanded to even their games. She also voiced strong doubts about the twelve he supposedly carried as a handicap. Dave ignored her grousing and whacked ball after ball through the thin mountain air.

Kate had to pull out all the stops to stay even on the front nine, and led by two strokes as they approached number seventeen. It was a par three, only about a hundred and twenty yards from tee to green. In between was a sheer drop of a thousand feet or more!

Of course, she shanked her ball and lost it in the dense undergrowth at the bottom of the gully. That cost her two strokes, putting them even for number eighteen. They both made the green in regulation and the game boiled down to the final putt.

Dave was closer to the pin, so Kate putted first. It took her two tries to sink her ball. Not bad, considering how far out she'd been, but she held her breath while Dave lined up his shot. If he made this putt, he'd win.

He stroked the ball gently. His putter made its distinctive little *ping*. The ball rolled right for the cup—and stopped an inch short. Shaking his head, he walked up and dropped it in. His eyes held a glint of pure devilry when he retrieved his ball.

"How do you like that? Another tie."

Kate eyed him suspiciously. "Did you short that putt on purpose?"

"What do you think?"

It was the same answer he'd given her the first time they raced, and she didn't like it any better this time than she had then.

"Get this straight, Scott. When I play, I play to win."

He tossed his ball a few times, catching it in his palm. "Could be we're just well matched."

Belatedly, she remembered her ex had given him an earful. "And it could be," she said carefully, fighting the memory of old hurts and recriminations, "you think I'll get all bent out of shape if I lose."

"Win or lose, Hargrave, you couldn't get bent out of shape if you tried."

"I'm serious about this. I don't like the idea you're toying with me."

His fist closed around the ball. He fingered the dimples for a few moments before answering. "I like to win as much as you do. What I don't like is when healthy competition turns mean."

Kate stiffened. "As I'm sure my former husband told you happened in our marriage."

"He implied something of the sort," Dave admitted with a shrug, "but I wasn't thinking of your marriage when I said that."

"Whose were you thinking of, then?"

"My brother's." His forehead creasing, Dave frowned at the ball still clutched in his hand. "My sister-in-law is on his case all the time. About money. About the kids. Who's doing a better job with both. Ryan takes it, but it's eating him alive."

"Why doesn't he walk?"

His gaze lifted and locked with hers. "He says he loves her."

"Funny thing about love." Kate managed to swallow the lump that suddenly formed in her throat. "Sometimes it just plain hurts."

"Well, I can't say I'm an expert on the subject, but I'll tell you this. I wouldn't walk, either, if I loved a woman as much as Ryan loves Jaci."

"What would you do?"

"Find some way to call it a draw, I suppose."

"Like this round of golf?"

His grin slipped out, quick and slashing. "Like this round of golf."

Kate wasn't sure, but she thought her heart did a funny little flip-flop at that point. How the heck could the man look so damned sexy with his cheeks singed red from the sun and his hair matted down from the ball cap he'd tugged on halfway through the game? Dragging her gaze from the tawny gold, she forced herself to concentrate as Dave offered a suggestion.

"Why don't we officially declare this game a tie and duke it out with another round tomorrow? If we arrange an early tee time, we can still make it back to the base by evening."

She breathed in the cool, clean air. Swept a glance at the riot of colors spilling down the mountain slopes.

Brought her gaze back to the man who, despite her best efforts to hold him off, had somehow breached her barriers.

"You're on."

Dave had figured she couldn't resist the challenge. Hiding a smile, he dropped his putter back in his bag and waited for her to settle in the golf cart beside him.

His conscience didn't so much as ping at him for dangling the bait of another match. Golf was the last thing on his mind at this point. That was occupied with schemes to finesse Lieutenant Commander Kate Hargrave into bed.

Tonight. Right after dinner. Or before, if he could manage it.

God, he wanted her! Their morning runs had been enough to tie him in knots. Kate Hargrave in stretchy tights could tie *any* man in knots. Yet working with her this past week had added an entirely different dimension to his craving.

Dave had dated his share of beautiful women. He'd also worked alongside a good number of smart, dedicated ones. But Kate's particular combination of gorgeous and intelligent and dedicated was fast pushing the memory of all other females right out of his head.

He was still trying to lay out his game plan for the rest of the evening when they entered the two-story lobby of the resort. The pride the Mescalero Apaches took in their heritage showed in the soaring pine beams, the massive circular stone fireplace and the artistry of the woven rugs and baskets decorating the walls.

If the woman at the front desk took note of the fact that neither Kate nor Dave carried any luggage, she was too well-trained to show it. Her black eyes warm, she greeted them courteously.

"Welcome to the Inn of the Mountain Gods. May I help you?"

Dave returned her friendly smile. "We don't have a reservation, but would like to stay tonight. Do you have any vacancies?"

"Yes, sir, we do." Her fingers flew over a keyboard. "I can offer you a choice of views. Rooms with lake views are a little higher priced than those that look toward the mountains, but you'll consider the extra twenty dollars well worth the cost when you see the sunset."

"A lake view it is then."

"Will that be one room or two?"

Dave turned to Kate. She chewed on her lower lip, and he decided he wouldn't rush her. Not until after supper. He turned back to the clerk, intending to inform her they'd need two rooms, when Kate preempted him.

"One room, please."

Just in time, Dave choked back his words.

"Yes, ma'am," the clerk replied, unaware the earth

had just rocked under his feet. "Would you prefer smoking or nonsmoking?"

"Nonsmoking."

"Two queen beds or one king?"

Dave sent a swift, silent prayer to the mountain gods.

They answered his prayer. Or rather, Kate did. With a small, private smile, she said the magic words.

"One king."

Short moments later, they headed for the elevator. Dave's blood was already drumming in his veins, but he had Kate wait for him at the elevators while he made a quick detour to the gift shop. He returned with a small paper sack bearing the inn's distinctive logo. Grinning, he responded to her look of inquiry.

"You said you needed a toothbrush."

He'd purchased one for himself, too. Along with a box of condoms. With luck, stamina and a little ingenuity, he and Kate would run through the entire dozen before they had to return to the site tomorrow.

Chapter 6

Dave put both his ingenuity and his stamina to the test the moment the door to their minisuite thudded shut. He got a brief glimpse through the floor-to-ceiling windows of the still, silver lake and the neon eagle soaring above the casino. Ignoring both, he tossed the paper sack on a chair and snagged Kate's wrist.

A single tug spun her around. One step and he had her backed against the wall. Her head came up. Surprise flitted across her face.

"I warned you," Dave reminded her gruffly. "After our last kiss. No 'nice' this time."

Laughter leaped into her green eyes. "That still stings, does it?"

"Like you wouldn't believe."

"Seems I recall another part of the conversation. Didn't I say I'd give the signal when I was ready for you to conduct another test?"

"You already gave the signal. Downstairs. When you opted for one king."

"You're right. I did. Okay, flyboy, you have my permission to rev up to full throttle."

He was already there, Kate discovered when she slid her hands up his chest to his shoulders. The hard, roped muscles under her palms thrilled her. The rock-solid wall of his body against hers sent an arrow of pure sensation straight to her belly.

And when his mouth covered hers, Kate knew instantly nice was the last thing she wanted. She craved this heat, needed this hunger. The raw sensuality of her emotions stripped away any need for pretense. Every bit as greedy as Dave, Kate locked her arms around his neck and arched her body into his.

She was lost in his kiss, feeling its punch in every corner of her body, when he dragged his head up. Red singed his cheekbones. His breath came fast and hard. She thought he was going to gentle his touch, slow things down, and had to swallow a groan.

She thought wrong. With a skill that had to have come from plenty of experience, he tugged her knit shirt over her head, popped the snap on her slacks and stripped her down to her bra and panties. To

Kate's intense satisfaction, though, he was the one who groaned.

"Oh, baby." A callused palm shaped her breast, cradling its weight and fullness. "You couldn't count the hours I've spent imagining this moment."

She pretended to give the matter serious thought. Not an easy task with his thumb creating a delicious friction as it grazed over her nylon-covered nipple.

"Let's see. You've been on-site all of six days. Spent at least ten hours a day in the simulator, another five to six poring over tech manuals. If we subtract two for eating and six for sleeping, that doesn't leave much time for— Oh!"

She broke off, gulping, as he bent and replaced his hand with his mouth. His breath came hot and damp through the thin fabric of her bra, his tongue felt raspy on her now-engorged nipple. Her gulp turned to a swift, indrawn hiss when his teeth took over from his tongue.

"That left," he growled between nibbles, "plenty of time. To imagine this. And this."

Keeping one arm wrapped tight around her waist, he planed his other hand down the curve of her belly. His palm was hot against her skin, his fingers sure and strong when they cupped her mound. Within moments, Kate was a puddle of want.

She wasn't the kind to take and not give, though. Somehow, she managed to find the strength to put a few inches between them and drag his shirt free of his jeans.

"My turn, cowboy."

Dave ducked his head, more than willing to let her take the reins. His entire body ached with wanting her and he wasn't sure he could stand straight for much longer, but the glide of Kate's hands and mouth and tongue over his skin was worth the agony.

When she unsnapped his jeans and slid her palm inside, though, he came too damned close to losing it to remain standing. Scooping her into his arms, he headed for the bedroom. The sand-colored walls, prints of Apaches mounted on tough little mustangs, and incredible vista of lake and mountains alive with color imprinted on a small corner of his mind. A *very* small corner! The rest was filled with Kate. Gorgeous, sensuous, Kissable Kate.

She stretched like a cat on the luxurious down comforter. Her smooth, sexy curves made Dave's throat go tight. While he peeled off the rest of his clothes, she wiggled out of her bra and panties. Her glance measured his length, smiling at first, then with a greedy hunger that fed Dave's own. Rock hard and aching, he joined her on the bed and gathered her under him. His knee had wedged between hers before he remembered the damned sack.

"Hell!" He rolled off the bed in one lithe movement. "I'll be right back. Don't move."

Yeah, right! Kate thought wryly. As if she could! Her heart hammered so hard against her chest she could hardly breathe, and everything from her waist down felt hot and liquid. She had a moment, only a moment, to wonder if she was crazy for tumbling into bed with a man who'd told her straight out he wasn't interested in any long-term relationships, before Dave was back with a full box of condoms. Kate's doubts disappeared on a gurgle of laughter.

"You don't really think we're going to need all those, do you?"

"A guy can only hope."

Opening the box, he dumped the contents on the bedside table. She was still chuckling when he rejoined her in bed. She welcomed him into her arms eagerly, hungrily, and into her body with a gasp of sheer delight.

Kate wasn't prepared for the intensity of the fire he stoked within her. He used his teeth and tongue and hard, driving body with a skill that soon had her writhing. The sensations piled one on top of each other, tight, hot, swirling. They came so fast and hard, Kate groaned out a warning.

"Dave! I can't…hold on!"

"So don't."

He flexed his thighs. His muscles in his back and butt went tight under her frantic fingers. Gasping, Kate tried to contain the wild sensations.

"I don't…want it to end…yet."

He lifted his head. His blue eyes held a wicked glint. "Oh, sweetheart, it's just beginning. I swore I'd pay you back for every jolt and sickening drop you put me through, remember? This is just payback number one."

He flexed again, the sensations exploded, and Kate lurched almost out of her skin.

After that first frenetic coupling and several more not quite as fast but just as furious, they came up for air long enough to order a late dinner from room service.

Dave hit the showers while waiting for the delivery. Kate took her turn next and made good use of the toothbrush he'd purchased for her. Luckily, she had a comb in her purse to drag through her tangled hair. Wrapped in one of the inn's luxurious terry-cloth robes, she joined Dave at the table beside the tall windows for a feast of crusty bread, crisp salad and mountain trout crusted with piñon nuts. A million stars glittered in the black-velvet sky outside, but Kate's mind wasn't on the spectacular nightscape. It was focused completely on the man across the table.

"Tell me more about your family," she asked him between bites. "Do you have any sisters or brothers besides the one you told me about?"

"Nope. There's just Ryan and me. Our folks died some years ago. How about you?"

"Both parents and three grandparents alive and well, along with three brothers, one sister."

"Are they all as good at what they do as you are?"

"Better," she said with a smile, thinking of all the support and encouragement her large, gregarious family gave each other. "My grandmother breeds and shows champion collies. My sister, Dawn, won a bronze in the Pan-American Games as a marathon runner and now coordinates the Special Olympics for a five-state region. One of my brothers is a fireman, another is on the pro tennis circuit. Josh, the baby of the family, is still in college. On a golf scholarship, I might add. I haven't beat him since his junior-high days, the stinker."

"So that's where you get it."

"Get what?"

"That mile-wide competitive streak. It's in your genes."

"Yes, it is."

She hesitated, reluctant to admit even now how much her inbred competitive spirit had played in the demise of her marriage.

"I tried to change," she confessed after a moment. "John—my former husband—interpreted my ambition and desire to excel as some sort of challenge to his masculinity. But the more I tried to hold back and suppress my natural instincts, the more I began to resent him for *wanting* me to hold back. There were other factors involved, of course."

Like a nineteen-year-old blonde, Kate thought sardonically.

"But the bottom line was he just didn't like being beat," Dave finished for her.

"That's about it." Kate laid down her fork. "Neither do you, or so you say. Yet every contest we've had so far has ended in a tie. Was that by chance or design?"

"You want the truth?"

"I asked, didn't I?"

"When we raced that first morning, I held back a little. *Only* because I was worried about your ankle," he added when Kate bristled. "I just about bust a gut trying to catch up to you the second time we raced."

That made her feel a little better.

"What about the putt you missed today?"

His mouth curved. "You didn't hear the four-letter words bouncing around inside my head after that stroke."

She tapped her fork against her plate, wanting to believe him. After her experience with John, she *needed* to believe him. There was no way she could change her basic personality and it was becoming increasingly important Dave know that right up front.

She was pushing a last, slippery little piñon seed around her plate when it occurred to her Dave couldn't change his basic personality, either. With a suddenly sinking feeling, she remembered her conversation with the weather officer at Luke.

"What about that?" she asked him, waving her fork at the rumpled bed. "How much of what just happened here is a game to you? One with tactical and strategic moves?"

"Oh, babe! All of it."

Grinning, he pushed out of his chair and came around the table. A tug on the knotted tie of her robe brought Kate to her feet.

"I started scheming ways to finesse you into bed three and a half seconds after I spotted that turquoise spandex coming at me out of the dawn."

"Why am I not surprised?" Kate drawled.

"You shouldn't be." Unrepentant, he dropped a kiss in the warm V between her neck and shoulder. "You, Lieutenant Commander Hargrave, are eminently finessable."

"Is that supposed to be a compliment?"

"Of the highest order," Dave assured her solemnly, his fingers busy with the knot at her waist. The ties gave, and he slid his hands inside the folds to stroke the long, smooth curve from ribs to hips.

"Now, about dessert..."

"Yes?"

"I was thinking of something hot and sweet."

Very hot and very sweet, he thought, his gut tightening as he slid his hand to the fiery curls at the juncture of her thighs. Slowly, he went down on one knee.

Kate woke to dazzling sunlight and the sound of running water. She rolled onto her side and watched Dave slide a plastic razor through the lather covering his cheeks with sure, clean strokes.

He must have taken another shower. The tawny gold of his hair was still damp and water drops glistened on his bare back above the waistband of his jeans. Kate swallowed a sigh as her glance lingered on his perfect symmetry. Broad, muscled shoulders. A nice lean waist. That tight butt.

No doubt about it. The man was beautiful.

He was also, she reminded herself, taking a new vehicle into the sky for the first time tomorrow. A shadow seemed to cloud the sun as she thought about the two Pegasus prototypes that had crashed and burned. The pilot had been killed in the first one. The crew had survived the second, but sustained severe burns.

Kate had lost friends and associates to the vicious weather they routinely flew into. In her line of business, the risks were as great as the rewards. Yet the thought of Dave battling a violent wind shear or an engine stuck in half-tilt position made her feel sick.

She managed a smile, though, when he caught her watching in the mirror. You didn't talk about the odds. You just lived with them. Toweling his face, he strolled into the bedroom.

"We slept right through our tee time this morning."

"Did we?"

Kate couldn't get excited about missing a rematch on the links. She'd stretched every muscle and tendon in her body last night, and then some. In fact, she wasn't sure she had enough strength to make it to the bathroom.

"We did," he confirmed, hitching a hip onto the side of the bed. "We also missed breakfast and lunch."

"Lunch?" Struggling up, Kate pushed the hair from her eyes. "What time is it?"

"Almost one."

"One?" she echoed incredulously. "As in p.m.?"

"As in p.m."

"Good grief!"

"Not to worry. I called down and arranged a late check-out." He waggled his eyebrows in an exaggerated leer. "So what do you want to do until two?"

"Well…"

By the time they finally abandoned their room and grabbed a late lunch in the hotel's dining room, it was after three. Yet Dave didn't seem any more anxious to end their stolen hours of freedom than Kate.

She'd checked in with her roommates by cell phone. Twice. Jill had already pinpointed their location via the tracking devices embedded in the IDs issued to both Kate and Dave, so there wasn't any use trying to deny they'd spent the night together. Promising to fill her and Caroline in later, Kate confirmed Captain Westfall hadn't returned from D.C. yet and hung up.

With no briefings or meetings pulling at them, she and Dave decided to take the slow way back to the site. From Ruidoso they headed south toward

Cloudcroft. En route, the road meandered through the high mountain ridges and produced spectacular color at every turn. To Kate's delight, it also produced a turnoff for Sunspot.

"Who or what is Sunspot?" Dave asked.

"It's the home of the National Solar Observatory. *The* premier research facility for solar phenomena in the country. I've been wanting to visit for years."

She took a quick look at her watch, another at the mile indicator on the signpost, and calculated they could squeeze in a quick visit.

"Think they're open this late on a Sunday afternoon?"

"Not to the general public, maybe. But I've done some work with the observatory's director. If I drop his name a few times, maybe they'll let us poke around."

The sixteen-mile drive up to the observatory took a half hour and climbed over four thousand feet. Considering they were already at five thousand, Kate felt as though they'd reached the top of the world when they arrived at the cluster of buildings that constituted Sunspot, New Mexico. There was no restaurant, no grocery store, no services of any kind, so she could only hope the pickup had enough gas in it to get them back down the winding twists and turns.

What Sunspot did have, though, was a searingly blue New Mexico sky known for its clarity and transparency. For this reason, the U.S. Air Force had asked Harvard University to design a geophysics center on the site back in 1948 to observe solar activity. They started with a six-inch telescope housed in a metal grain bin ordered from Sears Roebuck. The site had since developed into a complex that included two forty-centimeter coronagraphs, high-tech spectrographs to measure light wavelengths and the Richard B. Dunn Solar Telescope—an instrument that was thirty stories tall and weighed some two hundred and fifty tons.

Kate couldn't wait to see it. Being able to show Dave some of her world was an added excitement.

"Park there by the gate," she instructed. "Let's go name-drop."

As it turned out, the only name Kate had to drop was her own. The director wasn't available, but his deputy happened to be on-site and came personally to escort her. Fence-pole thin and tanned to leather by the high altitude and thin air, the scientist pumped her hand.

"Dr. Hargrave! I'm Stu Petrie. This is an unexpected pleasure. I read your paper on the effects of ionization on water droplets spun up into the atmosphere by hurricane-force winds. *Most* impressive."

"Thank you. This is Captain Dave Scott, United States Air Force."

The deputy greeted Dave with a polite nod, but it was clear his interest was in Kate. So was Dave's, for that matter.

"Are you here on business? I didn't see a request from NOAA to use the facilities, but maybe it hasn't reached my desk yet. Sometimes the paperwork takes weeks to process."

"No, this is strictly spur of the moment. Dave and I were driving down from Ruidoso and saw the sign for the observatory. I couldn't resist taking a quick peek."

"We can do better than a peek. Please, let me give you a guided tour."

Dave's travels had afforded him the opportunity to view a good number of the world's marvels, both ancient and modern. The Dunn Telescope certainly qualified as the latter. The telescope's upper portion was housed in a tall, white tower that rose some thirteen stories into the air. The lower portion lay underground. The entire instrument was suspended from the top of the tower by a mercury-float bearing. The bearing in turn hung by three bolts, each only a couple of inches in diameter. Thinking about those nine meager inches didn't make Dave feel exactly comfortable when he followed the two scientists out onto the observing platform.

"The telescope is set to look at the quiet side of the sun right now," Petrie said apologetically as Kate peered through its viewer. Dave took a turn and saw a dull gray ball.

"We use a monochrome camera to record the video image," Petrie explained. "This one is being taken in hydrogen alpha light, at about sixty-five hundred angstroms."

"Right."

Thankfully, Kate drew the scientist's attention with a comment. "You must use an electronic CCD to record the color images captured by your spectrographs."

"We do. With the Echelle Spectrograph we can measure two or more wavelengths simultaneously, even if they're far apart on the spectrum. We can also conduct near-ultraviolet and near-infrared observations."

Like most pilots, Dave had studied enough astrophysics to follow the conversation for the first few minutes. He knew near-ultraviolet and near-infrared light were just outside the visible range. After that, the two scientists left him in a cloud of dust.

He trailed along behind them, as fascinated by Kate's excitement and animated gestures as by her seemingly inexhaustible knowledge. She wasn't wearing a trace of makeup. She'd caught her hair back with a rubber band she'd snagged from the reservations clerk on the way out. Her knit shirt showed more than a few wrinkles from lying where Dave had tossed it the night before. She looked nothing like the spit-and-polish officer he'd worked with at the site. Even less like the runner in tight spandex.

Strange. Dave wouldn't have imagined she could

replace either image in his mind, but her lively questions and the impatient way she tucked a loose strand behind her ear gave him a kick to the gut. Not as big a kick as Kate all naked and flushed from his lovemaking, of course. But close.

Busy studying her profile, Dave missed the comment that drew her auburn eyebrows into a quick, slashing frown.

"How much activity?" she asked Petrie.

They were talking about sunspots, Dave realized after a moment. The real thing, not the town. Evidently the folks at the observatory had recorded a buildup of energy in the sun's magnetic fields.

"There's definitely potential for eruptive phenomena."

That sounded serious enough for Dave to display his ignorance. "What's going to erupt where?"

Stu Petrie gave him the high school version. "Sunspots occur when the magnetic fields on the sun start to twist and turn. This movement generates tremendous energy, which is often released in a sudden solar flare."

"How much energy are we talking about?"

"Roughly the equivalent of a million hundred-megaton hydrogen bombs all exploding at once. The radiation is emitted across virtually the entire electromagnetic spectrum, from radio waves at the long-wavelength end to optical omissions to X ray and gamma rays at the short-wavelength end. Given their tremendous speed, these waves can reach the earth in as little as eight minutes after a major flare and produce some very spectacular results."

"Like the lights of the aurora borealis," Dave finished, feeling somewhat redeemed. Maybe he hadn't forgotten everything he'd learned about astrophysics after all.

"Solar flares can cause more than just lights in the sky," Kate put in, giving him a severe reality check. "They can knock out power and fry electronics. In 1985, a flare blacked out Quebec. Another flare in 1998 knocked out the Galaxy 4 satellite and interrupted telephone pager service to some forty-five million customers."

That caught Dave's attention. He was only hours away from going up in an aircraft crammed with the most sophisticated electronic circuitry yet devised. He wasn't real anxious for it to get fried while he was in the air.

"So, Doc," he asked Stu. "What's the prognosis on this activity you're talking about?"

"We don't feel there's any cause for alarm at this point, but we're watching the energy buildup. Closely."

"So will I," Kate muttered under her breath.

She left the National Solar Observatory considerably less relaxed than when she'd arrived. Her day didn't totally turn to crap, however, until Dave stopped to gas up in Chorro.

Chapter 7

"**B**e right back," Kate said as Dave inserted his credit card into a gas pump. "I need to hit the ladies' room."

Busy squinting at the buttons in the dim glow cast by the moth-speckled overhead light, Dave nodded. Dusk had fallen while they were still on the narrow winding road down from the observatory, followed by one of New Mexico's clear, star-studded nights.

A glimpse of the gas station's single, dingy rest room had Kate opting for the restaurant across the street. As she pushed through the doors of the Cactus Café, Bar and Superette, she was still mulling over her conversation with Stu Petrie. Solar flares were a common enough occurrence. Nothing to become unduly alarmed about unless they gathered intensity and erupted with enough force to send huge pulses of energy hurtling through space. Then it was anyone's guess how much, if any, havoc the flares could wreak.

She'd stay in close contact with the National Solar Observatory over the next few days, Kate decided as she wove a path through the tables. Check their Web site regularly, just to see what was happening with those flares. That way she could...

"Hey!"

Jerked out of her thoughts, Kate turned to face a woman in tight black jeans, a puckered chambray top that left most of her midriff bare and dangling silver earrings. She held a plastic pitcher of iced tea in one fist. The other was planted on her hip.

"Did you just climb out of the pickup across the street?" the waitress asked Kate.

"Yes, I did. Why?"

The woman's glance flicked to Kate's left hand, noted the lack of rings, then shifted to the café's front window. It gave a clear view of the man at the pumps.

"I, uh, know the driver."

"Do you?"

"He stopped by the café a week or so ago. We hit it off, if you know what I mean."

Kate felt her limbs stiffen one by one. "I'm getting the picture."

"He had to leave early the next morning, said he

was late for some business meeting. He promised he'd call me. Never did, though." She shook her head, smiling despite her obvious disappointment that Dave hadn't followed through. "That was some night, I can tell you."

"Yes, I'm sure it was."

The waitress—Alma according to her name tag—heaved a long sigh. "Oh, well, maybe you'll have more luck with him than I did. The handsome ones are always the hardest to bring to heel."

"That's what I hear. Where's the ladies' room?"

"Back of the café and to your left."

"Thanks."

Kate kept a tight smile on her face until she gained the privacy of the one-stall rest room. Slamming the bolt, she propped both hands on the chipped porcelain sink and let the idiot in the mirror have it.

"You dope! You almost fell for the guy. Him and his macho, do-it-till-we-get-it-right attitude in the simulator. And those morning runs! You let him invade your space, your solitude and your head."

The eyes staring back at her from the mirror blazed with scorn.

"You are *so* pathetic, Hargrave. He told you right up front he wasn't interested in long-term commitments. Hell, last night he admitted that he'd been scheming to get you into bed since day one, that it's all a game to him."

He couldn't have laid things out any plainer! Yet just this morning Kate had gotten all warm and gooey inside and started thinking maybe, just maybe, she might have something going here.

"For a supposedly intelligent woman," she said in total disgust, "you sure don't display many smarts when it comes to men."

Furious with herself, Kate twisted the cold tap to full blast and splashed her face. The shock of the icy water and a thorough drying with rough paper towels went a long way to restoring her equilibrium. Forcing herself to get a grip, she leaned on the sink once more and lectured the face in the mirror.

"What the heck are you so mad about, anyway? You got off-site for a couple days. Shot a great round of golf. Indulged in some world-class sex. No promises of undying devotion were given or received, so there's no harm, no foul. On either side," she said sternly. "Now it's back to business. Strictly business. Got that?"

Okay! All right! She got it.

She jerked the bolt and started to march out, but remembered her original purpose for exiting the pickup. Locking the door again, she hit the stall.

Alma was behind the counter in the café when Kate sailed through. The waitress popped her gum and flashed a rueful grin.

"Good luck, honey."

Kate didn't need luck. She had her head back on straight. But she returned the smile.

"Thanks. How about two cups of coffee to go?"

"You got 'em."

Dave was just finishing at the pump when she stepped outside.

"I brought you some coffee," Kate said, proud of her nonchalance

"Thanks." He took the cup she offered and downed a cautious sip. "Sure you don't want to grab something to eat?"

And have Alma wait on them? Hardly!

"We'd better get back to the site. Last time I talked to Jill, they had an ETA of twenty-one-hundred for Captain Westfall. If we push it, we can beat him back."

Taking care not to splash the hot coffee, Kate reclaimed her seat. Dave did the same.

"Jill didn't indicate the old man wanted to brief us tonight, did she?"

"No."

"Then what's the hurry? We've still got our toothbrushes and a few emergency supplies."

The crooked grin didn't work this time. If anything, it grated on Kate's nerves like fingernails scraping down a blackboard.

"There's a motel down the road a bit," Dave added while she fought to hang on to her temper. "Nothing special like the Inn of the Mountain Gods, but clean and handy."

She just bet it was. No doubt Dave and Alma had made good use of it. Somehow, Kate managed to infuse her voice with just the right touch of amusement.

"Look, cowboy. This was fun, but playtime is over. It's time to get back to work."

"Fun?"

"Hey," she tossed off with a shrug, "fun is a big step up from nice. Let's go, Scott. It's getting late, I'm tired, and we both need to log in a good night's sleep before the flight tomorrow."

His eyes narrowed, but Kate was past caring. Her nonchalance meter had pegged out. Thankfully, he dropped the sexy, bantering tone and shoved the key in the ignition.

"Yes, *ma'am*."

She wasn't up for any more talk. Reaching out, she flicked the switch on the CD player.

They passed through the last checkpoint a little before 9:00 p.m. Kate shoved her ID back in her pocket and waited impatiently until Dave pulled up outside her quarters. The squat, square modular unit had never looked so good. She reached for the handle and was out of the pickup before Dave had killed the engine.

"I'll see you tomorrow," she said. "Thanks for… for everything."

That was lame. Really lame. But the best she could do at the moment.

Evidently Dave shared the same opinion. His door slammed shut a half second after hers. Stalking around the front of the truck, he intercepted her straight path to her quarters.

"What the hell's going on here?"

She had her answer ready. She'd been working on it all the way in from Chorro.

"Nothing's going on here. Nothing *will* go on here. We're back on-site. We declared this a no-fly zone, remember?"

"Sure felt like we made some changes to the rules last night."

"Last night we were off base," Kate said stubbornly. "We'd been ordered to relax, relieve some stress. We're back now and—"

"Relieve some stress!" he interrupted, his eyebrows snapping into a scowl. "Is that what you thought we were doing?"

His apparent anger surprised her. She would have guessed Dave Scott would be the first to argue that sex was the perfect antidote for everything. She couldn't resist getting a little of her own back.

"Come on, Scott. You have to admit you're a whole lot looser than when you left yesterday."

"I was," he retorted. "That looseness seems to have dissipated in the last half hour or so."

Feeling considerably better than when she'd walked out of the Cactus Café, Kate smiled. "Sounds like you've got a problem, cowboy. See you tomorrow."

Dave had a problem, all right. It was sashaying away from him at the moment. Folding his arms, he propped his hips against the fender of his pickup and tried to figure out what the heck just happened.

Kate couldn't be serious about this "not-on-site" stuff. Not after last night. Not to mention this morning. The mere memory of her smooth, slick skin and smoky taste had his throat going tight.

He was as serious about the mission as the next guy. More so. He was the one who'd put his life on the line when Pegasus lifted off, for Pete's sake. So where did Kate get off suggesting he was such a jerk he couldn't concentrate on her *and* on the mission at the same time?

And why did he want to?

That last thought brought him up short. Frowning, he stared at the door Kate had just disappeared through. Okay, they'd had some great sex. Better than great. He got a hitch in his breath just thinking about it. But the lady had made her druthers clear and Dave didn't usually push so hard or so long after being waved off.

Still frowning, he shoved away from the fender and headed for his own quarters.

"Please tell me it was awful," Cari begged as Kate dropped onto the sofa. "I've already wormed a report out of Jill and I'm not sure I can take being the only sex-starved female officer on-site. Tell me Scott's only so-so in bed."

"Scott is excellent in bed. He's also a total jerk. No, that's not right. I'm the jerk."

Obviously that wasn't the answer Cari expected.

Blinking, the Coast Guard officer laid aside her dog-eared paperback. "What happened?"

Kate blew out a long breath. "We drove up to Ruidoso, played some golf, hit the sack."

"And the problem with that sequence of events is…?"

"There wasn't any problem," Kate admitted wryly, "until we stopped for gas on the way back and I bumped into Dave's little bit of 'personal business.' The one who caused him to call in and delay his arrival on-site," she added at Cari's puzzled look.

"Uh-oh."

"Right. Uh-oh."

The brunette bit her lip. She knew Kate had good reason to be wary of too-handsome, love-'em-and-leave-'em types like Dave Scott. Still, anyone standing within fifty yards of the weather officer and the sky jock had felt the heat from the sparks they'd been striking off each other since the first day Scott appeared on the scene.

"In all fairness," she pointed out, "Dave obviously met that little bit of personal business, as you term her, before he met you."

"True."

"And he hasn't been off-site since he got here— except with you."

"Also true."

"So why do you think you're a jerk for having a nice steamy weekend fling with the guy?"

When her roommate didn't answer right away,

Cari's eyes widened. "We *are* talking just a weekend fling, aren't we?"

"Of course we are. I guess."

"Kate!"

"I know, I know! It's just… Well, for a crazy moment or two I was starting to think it might be something more. Stupid, huh?"

"Not necessarily," Cari countered, recovering from her surprise.

"Yes, it was. *Very* stupid. We'll only be here for another month at most, after which we'll all return to our respective units."

"So you go back to MacDill and Dave returns to Hurlburt. The two bases are both in the Florida panhandle, not more than a hundred or so miles apart."

"A hundred miles is a hundred miles," Kate said doggedly. "I learned the hard way that long-distance relationships don't work. Not for me, anyway. Besides which," she added with a shrug, "Dave made it clear his first or second day on-site he's not in the market for anything long term."

"He did?"

"He did."

Kate's ready sense of humor inched its way through the funk that had gripped her since her encounter with Alma.

"We got in one heck of a round of golf, though. I have to admit the man has a great swing."

"I'll bet."

"Oh, and we stopped at the National Solar Observatory on the way back."

"Golf, sex *and* the National Solar Observatory." Cari rolled her eyes. "What more could a girl ask for?"

Her amusement disappeared when Kate related the news about possible solar-flare activity. Having spent most of her career on the water, the Coast Guard officer had learned to pay serious attention to any unusual weather activity.

They were still discussing the potential impact on the Pegasus test program when Jill returned from one of the perimeter checks she ran at random times.

"Hey, you finally made it back," she said to Kate. "How was your, uh, golf game?"

"Terrific. How was yours?"

"Terrific," Jill replied, laughing. Tossing aside her fatigue cap, she raked her fingers through her blunt-cut collar-length hair. "So? What's the scoop? Is Dave Scott as good with his hands out of the simulator as he is in it?"

"Better. As I was just telling Cari."

Kate lifted her arms in a lazy stretch. She was fine now, over her brief spate of lunacy. She'd let down her guard for a few hours and Alma had jerked it back up. She owed the woman for that.

"And as I told Dave a few minutes ago," she continued, "the weekend was fun. But now it's over and we both need to concentrate on more important matters."

Jill's eyebrows soared. "Fun? You told him it was fun? How did our hotshot pilot take that?"

Not as well as Kate had expected, surprisingly. She supposed she could have phrased things a little more politely, but she'd been in no mood to stroke the man's ego at that point.

"He took it," she said dismissively, and deliberately changed the subject. "Did Captain Westfall get back?"

"He's twenty minutes out," Jill confirmed. "Rattlesnake Control just notified me. They also relayed a message from the boss. He wants the senior test-cadre personnel to convene at his quarters as soon as he touches down."

"Any idea why?"

"Not a clue. I've already notified Russ McIver. He'll pass the word to Dave. Consider this your official notification."

Kate surged off the couch. "I better scrub away some of this road dust and get into my uniform."

Cari was right behind her. They took turns in the tiny, closet-size bathroom and bumped elbows squeezing past each other in the narrow hall. Brushed, buffed and uniformed, they were ready when Rattlesnake Control confirmed the captain had returned to the site.

The three women walked the short distance to the captain's quarters. Dave and Russ were already there, along with the senior civilian test engineers. Kate gave the men a friendly smile, Dave included. He returned it, but a crease formed between his eyebrows and stayed there until Captain Westfall called the impromptu meeting to order.

"The good news is that the Joint Chiefs are pleased with the way we've gotten the Pegasus test schedule back on track. I told General Bates that was due in large part to your skill, Captain Scott."

Dave took the news that Captain Westfall and the air force's top-ranking four-star general had discussed his abilities with a nod.

"General Bates suggested our progress probably had more to do with your tenacity than your expertise," Westfall added, his gray eyes glinting. "He had a few words to say about your insistence on doing a task again and again until it gets done right."

"I was in the left seat when he took the Osprey up for the first time," Dave explained with a grin. "I failed him—on that check ride and the next."

"So he indicated."

Sobering, Westfall glanced around the group. They'd formed a tight bond, officers and civilians alike. Some tighter than others, he suspected. Normally he wouldn't tolerate fraternization within the ranks, but this small test cadre represented a unique set of circumstances. Although the six uniformed officers had chopped to him for the duration of the Pegasus project, they still reported to their respective services. More to the point, they were all experts in their fields. Each of them was vital to a project that had just jumped the tracks from fast to urgent.

"The bad news is that all hell is about to break loose in Caribe."

"Again?" Russ McIver shook his head. "The island has gone through three coups in two years, each one bloodier than the last. I thought the U.S. had poured enough money and troops into the area to keep this president in office for more than a few months."

"That's the problem. We poured in too many troops, some of whom are now needed on the other side of the globe. The Pentagon intends to withdraw elements of the 101st and the 2nd Marine MAF. They also want to speed up the air and sea trials of Pegasus. The thinking is that Pegasus would make a perfect insertion vehicle if it becomes necessary to go back into Caribe in a hurry."

"No problem with the sea trials, sir," Caroline said firmly. "I'll take a look at the test schedule and see what runs we can shave off."

"Good. Captain Scott?"

"Pegasus is ready to fly, sir. So am I. We'll test our wings tomorrow."

Chapter 8

Pegasus took to the sky like the mythical winged steed it was named for.

Two chase vehicles accompanied it. The first was the site's helo. Painted in desert colors, the chopper hovered like an anxious brown hen while Pegasus rose slowly from the desert floor. Russ McIver viewed the prototype's ascent from the chopper's cockpit.

"We've got you at fifty feet, Pegasus One. Seventy. One hundred."

"Confirming one hundred feet, Chase One."

His hands and feet working the controls, Dave held the hover. Sand blew up from the rotors' downwash and obliterated any view outside the cockpit windows, but he kept his gaze locked on the instruments and ignored the whirlwind.

Like the tilt-winged Osprey that was its predecessor, Pegasus was designed to lift off from small, unimproved patches of dirt, fly long and hard, and drop down in another small patch. Dave maintained the hover for a good ten minutes before taking the craft back down. Foot by foot, inch by inch, with the desert sand whirling in a mad vortex until the wide track tires just kissed the dirt.

After three more touch and go's, he was ready to switch to cruise mode. He brought the vehicle back up to a hundred feet, retracted the wheels into the belly of the craft, and ran through a mental checklist before sucking in a deep breath.

"Pegasus One, preparing to tilt rotors."

"Roger, One."

At ten degrees tilt, the test vehicle still handled like a helicopter. Dave nosed it forward, added speed and increased the tilt. The craft bucked a bit at thirty degrees, then the blades on the two engines began slicing air horizontally instead of vertically. Dave pushed the throttles forward and Pegasus took the bit. Within moments he had gained both altitude and airspeed.

Chase One kept up with them for the first few miles. Chase Two took over as the chopper fell behind.

"Pegasus One, this is Chase Two. We've got you in sight. You're lookin' good."

The C-130 Hercules and its crew were detached from the 46th Test Operations Group at Holloman AFB, New Mexico. The highly instrumented aircraft had been designed for just this purpose—observing and testing the latest in sophisticated weaponry. Kate and a team of evaluators were on board to serve as observers for the long-distance portion of the flight. Straining against her shoulder harness, she peered over the flight engineer's shoulder at the sleek white vehicle streaking through the sky. The Herc's pilot kept Pegasus just off his left wing.

"Look at that baby move," she heard him comment to his copilot. "He's approaching a hundred and fifty knots and still piling on the airspeed."

Kate's heart stayed firmly lodged in her throat as Dave pushed Pegasus to perform at maximum capacity. Both the test vehicle and its chase plane reached two hundred knots, with the desert sliding by below them in a blur of silver and tan. Two-twenty. Two-thirty.

"Control, this is Pegasus One."

Dave's voice came through Kate's headset, cool and calm above the background static.

"I'm feeling a vibration in the right aft stabilizer area."

Test Control came on immediately. "Are you showing any system malfunction or warning lights?"

"Negative, Control."

"Is the vibration such that it could affect the structural integrity of the tail section?"

Kate held her breath. That was a judgment call, pure and simple. An educated guess based on the pilot's expertise and familiarity with his craft. A sick feeling gripped her as she remembered that one of the first two prototypes had gone down after a structural stress fracture almost took off a wing. She could hardly hear Dave's reply through the pounding of her heart.

"Negative, Control. He's giving me a bumpy ride, but not trying to buck me off."

"Copy that, Pegasus One. We recommend you decrease your airspeed to two hundred knots. Let us know if the vibration continues."

"Roger."

Kate strained forward. Her harness straps cut into her shoulders. A vein throbbed in her left temple. She counted the seconds until Dave came on again.

"Airspeed now at two hundred knots and I'm not feeling the tail shudder."

The controller didn't try to disguise his relief. "Roger that, Pegasus One. Recommend you keep the airspeed below two hundred for the duration of this flight."

"Will do."

Gulping, Kate tore her gaze from the vehicle across a stretch of blue sky and checked the Doppler radar screen. It showed clear, no sign of weather within the projected flight pattern, but she used the satellite frequency assigned to her to call for regular updates throughout Pegasus's first flight.

It lasted for one hour and seventeen seconds. Dave took the craft in a wide circle over the New Mexico desert, testing the flight-control systems at various altitudes. By the time he slowed the vehicle, rotated the engines from horizontal to vertical and set down in the same patch of dirt he'd lifted off from, Kate was a puddle of sweat inside her flight suit.

The C-130 landed at an airstrip bulldozed out of the desert specifically for the Pegasus tests. The crew piled out as soon as the pilot shut down his craft, then boarded the waiting shuttle to take them back to Test Operations for the mission debrief. There they congratulated a sweaty, grinning Dave Scott.

"Good ride, Captain." The C-130's pilot pumped his hand. "You really put that baby through his paces."

The navigator, who had evidently flown with Dave before, pounded him on the back. "Sierra Hotel, Scott."

Kate hid a smile at the aviators' universal shorthand for shit hot, but her congratulations were every bit as sincere.

"You did good, Captain."

"Thanks, Commander." The tanned skin beside his eyes crinkled. The glint in their blue depths was intended for her alone. "How about we get together later this evening and review the flight-test data?"

With the thrill of success still singing in her veins, Kate had to force herself to remember Alma. And Denise. And who knew how many other women this man had charmed with that same wicked glint. Keeping an easy smile on her face, she sidestepped the invitation.

"I have a feeling Captain Westfall will want to pore over every bit of data right here, right now."

She was right. They spent the next three hours reviewing every phase of the flight and analyzing instrument readings. Captain Westfall was particularly concerned about the vibration and asked the engineers to examine every inch of the tail section before the next flight, scheduled for the following Thursday.

That was only four days away. Barely enough time to make any changes or corrections in either the instrumentation or the body of the vehicle itself if necessary. Chewing on her lower lip, Kate gathered her stack of computer analyses and stuffed them in her three-ring binder for additional review tomorrow. From her experience during the land phase of testing, she knew the euphoria from the flight would have subsided by then and reality would set in with a vengeance.

Dave and Russ were the first to arrive at the picnic table later that evening. Jill Bradshaw soon joined them. She'd spent the day racing across the desert in a souped-up Humvee, directing ground security for the flight. If Pegasus had gone down, she and her troops would have had to secure the crash site immediately. She was still in uniform and her cheeks showed a flush of red sun and windburn below the white patches made by her goggles.

"You look like you could use a cool one," Russ commented, pulling a beer from the ice chest.

"I could. A *long* cool one." She took the dripping can, popped the top and clinked it against Dave's. "In all the hubbub this afternoon, I didn't get to offer my congrats. Good flight, Scott."

"Thanks."

Caroline Dunn joined the group a few moments later, followed in short order by Doc Richardson and Captain Westfall. Isolated by the responsibility of command, Westfall didn't often unbend enough to gather with his subordinates. Tonight marked a definite exception.

Gradually, the tension that had held Dave in its grip since early morning slid off his shoulders. Just as gradually, a different kind of tension took hold.

"Where's Kate?" he asked Cari during a lull in the conversation.

"At her computer. She said she wanted to review the latest reports from the solar observatory."

Dave nodded and tipped his beer, but it didn't go down with quite the same gusto as it had before. Nor could he shake the urge to slip away from the crowd, rap on Kate's door, and sweet-talk her into a private little victory celebration. He could almost feel her curves and valleys against his body. Taste her on his tongue. He didn't realize his fist had tightened around the beer until the can crumpled and slopped cold liquid over his hand.

"Damn!"

Laughing, Cari passed him a paper napkin. "Good thing your hand was steadier this morning."

He gave the Coast Guard officer a sheepish grin and was about to reply, when her cell phone buzzed. Everyone on-site had been issued special instruments that picked up the signals from their personal phones and relayed them through a series of secure networks to the test site. Friends and relatives could still keep in touch, but no one would find any record of calls made to or from this particular corner of New Mexico.

Flipping open the phone, Cari put it to her ear. "Lieutenant Dunn. Oh, hi, Jerry."

She listened a moment and a smile come into her eyes. "No kidding? I bet that was something to see."

Holding her hand over the mouthpiece, she excused herself from the group and walked a little way away.

"Jerry again," Jill muttered to Cody. "I wish the man would get a life."

Cody nodded. Russ McIver frowned into his beer. Obviously the only one in the dark, Dave voiced a question.

"Who's Jerry?"

"A navy JAG," Jill answered. "He calls Cari every few days."

Dave lifted an eyebrow. "Sounds serious."

"He'd like it to be."

"But?"

Jill hesitated, obviously reluctant to discuss her friend's personal life. Once again, Dave sensed he was still an outsider, that the rest of the group had yet to fully accept him into their tight little circle. It was left to Doc Richardson to fill in the gaps.

"Commander Wharton has three kids by an ex-wife. Evidently he has some reservations about starting another family while he's still on active duty."

Dave could understand that. He'd seen how tough it was for air force couples to juggle assignments and child care. Throwing long sea tours into the equation would make it even tougher.

Russ McIver voiced the same reservations. "The guy has a point. Be hard to raise kids with one parent at sea and the other deployed to a forward area."

"I've seen it done," Captain Westfall said calmly. "It takes a lot of compromise and a couple as devoted as they are determined."

Mac was too well trained to contradict his superior, but his disagreement showed on his face as he eyed the small, neat figure some yards away.

The gathering broke up soon after that. Still too hyped from his flight, Dave wasn't ready to hit the sack. The urge to rap on Kate's door and coax her out into the night was still with him. He managed to contain it with the knowledge he'd have her to himself tomorrow morning when they went for their run.

She didn't show.

Dave waited in the chilly dawn while reds and golds and pinks pinwheeled across the sky. Arms folded, hips propped against the fender of his pickup, he watched the glorious colors fade in the slowly brightening sun. They seemed to burn brighter and take longer to dissipate, just as the minutes seemed to drag by. Finally he shoved back the sleeve of his sweatshirt and checked his watch. If he pushed it, he'd have time to get in a quick five miles before breakfast and the round of postflight briefings scheduled for 0800.

He worked up a solid sweat and a fierce hunger on the punishing run. A dark V patch arrowed down the front of his shirt. His drawstring sweatpants felt damp at the small of his back. Swiping his forearm over his face, Dave made for the dining hall. He'd scarf up some of the cook's spicy Mexican scramble, hit the showers and track Kate down before the meeting to find out why she'd missed her run.

He didn't have to track far. She came out of the dining hall just as Dave was going in. He stopped, frowning as he took in the towel draped around the neck of her warm-up suit and the perspiration glistening on her cheeks and temples.

"What's going on? Did you change your exercise routine?"

"It's getting a little too cool in the mornings for me. I decided to use the treadmill in the gym instead."

"You could have told me about the change in plans. I waited a half hour for you."

"Sorry."

She looked anything but. Dave's jaw tightened. He had received his share of brush-offs, but none of them had left him both angry and frustrated. Kate was doing a helluva job at both.

"We need to talk about the other night," he told her brusquely.

"No, we don't."

"C'mon, Kate. I'm not buying this on-site, hands-off crap. What's the problem here?"

She opened her mouth, shut it, then tried again.

"The problem is me. I've discovered I can't combine fun and work without one slopping over into the other. So one has to give."

"When did you make this big discovery?"

"After talking to Alma."

"Who?"

She stared at him for long moments. "Never mind. She's not important. What's important is Pegasus. That's why we're here, Dave. And that's why the on-site, hands-off rule will stay in effect."

She issued the edict as if expecting him to snap to, whip up a salute and bark, "Yes, *ma'am!*"

Dave wasn't about to bark anything. Cocking his

head, he weighed his options and chose the one he suspected she would least expect.

"You don't have to cut out your morning run. I'll take mine in the evenings. In exchange, you stop treating me as though I'm some plebe at the academy who needs to be reminded of his purpose in life every hour on the hour."

Her startled expression had him shaking his head.

"It's called compromise, Hargrave. I give a little. You give a little. Before you know it, we've found a satisfactory solution to this problem we appear to have."

He left her at the door, feeling pretty smug. It was good to see *her* knocked off balance for a change. She'd sure as heck kept Dave flying a broken pattern almost from the day he'd arrived.

He didn't realize how broken until two nights later.

The compromise he'd proposed wasn't working. Not for him, anyway. He missed his early-morning runs with Kate and her collection of spandex. He even missed her officious tone when she'd tried to pull rank or put him in his place. All he got from the woman now were cool smiles and polite nods that left him edgy and frustrated and hungering for the fire he knew smoldered inside her.

It took a call from his brother to open his eyes to the truth. Like Caroline's JAG, Ryan was patched through a series of relay stations that gave him no clue where Dave was. Not that Ryan particularly cared. He was too used to his brother's nomadic lifestyle—and on this particular occasion too drunk—to question his whereabouts.

"Hey, bro," he got out, the slur thick and heavy. "I thought I'd better call you and give you the news."

Dave propped himself up on an elbow and squinted at the bedside clock: 2:30 a.m. New Mexico time. Four-thirty back in Pennsylvania. Alarm skittered along his nerves. Ryan drunk was a rare occurrence. Ryan drunk and out all night had never happened before. Not to Dave's knowledge.

"What news, Ry?"

"Jaci and me. We're calling it quits."

"Aw, hell!"

"That's what I said. Right before I walked out."

Ryan burped, thunked the phone against something and cursed.

"I couldn't take it anymore," he said a moment later. "I tried. The Lord knows, I tried."

"Yeah, you did. Where are you now?"

"I'm at my office."

It figured. Over the years Ryan's office had become more than a workplace or source of income. It had become his refuge, his retreat when the arguments got too heated and too hurtful. Struggling upright, Dave punched the pillow behind him and tried not to wince when a pitying whine crept into his brother's voice.

"I still love her. That's the rotten part. I can't imagine life without Jaci and the kids."

"So don't imagine it."

"Huh?"

"You're drunk, Ry. You need to sleep this off, then go home and talk to your wife. See if you can't work a compromise."

"What kind of compromise?"

"Hell, I don't know. Maybe if you spend a little less time at the office and a little more with Jaci and the kids, she'll get off your back some."

"Thass what she says."

Another morose silence descended, interspersed with some heavy breathing.

"Dave?"

"I'm here."

"I'm drunk. I'm going to sleep it off."

"Good idea."

"Dave?"

"What?"

"Have you ever wanted a woman so bad you ached with it?"

All the time, bro.

His brain formed the flip reply, but the words stuck in his throat. The truth came out of the darkness and hit him smack in the gut.

"As a matter of fact, Ry, I'm kind of in that situation now."

He waited for a response. All that came over the phone was a loud snore.

"Ry! Hey, Ryan!"

"Huh?"

"Hang up the phone, man. Then get some sleep and talk with Jaci in the morning."

"Yeah."

The receiver banged down. Wincing, Dave flipped his cell phone shut and dropped it on the bedside table. He took a long time going back to sleep. Worry for his brother was a habit that went deep. Ryan and Jaci had been going at each other for a long time. Dave only hoped they'd find a way to patch things up.

In the meantime, he had another problem to keep him awake. One that came packaged with flaming copper hair, a mouth made for kissing and a bone-deep stubborn streak.

Here, alone in the dark, Dave could admit the truth. He ached for Kate. Physically *and* mentally. The feeling was as unsettling as it was unfamiliar.

Hooking his hands behind his head, he stared up at the ceiling and tried to figure out when lust had slipped over into something deeper, something he wasn't quite ready to put a name to yet.

He couldn't pinpoint the exact moment, but to his surprise he suspected it had happened well before their weekend in Ruidoso. He'd wanted Kate in his bed, sure. He *still* wanted her in his bed. Looking back, though, he realized he'd come to crave her laughter and her company as much as her seriously gorgeous body.

The realization had him scowling up into the darkness. Okay, he wanted Kate. All of her. Like he'd never wanted another woman. The problem now was what the hell to do about it.

Chapter 9

Dave made his move the next evening.

The timing was iffy. The entire test cadre had been going full out for three days to analyze the data from the first flight and prepare for the second. The engineers hadn't been able to pinpoint what caused the vibration in the tail section. With the second flight scheduled for tomorrow afternoon, Dave had insisted on more hours in the simulator to practice emergency responses to possible structural failures. By the time he climbed out around six that evening, he felt as though he'd been ridden hard and put away wet.

A long shower and a hearty meal of steak and home fries revived him. So did the prospect of getting

Kate alone for an hour. He caught her on her way back to Test Operations. Unlike Dave, she was still in uniform. The sky blue of her zippered flight suit formed a perfect foil for the fire of her hair.

"I thought we were done for the day," he commented, falling in beside her.

"I thought so, too. But tomorrow's flight is going to take you into the mountains and I want to review the wind patterns one more time. I wouldn't want you to run into another katabatic wind," she added, her lips curving.

It was the first real smile Dave had received from her in days. He felt like a kid who'd just been handed a fistful of penny candy.

"Trust me, I have no desire to get hit with another whammy like that one. Think it's possible?"

"Highly unlikely. The air temperatures at the higher altitudes are dropping significantly, but there's no snow on the peaks yet. You could experience some severe downdrafts, though."

"I'm wondering if that's all I'll experience. Did you notice a greenish glow in the sky when you were running this morning?"

She threw him a sharp look. "No."

"I saw it last night while I was running along the perimeter road. It was hanging low in the northern sky. I just caught a glimpse of it through the peaks."

"What time was that?"

"About eight-forty."

Her eyebrows drew into a frown. "I didn't see any reports of unusual light patterns on the weather sites this morning."

"The glow only lasted for a short while, maybe two or three minutes."

Dave wasn't lying. Not exactly. He *had* noticed a dim glow, but it was more smoky than green. Anything could have caused it. A dust cloud thrown up by a passing vehicle. A low-hanging storm cloud scudding across the sky, lit from within by the moon. Given the recent reports of possible solar-flare activity, though, he'd figured Kate would want to check it out.

Sure enough, she took the bait. Still frowning, she checked her watch. "It's eight-fifteen now. Can you show me where you spotted this glow?"

"I'll get my truck and drive you out there. We should just make it."

The pickup jounced along the unmarked dirt track that served as the site's perimeter road. Dave checked the odometer, squinted at the dark shapes to the north and pulled over.

"This is about where I spotted the lights." Leaning across Kate, he pointed to the jagged ridgeline. "Over there, through those peaks."

She reached for the door handle, but Dave stilled her with a quick warning. "We'd better notify Security before we climb out. We're right on the perimeter.

Their sensors are probably already flashing red alert."

All it took was a quick press of one key on his specially configured cell phone to connect him with Security Control.

"This is Captain Scott. I'm out along the perimeter road, 3.2 miles into the northwest quadrant."

"We've got you on the screen, Captain Scott."

"Commander Hargrave is with me. We're going to step out of our vehicle."

"We'll track you. Watch where you walk. You don't want to put your boot down in a nest of diamondbacks."

Dave didn't take the warning lightly. He'd heard that one of Jill Bradshaw's cops had done exactly that before he'd arrived on-site.

Kate was doubly cautious. "I listened in via the radio net with the rest of the test cadre that night when Jill and Doc Richardson jumped a chopper and raced to the injured cop. That wasn't an experience I'd want to see repeated. We'd better not stray too far from the truck."

That suited Dave just fine.

"No problem. I'll just back it around and let down the tailgate. We can perch there while we wait for the show."

With the truck in position, he and Kate climbed out. They couldn't have asked for a better night for star watching. Above the black mass of the mountains, the sky was deep and dark. A couple of million stars shone with the brilliance only visible at these high altitudes. The nip in the night air had Dave reaching into the back seat for a worn leather bomber jacket. When he offered it to Kate, she declined.

"You'd better put it on. My flight suit will keep me warm."

When Dave lowered the tailgate, Kate propped her hips on the edge. He opted to stand and watch the northern sky for signs of unusual activity. The moments slid by with only the still, dark night around them. Kate checked her watch a couple of times. Dave couldn't tell from her expression whether she was relieved or disappointed that nothing happened.

"I got a call from my brother last night," he said after a while.

She angled her head around. "The one having problems with his marriage?"

"That's the one. Ryan said he and Jaci are calling it quits."

"Ouch." Her face softened in sympathy. "Been there, done that. It's not fun."

"Didn't sound like it from Ryan's perspective."

"What made him finally decide to walk?"

"I'm not sure. He was pretty drunk when he called. I couldn't get much out of him."

"You said they love each other despite their problems. Maybe they'll patch it up."

"Maybe." He hadn't forgotten her remark that love can sometimes hurt. "What about you? What made you decide to walk?"

Her mouth twisted into a rueful grimace. "A nineteen-year-old blonde. Evidently she was just what my ex needed to stroke his ego after the way I'd pounded it into the dust. His phrasing, not mine, by the way."

"In other words, he couldn't keep up with you on the golf course."

"Or off it." Her shoulders lifted under the blue Nomex of her flight suit. "Took me a while to stop feeling guilty about that."

"Is that why you skittered away from me after we got back from Ruidoso? You were afraid I couldn't keep up with you on or off the course?"

"I didn't skitter away. I merely redrew the lines we had already established."

"The lines *you* had established. I've been thinking about those."

He pushed away from the fender. A single step placed him in front of her. His hands slid up her arms, gliding over the smooth fabric of her flight suit. With a gentle tug, he pulled her to her feet.

"Dave, we agreed. Not on-site."

"Well, technically we're off-site. I angled the truck around. The tail end is sticking clear over the perimeter road."

Anger flared hot and quick in her eyes. Planting her palms flat on his chest, she stiff-armed him. "So this was all a ploy? A ruse to get me out here?"

"Partly. I did see a strange glow last night. I also

wanted to get you back on neutral ground, so we can rekindle the fires we lit last weekend."

"We can't." Jerking free of his loose grip, she folded her arms. "And even if we could, I don't want to compete with Denise and Alma."

"Denise I remember," Dave said, exasperated, "but only because you keep bringing her into the conversation. Who the heck is Alma?"

"She's a waitress at the Cactus Café. About five-five. Brown hair. Lots of mascara. Remember her?"

"Now I do," he replied with a sheepish grin.

Talk about ironic. Dave had been sure he'd never forget that wild night. Since tangling with Kate, though, he could barely remember his name at times, let alone his carefree days before he arrived on-site.

"Let me guess," he said wryly. "You bumped into Alma when we stopped to gas up in Chorro."

"Bingo."

"And she's the reason you've been giving me the deep freeze all week?"

Arms still folded, she tapped a foot and considered her answer. Dave had spent enough time with her by now to know she wouldn't dodge the issue.

"Alma is part of the reason," Kate admitted at last. "Only because she made me face up to hard, cold reality. The problem is it's impossible to keep personal feelings from slopping over into our professional situation. For me, anyway. The thought of being the latest in your string of weekend flings made me furious until—"

"I'm not keeping score," Dave interrupted dryly. "You can check my bedpost. You won't find any notches carved there."

"Until I realized I had no right to be angry," she finished firmly. "We had some fun, that's all. Neither one of us made any promises. I had no reason to feel hurt or jealous. More to the point, I don't *want* to feel hurt or jealous. Not again."

"I can't change the past, Kate. Nor am I going to apologize for it. But did it ever occur to you I might just be looking for the right woman?"

"You have my permission to keep looking, cowboy."

"Funny," Dave mused, "I wouldn't have pegged you as a coward."

Stiffening, she lifted her chin. Before she could lash out at him, he offered his own take on the situation.

"I don't think you're afraid of feeling hurt or jealous. You're afraid of failing. You like to win, Kate. You want to be the absolute best you can be at everything. Golf. Work. Marriage."

"And that's bad?"

"No. That's good. Very good. You go into everything heart first."

She was still stiff, still a little torqued at being called a coward. Smiling, Dave brushed a knuckle down her cheek.

"The problem is, there are no guarantees when it comes to this love business. Not for Ryan and Jaci. Not for us."

"Who's talking about love?"

"I am. I think."

At her look of astonishment, his smile took a lopsided tilt.

"I know. Half the time I'm convinced it's only plain old-fashioned lust. All I have to do is picture you in turquoise spandex and my throat goes bone dry. Then I watch you at work, see the sweat and long hours you put into this project, and lust gets all mixed up with admiration and respect and something I've had a hard time putting a name to."

"Dave, this is crazy. You can't… You don't…"

She stopped, drew in a slow breath, and adopted the gentle tone of a nurse addressing a seriously ill patient.

"Respect and admiration I appreciate. Lust I understand. I've felt more than a few twinges of all three myself where you're concerned. But love… Well…"

She glanced to the side, as if expecting the right words to materialize on the cool, crisp air.

"It's okay." A grin stole into his voice. "The idea kind of gives me goose bumps, too."

It gave Kate more than goose bumps. It shook her right down to her boot tops. She'd worked so hard at convincing herself she was just another trophy in his collection, that one torrid weekend defined the parameters of their relationship. It stunned her to hear his feelings went deeper. And that they had confused him as much as Kate's had confused her.

But love…

Her face must have expressed her welter of uncertainty, doubt and wariness. Chuckling, Dave stroked her cheek again with the back of a knuckle.

"I don't figure we'll sort this out tonight. Or next week. Let's just take it a step at a time. See where it goes."

"Where can it go?" Kate asked, echoing her conversation with Cari. "Once Pegasus proves his stuff, we all head back to our separate units. Unfortunately, I've discovered I'm not real good at long-distance relationships."

"So you stumbled once. You didn't win. Does that mean you won't ever get back in the race again?"

He knew what buttons to push, she thought ruefully. She hadn't liked being called a coward. Nor was it in her to run away and hide from a challenge. Particularly when the stakes were as high as these.

Could she love this man? Did she want to?

The answer was staring her right in the face.

"Okay," she conceded with something less than graciousness. "Consider me back in the race."

"Good." With a satisfied smile, he slid a palm around her nape. "Just to make it official, here's the starting gun."

"Hey!"

That one startled yelp was all she managed to get

out before his mouth came down on hers. He kissed her hard and long, apparently determined to make up the ground he'd lost over the past few days.

His taste and his tongue sent little sparks of pleasure through Kate, heating her skin as they traveled her length. Dave added to the sensations by tunneling one hand into her upswept hair, wrapping the other around her waist and bringing her hard against him.

She curled her fingers into the soft, worn leather covering his shoulders. Her head went back, her chin tilted to find just the right angle. Within moments, she was breathless. Moments more, and she had to drag in big gulps of air when Dave broke off the kiss. She was still gulping when he reached down, hooked an elbow under her knees and deposited her on the tailgate with a small thump.

His skin was stretched tight across his cheeks, and his wicked grin signaled his intent even before he reached for the zipper tab at the neck of her flight suit.

"Dave!" She grabbed his hands, stilling them. "This is your idea of taking it slow?"

"I didn't say slow. I said one step at a time. And this, my very Kissable Kate, is the next step."

He tugged free of her hold, got the zipper halfway down, and bent to nuzzle her breasts. The warm, damp wash of his breath came through her cotton T-shirt. Shivers rippled over every square centimeter of Kate's body. Sighing, she gave herself over to the pleasure.

Her sigh got stuck in her throat as he took little nips through the soft cotton. Pleasure gave way to hunger and Kate knew she was in trouble. But when he eased the fabric off one shoulder, common sense told her it was time to put the skids on. Unfortunately.

"Surely you're not thinking we'll get naked out here in the middle of nowhere, are you?"

"Oh, babe," he muttered against the curve of her shoulder, "I'm way past the point of being able to think."

"Dave! One of Jill's patrols could come cruising by at any moment."

"Nah." He nibbled his way back up to her throat. "I said a silent prayer to the mountain gods. Worked like a charm last time."

"Dave, we can't. It's too cold out here. And I want an official measurement. I'm not sure this truck bed is really over the perimeter line. We might have to—"

Suddenly, she went stiff. Her breath left on a gasp.

"Omigod! There it is!"

With his face buried in the silky skin of her neck and his senses already close to overload, it took Dave a second or two to realize she wasn't referring to a hidden sweet spot he'd triggered by accident.

"Look!" Kate exclaimed, thumping him on the back with a fist. "Over there! One o'clock high."

Swallowing a groan, Dave dragged his head up and threw a look over his shoulder at the faint green glow just visible between the peaks.

"Now it shows," he growled, not at all happy to have his reasons for driving Kate out into the desert vindicated. She, on the other hand, could hardly contain her excitement. Wiggling free of his hands, she yanked at her zipper.

"We've got to get back to the site. I need to access the solar observatory database, see if they're taking readings on this."

Regret knifed into Dave at the disappearance of her lush curves. Despite her desire to return to the base, though, she couldn't seem to tear herself away. She stood transfixed, her gaze locked on the distant haze. Dave guessed she was trying to calibrate the intensity of the light waves dancing in the atmosphere and causing those weird, moving shadows.

He had to admit they were pretty riveting. He'd pulled some temporary duty at Elmendorf AFB in Alaska, had been treated to the spectacle of the northern lights. These weren't anywhere near as intense, but they gave Dave some insight into why the rumor had persisted for so many years that aliens had landed near Roswell, New Mexico. Folks had probably spotted a green glow much like this one and let their fears prey on them. They wouldn't have had the benefit of scientific data regarding sunspots and magnetic energy and solar flares. Kate and Stu Petrie had treated Dave to an extended discourse on the phenomena, yet the dancing lights still sent prickles of unease down his spine.

"Do you think that eerie glow will impact tomorrow's flight?"

The casual question masked a dozen different concerns. That the team maintain the tight test schedule. That they wrap up the air portion and move on to the sea trials. That Pegasus get a chance to strut his stuff before being harnessed for plow duty in the trenches. If things turned sour down in Caribe, the Pentagon might have to move troops in and noncombatant civilians out pretty quick.

Kate gave the haze a final, frowning glance. "At this point, I can't say what the impact will be. All I can do is check the data and see if the observatory is projecting any significant activity in the earth's ionosphere. We don't want to take any chances with you or with Pegasus."

She started for the passenger door, stopped, and spun around. Grabbing his jacket collar, she yanked him down for a hard, fast kiss.

"Particularly with you, flyboy."

Chapter 10

Kate didn't sleep at all that night.

She spent hours hunched over her computer collecting reports from every possible source. The solar observatory in Sunspot had recorded an increase in ionization in the earth's upper atmosphere, but no disruption of satellite or radio communications as yet.

By morning, she was hungry, hollow-eyed and more nervous than she'd ever been before jumping aboard one of NOAA's planes to fly into the eye of a howling storm. She knew every piece of equipment aboard the specially modified P-3, knew just how it would respond when buffeted by hurricane-force winds.

In contrast, Dave was going up in a new vehicle with only one operational test flight to its credit. The contractor representatives were confident they'd shaken the bugs out of Pegasus during the research and development phase—particularly after analyzing the data from the loss of the first two prototypes and incorporating design changes. But there was a good reason why the military didn't accept ships or aircraft or other highly sophisticated weapons systems without extensive field tests. Real-world conditions too often caused failure of systems that operated flawlessly in a controlled R and D environment. And high-energy solar explosions were about as real world as it gets.

As a result, Kate approached the 8:00 a.m. pretest meeting with considerably less confidence than she had previous such meetings. She was one of the first to arrive at the small conference room in the Test Operations building. Depositing her laptop and stack of briefing books on the table, she nodded to Russ McIver.

"'Morning, Mac."

"Hi, Kate."

"Are you going to load Pegasus with the equivalent weight of a full squad this morning?"

"That's the plan. Any reason to change it?"

Kate bit her lip. Pegasus was designed to carry a maximum of twenty fully-equipped troops or their equivalent weight in cargo. This would be the first test of how the vehicle performed fully loaded.

"No," she said slowly, thinking of all the weight

and drag Dave would have to compensate for, "no reason to change it at this point."

The marine went back to flipping through the PowerPoint charts he'd prepared for the prebrief. Too restless to sit, Kate poured coffee into a mug emblazoned with the Pegasus test-cadre shield. Dave arrived a few minutes later and joined her at the pot.

"You look dead," he commented, eyeing her drawn face. "Gorgeous, but dead."

"Thanks."

By contrast, she thought wryly, he looked good enough to eat. His blond hair still gleamed from his morning shower, and his blue eyes showed none of the red tracks Kate's did.

"Did you get any sleep last night?" he asked her.

"Not much."

One corner of his mouth kicked up. "Me, neither. That bit of unfinished business we started out on the perimeter kept me tossing and turning all night. We *are* going to finish it, Hargrave."

Kate didn't argue. Sometime during the long hours of the night she'd accepted Dave's challenge. She was back in the race. Despite the tension that knotted the muscles at the base of her skull, she flashed him a ten-gigabyte smile.

"If you say so, Scott."

The rest of the cadre filed in, dumped their briefing books and hit the coffee. Everyone was in place when Captain Westfall arrived at precisely 0800. Chairs scraped back. Officers popped to attention. Even the civilians stood as a mark of respect for the naval officer whose drive and determination fed their own.

"Good morning, ladies and gentlemen. Take your seats, please."

After another shuffle, **an** expectant silence settled over the room. Westfall's glance moved around the U-shaped table and settled on Kate.

"Before we get into the actual mission prebrief, I've asked Commander Hargrave to give you an update on recent solar activity. We'll make the go/ no-go decision for today's flight after we hear what she has to tell us. Commander."

Kate took the floor. The data she'd pored over last night was pretty well burned into her brain. She could talk her subject from memory, but had prepared a computerized slide presentation for the test team's benefit. Her palm slick from a combination of worry and nerves, she pressed the remote. The first slide cut right to the heart of the matter. It showed a soft X-ray image of the sun's "busy" side, with swirls of black clearly visible against the brilliant red corona.

"The National Solar Observatory at Sunspot, just a little over a hundred miles from here, has been monitoring a buildup of energy in the sun's magnetic fields. This increase in energy could lead to a solar flare, such as the one shown on this slide. This particular flare is in what we call the precursor stage, where the release of magnetic energy has been triggered."

Kate hit the remote again and brought up another slide. In this one, the dark swirls all but obscured the red ball.

"In the second or impulsive stage, protons and electrons accelerate to high energy and are emitted as radio waves, hard X rays and gamma rays."

The next slide depicted a glowing red ball with only a few black swirls.

"In the final stage, we can measure the gradual buildup and decay of soft X rays. Each of these stages can last as little as a few seconds or as long as an hour."

She had their attention, Kate saw. Dave had received much of this information during their visit to the observatory. It was new stuff for the others.

"Solar flares are the most intense explosions in the solar system," she continued, bringing up the next slide. "The energy released may reach as high as ten-to-the-thirty-second-power ergs. That's ten million times greater than the energy released in a volcano, and we all know the devastation that resulted when Mount St. Helens erupted.

"The problem is when the intense radiation from a solar flare enters the earth's atmosphere. It can disrupt satellite transmissions, increase the drag on an orbiting vehicle and generally wreak havoc with anything electronic."

"Oh, great!"

The muttered exclamation came from Jill Bradshaw, but Kate saw the same concern reflected in every face at the table. A click of the remote brought up a bar graph charting the sun's magnetic-field activity for the past two decades.

"Solar flares generally occur in cycles," she informed her audience. "As you can see, 2000 and 2001 were peak years. This was predicted and planned for."

"Planned for how?" Russ McIver wanted to know.

"A 1998 flare knocked out the Galaxy 4 satellite and disrupted some eighty percent of commercial cell phone and pager use in the United States. As a result, military and civilian communications agencies took a hard look at systems dependent on satellite signals and built in more redundancy. For example, radio, television, bank transactions, newspapers, credit card systems and the like are now spread across a wider spectrum of low- to mid-altitude satellites. Some might get knocked out, but the others would be at different points in their orbit and be protected from the solar blast by the curvature of the earth."

Caroline Dunn sat forward in her chair. Her brown eyes grave, she studied the bar graph. "Looks like flare activity has been minimal since 2001. Are you saying there's a chance that could change in a hurry?"

"I'm saying there's a possibility," Kate replied carefully. She had to walk a fine line between predicting something that might not happen and minimizing the potential, only to have it blow up in her face. "Some of you may have noticed a green glow in the sky, similar to the northern lights only much less intense. It's caused by higher than normal ionization levels in the upper atmosphere."

"High enough to disrupt communications or interfere with the instrumentation on Pegasus?"

Kate answered Dave's question as truthfully as she could. "Not at present."

"But you're concerned another burst of ergs will come zinging my way?"

"Yes."

They were speaking one-to-one now. The others were still there, within their field of vision, but relegated to the background.

"Pegasus comes equipped with a lot of that redundancy you mentioned," Dave reminded her. "Backup communications, laser-guided navigational systems, fly-by-wire manual controls in the event of hydraulic failure."

"I know."

"There's also the fact I'm a test pilot. I've logged over a thousand hours in both fixed-wing and rotary-wing aircraft." His lips tipped into a grin. "I also survived almost every natural and unnatural disaster you threw at me during those hours in the simulator."

"It's the 'almost' part that worries me."

"That part worries us all," Captain Westfall

interjected dryly. "I need your best professional guesstimate, Commander Hargrave. On the basis of the data available to you at this point, do you recommend we press on with the mission or scrub it?"

Kate fingered the remote. She knew the situation in Caribe had added to pressure on the captain. On them all. She also knew how little room there was for a slip in the schedule even without the Pentagon's latest worries.

She had to accept the possibility that one of the swirling sunspots could generate enough energy to fry every circuit aboard Pegasus. There was also the chance Dave and his craft could wing across a clear blue sky.

She didn't look at Dave. This was her time in the box. Captain Westfall would ask for his input in a few minutes.

"Based on all data currently available, sir, I recommend we continue the mission. I'll monitor the situation continuously. If I receive any indication of increased solar activity, we can terminate immediately."

The naval officer accepted her judgment with a nod and turned to Dave.

"Captain Scott, you're in command on this mission. You've heard the risk assessment. You're also fully aware that you're taking up a craft that's still in the test stage. The call is yours."

"I understand, sir. Taking educated, calculated

risks is an inherent part of the test business. I agree with Commander Hargrave. As far as I'm concerned, the mission is a go."

A small silence gripped the room. Although Westfall had deferred to Dave, none of the officers present thought for a moment the captain couldn't—or wouldn't—pull rank and overrule the pilot if he so desired. Kate held her breath, half hoping he'd exercise that authority.

But when he stood and moved back to the podium, Westfall gave the green light. "Look sharp, people. We've got a mission to fly."

They finished the prebrief just before eleven. Pegasus was scheduled to fly at noon. Dave skipped lunch to conduct a final walk-around of his craft.

Kate found him in the hangar. He and the crew chief assigned to the craft were inspecting the tail section yet again. The engineers hadn't been able to determine the source of the vibration Dave had experienced on the first flight and Kate knew it worried him.

She stood beside a rack of equipment, waiting for them to finish. Her recommendation to proceed with the mission hung like a rock around her neck. It was the right recommendation given the available data, but if anything happened to Dave...

Her stomach lurched. A tight ball of fear lodged in the middle of her chest. The stark, unremitting fear forced her to admit what she'd tried so hard to deny these past weeks.

She'd fallen for the guy. Big-time. Despite her doubts. Despite Denise and Alma. Despite the need to focus strictly on the mission. Sometime between the moment she'd spotted the long rooster tail of dust churned up by his pickup the very first morning he arrived on-site and their soiree out under the stars last night, she'd tumbled smack into love.

And now Kate was about to send him up into a sky that could go supercharged with as little as eight minutes' warning.

Swallowing the acid taste of fear, Kate waited until he and the crew chief had finished with the tail section and had worked their way up to the nose. They had their heads buried in a tech manual when she stepped forward.

"Got a minute?"

His smile was quick and for her alone. "Sure."

She couldn't say what she wanted to in front of the mechanic or the rest of the hangar crew.

"I need to talk to you." Snagging the sleeve of his flight suit, she tugged him across the gleaming, white-painted floor. "In here."

"Here" was the men's room, the closest private spot in the huge hangar. Lifting an eyebrow, Dave followed Kate inside. Luckily, no one was at the circular urinal.

The latrine was as spotless as the rest of the hangar, but if Kate had had time, she would have chosen a better spot than a rest room smelling strongly of Lysol to let him know how she felt. The fact that time was fast ticking away made the place and the scent irrelevant.

"What's up?" Dave asked.

The smile was still in his eyes, but Kate sensed the edge behind the question. No doubt he thought she'd come to tell him the sun was still acting up and the mission had been scrubbed.

If only!

"I've been thinking about last night," she said slowly.

"That's funny. So have I." Reaching out, he snagged her waist and pulled her closer. "Finishing what we started out there under the stars tops my to-do list for after this mission. Unless…"

He skimmed a glance over his shoulder.

"We're in luck," he said with a hopeful waggle of his eyebrows. "The door locks."

"Cool your jets, cowboy. I didn't drag you in here to make mad, passionate love to you."

"Well, damn! And here I thought I was going to lift off with a smile on my face. Okay, I'll bite. Why did you drag me in here?"

"I wanted to tell you… That is…"

Even now it was hard for her to say the words. She was still confused by the feelings this man generated in her, still unsure of where they'd go from here. But she couldn't let him take off without letting him know she'd had a change of heart. She wasn't just back in the race. She wanted very much to win this one.

"Come on, Kate," he prompted, as curious now as he was amused by her temporary loss for words. It didn't happen often. "Spit it out."

"All right, here goes. I think… No, I'm pretty sure I love you."

Surprise flickered in his blue eyes for a moment, followed in short order by laughter and delight.

"Well, well! That makes two of us who are pretty sure. What do you propose we do now?"

"This, for starters."

Wrapping her fists around the collar of his flight suit, she yanked him down for a kiss.

It took him all of a second to get into the act. Wrapping an arm around her waist, he dragged her up against him. They were hard at it, lost in each other's taste and touch, when Kate registered the thud of a palm hitting the rest-room door.

"Oh! 'Scuse me, folks."

"Use the latrine across the hangar," Dave growled without lifting his head. "This one's busy."

"Right."

There was a hurried retreat, the sound of the door swishing shut. Kate closed her mind to the small sounds, the astringent tang of Lysol, to everything but Dave.

Finally, she had to let him go. He still needed to run through his preflight checklists and she had to pull herself together enough to face the rest of the crew. She couldn't believe how difficult it was to ease out of his arms.

"I'd better get back to Test Operations. I want to have a front-row seat when you take off."

"Aren't you going up in the chase plane?"

"Not this time. I want to make sure I have a land link to the solar observatory."

In case the satellite links took a hit.

She didn't finish the thought. She didn't have to. With a crooked grin, he reached up and tucked a stray tendril behind her ear.

"Don't worry, Commander Hargrave. You'll be right there with me, in my head."

And in his heart, Dave thought with a funny little jolt.

So this is what it felt like. As if he'd stepped into a zero-gravity chamber a half second before the floor dropped out from under him. For the first time in his admittedly varied experience, he found himself floundering, not quite sure how to propel himself forward.

He'd figure that out after his flight, he decided. When he had Kate alone, in the dark, in some place that didn't stink of industrial-strength disinfectant.

Chapter 11

Kate left Dave at the hangar and returned to the dun-colored modular building housing Test Operations. Inside was the small room lined with digitized display boards that functioned as the site's command-and-control center during tests.

Using her laptop, Test Ops' high-speed computers and a battery of communications devices, she set up a series of redundant links to various weather sources. A voice link to Stu Petrie confirmed her real-time access to data being fed back through the solar observatory's array of equipment.

"We've reoriented the Dunn Telescope," the scientist informed her. "We're recording every burp and bubble of energy emitted by the magnetic fields.

So far, the propulsive activity has remained relatively stable."

So far.

The caveat didn't reassure Kate. As Stu himself had pointed out to Dave, intense bursts of energy from the sun didn't take long to reach the earth.

"I appreciate you allowing me to tap into your data system, Stu."

"There wasn't much 'allowing' involved," the scientist responded with a chuckle. "The order came straight down from the top."

Kate could hear the curiosity behind the comment. The observatory had been read in on the need for real-time information, but not the reason behind it. Neither Dr. Petrie nor his boss had been briefed on the specifics of the Pegasus project.

"I want to keep that data line open for the next few hours," Kate told him. "I've also got landlines and radio communications available as backup."

"Don't worry. We'll get the data to you if I have to bicycle it down the mountain myself."

Kate bit back the reply that bicycling would get the information here too late for it to do any good.

"Thanks, Stu. Let's hope it doesn't come to that."

Her glance went to the digital time display on the wall of Test Operations. Eleven-twenty. Dave would be airborne in less than an hour and back on the ground by 4:00 p.m. if nothing went wrong.

Her mouth set, Kate grabbed her mug and filled

it to the brim with black coffee. The coffee wouldn't help the acid already churning away inside her stomach, but she needed something to take her mind off the clock.

Cari joined her and grimaced at the residue left in the bottom of the carafe. "I'd better brew a fresh pot. This looks to be a long afternoon."

"No kidding."

"He knows what he's doing, Kate."

That was the best the brunette could offer. She didn't try to minimize the risks. She couldn't. If Pegasus proved his capabilities in the air, Cari would be the next one in the hot seat. Responsibility for the sea trials rested squarely on her slender shoulders.

With the brisk efficiency that characterized her, she filled the pot, poured the water into the well and added a prepack of coffee. When the water had started to gurgle, she turned to Kate.

"Remember what Dave said. He's a test pilot. He's been trained to think fast and respond instantly."

Kate nodded.

"We'll bring him home." Cari gave her arm a gentle squeeze. "We have to. I'll be darned if I'm going to miss my ride."

By three-fifteen Kate was almost beginning to believe they'd make it. Her eyes ached from staring at the computer screens nonstop, her neck had a knot in it that wouldn't go away, and her stomach was pumping acid by the gallon. With one ear she listened to every beep and blip of the computers. With another, she monitored Dave's voice as it came over the loudspeakers.

"Chase One, this is Pegasus One."

"Go ahead, Pegasus."

"I'm climbing to thirty thousand feet."

"Roger, Pegasus. We're right with you."

Kate's glance flew to the computerized tracking board. The last test objective yet to be met was to ascertain the vehicle's performance with a full load at, or close to, its maximum ceiling. To accomplish that, Dave was now taking his craft in a wide, ascending circle high above the same resort the two of them had golfed in.

And made love in.

They'd have to go back to the Inn of the Mountain Gods, Kate thought, once this mission was over and she could breathe again. Dragging her gaze from the tracking board, she scanned the screen in front of her.

Suddenly, she froze. Her heart stopped dead, kicked in again with a painful jolt. Her horrified gaze ripped across the numbers painting across the screen once, twice. Then she was shouting for Captain Westfall.

"Sir! I'm declaring a weather emergency. We've got to get those planes down!"

His steely-gray gaze shot toward her. She didn't have time to explain.

"Now, sir!"

He nodded once and keyed his mike. "Pegasus One, Chase One, this is Test Control. Terminate your mission and return to base immediately. Immediately. Do you copy?"

"This is Chase One. We copy."

Kate's pulse thundered in her ears until Dave responded.

"This is Pegasus One. I copy, too, Control. How long have we got?"

Westfall looked to her. Hitting the switch on her mike, Kate delivered the dire news.

"Seven to eight minutes. If you're lucky. Get that baby on the ground!"

"Roger that."

After an instant of frozen silence, the entire test cadre shifted instantly into emergency mode. The engineers sent their fingers flying over keyboards to back up every bit of flight data. Captain Westfall ordered the crash recovery team to stand by. Doc Richardson alerted his medical personnel. Jill Bradshaw instructed Rattlesnake Ops to yank every off-duty military cop from his or her bunk and prepare them to secure a possible crash site.

Kate heard their voices, felt their tension jump through the air like some evil demon, but she focused every atom of her being on the computer screen in front of her.

The numbers were off the charts now. The energy burst was coming and it was coming fast. All indications were it would hit right above them.

She forced herself to think, to clamp down on the terror icing her veins and *think!* The whole upper ionosphere was about to go supercharged. Dave couldn't get above it. He couldn't get around it. His one chance, his only chance, was to find a protective shield.

The mountains! He could use the mountains! If the burst occurred over the desert, as was now looking more and more certain, the mountains *might* act as a shield. The high peaks had certainly contained the green haze Kate and Dave had observed last night.

Every nerve center in her body screaming, Kate raced to Captain Westfall. Somehow she managed to spill out a succinct, coherent version of her theory. The captain took all of thirty seconds to weigh the pros and cons. His jaw tight, he keyed his mike.

"Pegasus One, Chase One, this is Test Control. You have two minutes to possible system shutdown. We recommend you change course and drop down behind the Sierra Blancas. Use the mountains as a shield."

"Test Control, this is Chase One. We copy and are banking hard left."

"Roger, Chase One."

One of the dots on the tracking screen turned sharply. The other remained on a straight course. Westfall keyed his mike again.

"Pegasus One, do you copy?"

"Roger, Test Control. I'm initiating..."

The transmission ended in a screech of static.

Kate's heart jumped straight to her throat as the lights in the control center flickered. Computers beeped. Displays went fuzzy.

A second later, the entire facility went dark.

Chapter 12

Deep, impenetrable blackness surrounded Kate. There was no light, not so much as a glimmer of a shadow, to give depth or definition to the windowless operations center. She heard a thump. A curse. A terse order for everyone to remain still until the emergency generators powered up.

Her heart measured each second with hard, excruciating thumps. After what seemed like a lifetime, a muted hum signaled that the backup generators were kicking in. Seconds later the lights blinked on.

The scene inside Test Control could have been crafted for a wax museum. Lifelike figures were frozen in different poses, their faces registering shock, dismay, determination.

Kate wrenched her gaze to the computerized tracking board. It was blank. Completely blank. Both aircraft had disappeared from the screen.

"Oh, God!"

Her agonized whisper seemed to break the spell. Suddenly everyone moved at once. Captain Westfall's deep, gravelly command brought instant order to the chaos.

"All right, people, listen up! Control, get on the radio and see if you can raise Pegasus and/or Chase One. The rest of you check your data terminals. I want to know if any of the computers aboard either aircraft are still transmitting."

Officers and civilians scrambled to power up their computers. Kate had no sooner toggled the key on her laptop than the loudspeaker in the control center crackled. She spun around, her heart in her throat, as the loudspeakers emitted a loud burst of static. A few seconds later, a voice broke through the noise.

"...declaring an in-flight emergency. Do you copy, Test Control?"

Kate's nails gouged into her clenched fists. The voice wasn't Dave's. The transmission was coming from Chase One. Her momentary panic quickly gave way to a sharp, stabbing relief. If the C-130 was still in the air, there was a good chance Pegasus was, too.

The pilot's transmission was still echoing through

the control center when Captain Westfall spun around and barked at the communications tech.

"Can you raise them?"

"No, sir. Not yet."

His jaw tight, Westfall could only listen with the others as the C-130 pilot tried to reach them again.

"Test Control, this is Chase One. We're transmitting on guard 121.5, using our backup battery."

Kate bit down hard on her lower lip. She'd spent enough time in the air to know 121.5 was a guarded frequency monitored around the clock by the FAA. It was always open, available for use by everyone from crop dusters to stealth aircraft in emergencies. The fact that the chase plane was transmitting via an open frequency told her instantly his secure communications had failed.

In the next moment, Kate and the rest of the team knew that the 130's comm wasn't all that had failed.

"Be advised we're declaring an in-flight emer_gency," Chase One repeated. "Our airspeed and altitude gauges are spinning like roulette wheels, the secure communications are fried, and we're flying by the seat of our pants. We're transmitting using our backup battery."

As Kate was all too aware, the backup battery contained only about thirty minutes of juice. The C-130 would have to go silent soon to conserve power for his landing.

"We had the target on our left wing…"

The transmission fuzzed, cut off for a moment, came back over the loudspeaker.

"...so we overshot the vehicle. Last reported sighting was at tango 6.2. I repeat, Control, tango 6.2."

Pegasus! He was referring to Pegasus. Kate's gaze whipped to the wall map that divided the vast site into specific patrol areas. Tango 6.2 was to the southeast, where the mountains trailed off into desert.

"This is Chase One, terminating transmission."

Kate chewed on her lip again until she tasted blood. A hundred unanswered questions thundered through her head. Had Dave made it to the mountains? Had the peaks shielded him, as they apparently had the C-130? Or had the chase aircraft overshot its target vehicle before Pegasus reached the granite peaks?

That question, at least, was answered a long, agonizing twenty minutes later.

The burst of solar energy fried communications towers and knocked out commercial radio, TV and cell phones in most of southern New Mexico. Buried cables were protected, although the switchers that routed calls took severe hits. Some calls went through. Others ended in static.

Hardened military communications fared considerably better. Jill used her radio to direct her people to activate the site's disaster-response plan. Within moments, each of the senior test-cadre members was supplied with a hand radio and could communicate with their counterparts in other agencies.

After several frustrating tries, Kate managed to get through to the National Solar Observatory. She was taking a fix on the exact area affected by the burst when Jill came rushing back into the control center. Her face set in tight lines, the military cop relayed the news they'd all been dreading.

"A local sheriff just notified the FAA of a possible downed aircraft. The air force picked up on the notification and relayed it to us. The craft was spotted going in just before the sky turned green."

Kate's chest squeezed. She couldn't move, couldn't breathe.

"The sheriff reports a column of black smoke rising from the approximate location," Jill continued grimly.

Captain Westfall clenched his fists. "Where?"

"Sector tango 6.2, sir."

Since the energy burst had fried the instruments in the chopper assigned to the Pegasus site, the initial disaster-response team was forced to employ land vehicles. Kate's duties didn't call for her to be part of the team, but no one, Captain Westfall included, challenged her determination to join the convoy. She raced out of Test Operations to retrieve her sidearm and survival gear.

Two paces outside, she skidded to a stunned halt. Jill was hard on her heels and almost ran over her.

"Some show, isn't it?"

Swallowing, Kate took in the green and yellow waves undulating across the sky. Normally the scientist in Kate would thrill at such a unique display. At the moment, she could only curse herself for underestimating their potential severity.

Sick over her miscall, she gathered her gear and ran to Rattlesnake Ops, where the convoy had already formed. Two Humvees, a wide-track fire-suppression unit, and specially modified all-terrain vehicles with machine guns mounted on the hood.

"I'll take the lead ATV," Jill informed the hastily-assembled response team. Her blond hair was swept up under a Kevlar helmet. She wore a bullet-proof vest under her battle-dress uniform. Her sidearm was holstered on her belt, and she'd slung an assault rifle over one shoulder.

"Our navigational and comm systems depend on satellite signals," she said tersely, "so we'll have to do this the old-fashioned way, using maps and compasses. Rattlesnake Four, you and your squad take the first Humvee. Doc, your medical response team have the second. Commander Hargrave, you're with the medical team. Mount up."

Jill had worked a deal with the military cops up at Kirtland Air Force Base in Albuquerque to modify the Hummers' engines. They'd required the increased speed to keep up with Pegasus during his land runs. Even with their modified engines, though, the vehicles couldn't chew up the desert fast enough for Kate. It took the small convoy almost thirty minutes to reach the foothills of the Sierra Blancas, another twenty to hump through them to reach Tango Sector.

Less than two hours had passed since they'd lost contact with Pegasus. Every minute of those hours was etched into Kate's soul. She felt as though she'd aged a hundred years by the time the driver of her vehicle shouted to the passengers in the back.

"We're seeing a plume of black smoke dead ahead. It appears to be rising from a narrow gully."

Cody Richardson shouted back the question that burned in Kate's throat. "Any sign of the vehicle or the pilot?"

"Negative, sir. Major Bradshaw has just signaled to us to kick into overdrive. Hang on to the side straps, folks, it's going to get bumpy."

Ten bone-rattling moments later, the Humvee jolted to a halt. Kate was almost snarling with impatience as she waited for the rear tailgate to let down and the others to pile out. Disregarding the hand Cody held out for her, she jumped out and hit the ground with a jar.

Even before she raced around to the front of the Hummer she could smell the burning engine fuel. No one who'd ever survived a crash—or assisted at a crash site—could mistake that oily, searing stink. Her first glimpse of the dense black tower of smoke billowing into the sky sent her heart and her last faint hope plunging.

"Oh, God!"

The billowing cloud blurred. Hot tears burned Kate's eyes. A scream rose in her throat, aching to rip loose.

Shuddering, she fought it back. She had work to do. They all did. She swiped an arm across her eyes, swallowed the sobs that tore at her throat and reached a shaking hand into the pack containing a small, portable respirator and an oxygen pack. Anyone going within a hundred yards of that raging cloud of smoke would need both bottled air and protective clothing.

The crash-recovery team was already dragging on their shiny silver protective gear. Suddenly, one of them jerked an arm toward the fire.

"Isn't that Captain Scott?"

Kate spun around, terrified he was pointing to a charred, blackened body. She couldn't believe her eyes when she saw Dave scrambling down the side of the gully.

"'Bout time you folks got here!"

Keeping well clear of the smoke, he broke into a long-legged lope. Kate wasn't as restrained. She dropped her gear bag and charged toward the gully full speed.

The idiot was grinning!

Grinning!

That was the only thought she had time for before she plowed into him. He rocked back, steadied and wrapped his arms around her.

The sobs Kate had forced down just moments ago ripped free. She couldn't hold them back, any more than she could keep from gripping his flight suit with both fists, as if to make sure he didn't disappear into that black cloud.

"I thought you were dead!" she wailed against his chest.

"It was touch-and-go there for a few minutes," he admitted, his voice a deep rumble in her ear. "But I'm okay, babe. I'm okay."

She didn't know whether it was his steady assurances, the knuckle that rubbed gentle circles on her spine or the abrupt arrival of the rest of the team that made her realize she had to get herself under control. Gulping, she pushed the sobs back down her raw throat and swiped her forearm across her eyes again. Dave kept one arm around her as the others peppered him with questions.

"How did you get down?"

"Did you have to bail?"

"Have you sustained any injuries?"

The last came from Cody Richardson, and Kate's euphoria took a swift nosedive. He'd insisted he was okay, but in tough, macho pilot lingo, that could mean anything from scratch-free to protruding bones. She pulled away to take a closer look while Dave parried their questions with one of his own.

"Did the C-130 crew land safely?"

"As far as we know," Jill informed him. "They declared an in-flight emergency and were flying by wire, but we've received no reports of a downed aircraft other than yours."

Dave let his breath whistle out. "Good. They were a couple of hundred feet above me when the sky lit up. I was afraid the mountains didn't give them the same protection they did me."

"Some protection," Jill murmured, her glance going to the burning funeral pyre.

"That was a hell of a call on Captain Westfall's part," Dave commented, "sending us down behind the hills like that."

"Captain Westfall didn't make that call," Jill informed him. "Kate did."

"No kidding." He squeezed her waist. "Thanks for saving my butt, Hargrave."

"To paraphrase a certain pilot I know, your butt is eminently savable, Scott. I'm just sorry I couldn't save Pegasus, too."

"You did."

"Huh?"

That less-than-intelligent response won her a quick grin.

"I lost some instrumentation, but I managed to bring him down. He's parked about a hundred yards down the gully."

Kate's gaze whipped to the noxious black column. "But the fire… The smoke."

"My communications were fried. I didn't have any way to signal my location, so I emptied some fuel from the vehicle, piled up brush and started my own personal bonfire. I figured someone would spot the smoke."

Kate couldn't quite take it in. Dave had survived. So had Pegasus. They'd both come within a breath of having their wings permanently clipped, but both had survived.

"Now what do you say we put out the fire," he suggested briskly, "throw a security cordon around the craft until we can get it back to base, and make tracks. I didn't have any lunch. I'm hungry."

Still in a daze, Kate shook her head. "He's hungry," she echoed to Jill. "He wants food."

"So feed him," the cop replied with a grin. "Doc, one of my troops will drive you, Kate and Dave back to the site. I'll stay with the craft until it's secured."

Dave released her long enough to retrieve the gear bag he'd stashed well away from the fire before rejoining her at the Hummer. Kate ducked her head and prepared to scramble inside. He helped her with a firm hand under her elbow and a whispered promise that raised instant goose bumps.

"Food isn't all I'm hungry for, my very, very Kissable Kate."

Chapter 13

It was long past midnight before full communications and power were restored at the base, Dave had finished debriefing his extraordinary flight, and Pegasus was once again bedded down in his gleaming white stall.

Two days, Captain Westfall announced to his weary staff, before the maintenance crew could replace every circuit that had blown in the test vehicle.

"That puts us behind the eight ball again on the sea trials. We'll have to cut the water-test phase to the bone," he instructed Cari. "I want you and Major McIver in my quarters at oh-seven-hundred with a restructured schedule."

Cari gulped. "Yes, sir."

"You can work here," Westfall said. "We'll clear the conference room and let you have it. The rest of you…" His glance roamed the circle of military and civilian personnel. "Get some rest. You'll need it, because once we leave for the coast and begin water trials, the pace is going to pick up considerably."

Kate couldn't imagine how! In the past two months, their tight-knit group had warded off an attack by a mysterious virus, lost one of their members to a heart attack and survived a megaburst of solar energy. Oh, yes, they'd also proved Pegasus could run like the wind and fly with eagles.

She muttered as much to Jill as the group dispersed. With a shake of her head, the site's chief of security agreed the pace was plenty fast enough for her.

"At least I'll get a break when we move down to Corpus Christi. We'll be operating out of a navy base, so they'll have overall responsibility for security. All I'll have to do is keep unauthorized visitors away from our little corner of the base."

"Wish I could look forward to a break. We'll be arriving at Corpus smack in the middle of hurricane season. Cari might just get stuck swimming Pegasus through gale-force seas."

"If anyone can do it," said a deep voice behind them, "Cari can."

Both women turned to find Doc Richardson waiting patiently for Jill to finish her conversation. Kate looked past him at the still-dispersing group.

"If you're looking for Dave," the doc commented, "he said to tell you he had something he wanted to take care of and he'll see you later."

"Later?"

It was close to 2:00 a.m. Kate hadn't slept more than an hour or two last night. Worry over that damned solar flare had kept her tossing and turning. That, and Dave's challenge that she get back in the race.

"Did he say how much later?"

"No." The doc's cheeks creased in a grin. "But he did ask me to keep Jill occupied for an hour or two."

"And your reply was?" Jill wanted to know.

"I told him I'm here to serve. Come with me, Major, and I'll let you look through my microscope."

"The last time I did that, I ended up flat on my back. With a virus," she tacked on dryly, but she didn't protest when Cody steered her toward the dispensary.

With a surge of excitement that chased away her weariness, Kate headed for her quarters. She had a good idea why Dave had asked Cody to keep Jill busy for an hour or so. If she moved fast, she could get in a quick shower and change out of the flight suit she'd been in for going on twenty hours now before the man arrived at her quarters.

She should have known she couldn't outrun a sky jock. Dave was already there. In her bed. Wearing nothing but a grin and his watch.

"What took you so long?" he complained.

Laughing, she leaned against the doorjamb. "How the dickens did you beat me here? Cody said you had some business to take care of."

"I did."

With a jerk of his chin, he indicated the box of condoms he'd invested in at the Inn of the Mountain Gods. They'd run through a respectable number of them, but there had to be at least five or six left.

"After our little adventure today, I just wanted to make sure we had plenty of backup and redundant systems."

Kate groaned. "That's the worst attempt to get a girl in the sack I've heard yet."

"I can do better," he assured her. "Come here, KK, and let me whisper in your ear."

"KK?" she asked, then remembered the nickname he'd bestowed on her. "Never mind, I got it. Move over, DD. Give me room to sit down and take off my boots."

He obliged, edging his hips to the far side of the twin bed. Kate sat on the edge, brought her foot up and let her glance sweep the length of his lean, muscled body. Her bootlace snapped in her fingers.

Dave didn't help matters by propping his head in one hand and playing with her hair while she shucked her boots and socks.

"DD, huh? Let me guess. Darling Dave, right?"

"Wrong."

"Daredevil Dave?"

"Not even close."

"Gimme a hint."

"No hints. You have to figure it out for yourself."

Kate stood, unzipped her blue flight suit in one fluid move and stepped out of it. Her sports bra and panties followed her cotton T-shirt to the floor.

"In the meantime, cowboy, why don't we see just how redundant your systems are."

Very redundant, Kate decided some hours later.

She lay flopped across Dave's chest, boneless with pleasure and so sleepy she couldn't pry up even one eyelid. A dozen solar flares could have burst above her and blazed across the night sky and she wouldn't have seen them.

She did, however, hear Dave's soft whisper as he eased her off his chest and into the crook of his arm.

"This is one race we'll both win, Kate."

* * * * *

WRONG BRIDE, RIGHT GROOM

To my mom, Alyce Thoma,
who packed up her house and her kids
and her dreams every time Dad got transferred.
You made a home filled with love and laughter
for us wherever we ended up.
Thanks, Mom, for all that and so much more.

Prologue

A long, melodramatic sigh carried over the clatter of keyboards and distant mutter of travel agents caught up in the frenzy of last minute Thanksgiving bookings. Lucy Falco, office manager of Gulliver's Travels, tugged her gaze from her flickering computer screen and smiled at the travel agent hovering just outside her office.

"What's up, Tiffany?"

A slender woman with a wild mane of silver curls strolled into the office, her pale gray eyes dancing under a layer of rather startling plum eye shadow. With a girlish grace that belied her sixty-plus years, Tiffany Tarrington Toulouse settled into a tall wingback chair.

"I've worked out the honeymoon package Mr. Gulliver asked us to put together for Abigail Davis's sister." She paused dramatically. "I got them the honeymoon cottage at the Pines."

Lucy's dark brows soared. "The Pines Resort?"

"And at a substantial discount, too."

"How in the world did you manage that?"

"Not very easily! But Abby performed such miracles with our offices, I was determined to come up with something special for her sister."

Tiffany's appreciative gaze roamed Lucy's office, recently redecorated by Abby Davis. The young estate appraiser and antique dealer had transformed Lucy's functional work center into an inviting haven with hunter-green walls, gilt-framed prints, wingback chairs and an antique leather-topped desk in burled cherry. She'd worked the same magic on the rest of Gulliver's Travels, including Tiffany's corner suite, which was why the older agent had worked so hard to put together a special package for her.

"Poor Abby," she said with a shake of her silver curls. "Her sister sprang this wedding on her less than a week ago, then dumped all the arrangements in her lap. I had a time pulling it all together, I can tell you. Every first-class inn and hotel within a hundred miles of Atlanta has been booked up for months, because of the big football game."

Lucy nodded sympathetically. The holidays were always their busiest time. The Georgia-Georgia Tech shoot-out on Thanksgiving Day only added to the chaos. Tiffany had pulled off a real coup by booking the honeymoon couple into the exclusive Pines Inn and Golf Resort, just fifteen miles north of Atlanta.

Still, remembering the near-disastrous Halloween honeymoon package Gulliver's Travels had put together for another couple recently, Lucy wanted reassurance.

"You're sure everything's confirmed?"

"I'm sure."

"You got it in writing?"

"Every detail."

Holding up a ringed hand, the older woman ticked off the arrangements.

"The groom arrives this afternoon. It took some doing, but between us, Beth and I got him an upgrade on a flight out of London. The wedding takes place this evening. The Pines helped us track down a justice of the peace who'll perform the ceremony."

"A real one, I hope," Lucy interjected, the Halloween fiasco still fresh in her mind.

Silvery locks bouncing, Tiffany nodded. "A real one. Afterward, they'll enjoy a private dinner prepared by the inn's world-class chef. Then—" she handed Lucy a colorful brochure "—a honeymoon cottage, complete with wet bar, Jacuzzi, wood-burning fireplace. And one very huge, very decadent bed."

Lucy's dark eyes lit with laughter as she studied the picture. "It's certainly huge, anyway."

"And tomorrow," Tiffany continued gleefully, "the Pines's year-in-advance-reservations-only gourmet Thanksgiving dinner, delivered to the cottage, compliments of Gulliver's Travels."

Smiling, Lucy handed back the brochure. "You and Abby certainly went all out. I hope her sister appreciates your efforts."

"I'm sure she will. This is one honeymoon the bride and groom will never forget!"

Chapter 1

"What do you mean, you can't marry him?"

Abigail Davis gripped the handle of the 1930s-style white plastic phone and fought to control her exasperation. Losing her temper never did any good. Not with Beth.

"I just can't." Panic laced her younger sister's voice. "I...I don't know him."

Turning her back on the two well-dressed matrons browsing through the antique shop, Abby rolled her eyes. *She'd* said exactly the same thing—several times!—when Beth called to announce that she'd met the man of her dreams during an unexpected crew layover in England. By the time her flight crew had been assigned to another international run, the impetuous, impulsive Beth had fallen passionately in love. For the umpteenth time.

Now, after begging Abby's help in arranging a wedding during the brief window of opportunity when she and her air force fiancé would both be in the States, Beth was backing out. Again.

"I'm sorry, Abby. I know how much trouble you went through to set this up for me."

An understatement if ever there was one! Abby bit back a groan, thinking of the frantic phone calls she'd made to Tiffany, not to mention the substantial deposit she'd already paid the Pines to guarantee the honeymoon cottage and the wedding supper. If the wedding was canceled now, she'd be lucky if all she lost was her deposit.

Still, she'd rather forfeit the entire cost of the wedding than see her sister make a serious mistake. Swallowing her irritation, she softened her tone.

"I'm glad you had the courage to face your doubts before the wedding, instead of after."

Relief added a breathless baby-doll quality to Beth's voice. "I knew you'd understand."

"I just hope your groom does."

"He will…when you explain it to him."

"What?" Abby shook her head, setting the tendrils of her loosely piled honey-blond hair dancing. "No way, kiddo! I'm not bailing you out of this one."

Her sharp retort drew startled glances from two browsers and a frown from her boss. Marissa DeVries maintained a standing rule against her employees taking personal phone calls while on the floor. That was only one of the many reasons Abby was looking forward to terminating her employment at Things Past.

"Please, Abby."

She hardened her heart against the plea in her sister's voice. "No, Beth."

"Just go to the airport this afternoon and meet Jordy's plane. I…I can't face him."

At the small, hiccuping sob, a hint of amused exasperation came into Abby's brown eyes. She'd heard that pathetic little sound many times over the years. Usually just before Beth confessed to some childish prank or another, which Abby would end up taking the blame for.

But Beth wasn't a child any longer. And running out on her groom the day of their wedding hardly qualified as a childish prank.

"I won't do it," Abby stated in her best no-nonsense big-sister tone. "If you insist on getting engaged every time you date a man more than once, you can darn well learn to get yourself unengaged."

"You *know* how I hate to hurt anyone's feelings…."

"For heaven's sake, Bethany! We're not talking about just anyone. The man is on a plane at this very moment, flying in from England to marry you."

"I know, I know!" Beth wailed.

"You have to meet him and tell him about your change of heart."

"I can't." There was a small silence, followed by a rushed, guilty admission. "My flight leaves in twenty minutes."

"Flight?" Abby squawked. "What flight?"

"I volunteered to fill in on a Paris-Cairo-Singapore run."

"Beth!" The irritation Abby had squelched just moments ago came rushing back in full force. "Don't you dare skip out on your fiancé. Or on me!"

"Talk to him, Abby. Tell him I'm sorry. Tell him I'll write and explain things."

"No. Absolutely not. I won't—"

"They're calling my flight. I love you, Sissy."

"Don't 'Sissy' me. Not this time. Beth? Bethany?" Abby stretched the receiver out at arm's length, glaring at the marble-grained white plastic.

She couldn't believe it! Beth had done it again. Slipped away and left her to clean up yet another mess. She knew darn well Abby wouldn't let Sergeant Doug Jordan wander Atlanta's busy airport, searching hopelessly for his missing bride.

Dammit!

"If you're quite through with your personal calls, Abigail, you might think about getting back to work."

With some effort, Abby refrained from slamming the receiver into its cradle. She dragged in a steadying breath and turned to face her employer.

As she met Marissa's haughty stare, she told herself she should be grateful to the woman. She'd given

Abby a job when she arrived in Atlanta five years ago with her younger sister, a self-taught knowledge of antiques and a burning desire to put down roots.

Abby had always known exactly what kind of roots she wanted. The old-fashioned kind. The kind that went way down deep and included two, or maybe three, generations taught by the same fourth-grade teacher. Sunday-morning pancake breakfasts at the local fire station. A house that wore its age like a welcome mat. Rooms of lovingly polished furniture proudly displaying their scars of use.

The job at Things Past had been Abby's major step toward achieving her dream. At the time, her knowledge of antiques had consisted entirely of a wealth of information gleaned from books and a deep, intrinsic love of all things that possessed the past she and Beth lacked.

Since then, however, she'd learned the business inside and out, been licensed by the state insurance board as an appraiser and increased the shop's inventory through ever more skillful buys. In the process, she'd also worked more hours than any other employee, with marginal recompense and even less recognition. Marissa wasn't the kind of woman to acknowledge anyone's efforts but her own.

"You're taking off early this afternoon to help your sister prepare for her wedding," the raven-haired shop owner said icily. "Do you think you might give Things Past a little attention until then?"

Abby wasn't ready to explain the latest development in the on-again, off-again wedding to her employer, who resented Beth's demands on Abby's time almost as much as the younger woman disliked the supercilious shop owner. Abby suspected one of the reasons her sister had insisted on a small, intimate, family-only wedding was to avoid inviting Marissa.

"Actually," she told her boss, "I need to take off earlier than anticipated. I've got to meet Beth's fiancé at the airport."

"That's out of the question. Your sister knows very well the holiday season is our busiest time of year." Lowering her voice, Marissa nodded toward the two women examining a case of pink Depression glassware. "What's more, the football game is bringing in all kinds of wealthy alumni. I need you here."

"I only came in at all as a special favor to you," Abby reminded her patiently. "I have a lot to do today."

Like cancel a wedding.

Marissa's sharp, elegant features took on a peevish cast. "Beth knew how busy we'd be today. She should have exhibited a bit more consideration in making these hasty wedding plans."

"I doubt if Beth was thinking about the shop when she fell in love and decided to get married," Abby said dryly.

Or when she fell *out* of love, she added with a silent grimace.

While Marissa huffed and complained a bit more, Abby stole a quick glance at her watch. She didn't have the time to humor her humorless employer. Or the patience.

Maybe this little confrontation was for the best, she decided. She was ready to cut the cord. She'd planned to wait until after Beth's wedding to give notice, but she might just as well do it now.

Her sister might have changed her plans for the future. Abby hadn't.

"I'm sorry," she said firmly, interrupting her employer in midcomplaint. "I can't give you any more time today. Or any other day, after the first of December."

Marissa's penciled brows sliced sharply downward. "What do you mean?"

"I told you a few months ago I was thinking about starting my own business."

"Don't be ridiculous. You don't have the capital or the expertise to launch yourself in this business."

"Yes, I do."

The calm rejoinder took the older woman aback. Her heavily mascaraed eyes narrowed as she stared at her employee.

"I've made an offer on a house on Peabody Street," Abby said evenly, hugging to herself the tingle of excitement just saying the words aloud caused. "If the offer's accepted, as the Realtor assures me it will, I plan to open the Painted Door just after the first of the year."

Abby didn't expect congratulations or good wishes, which was just as well, since she received neither. Marissa's lips tightened to a thin scarlet line. Without an-other word, she turned and walked back to the customers.

Torn between relief at having given notice, simmering exasperation with Beth and near panic at all she had to do in the next few hours, Abby headed for the room at the back of the shop. Another quick glance at her watch told her she'd didn't have time to call Gulliver's Travels and get Tiffany working on the cancellation. Maybe she could reach her from the airport.

She grabbed her purse from the middle drawer of the rolltop desk, then swirled a long black wool cape over her lacy-collared dress. A treasured find at an estate sale some years ago, the cloak served both everyday and evening duty during the chill winter months. Throwing one edge of the cloak over her shoulder, she dashed for the back door.

The moment she stepped outside, icy rain hit her in the face. Gasping, Abby huddled under the overhang, buried her nose in the cape's soft mohair lining and viewed the pelting sleet with dismay. Every few years, a horrendous winter storm swept down from the Great Smoky Mountains to the north and paralyzed the entire Atlanta area. She only hoped this gray, icy drizzle wasn't the precursor of another monster.

The narrow heels of her high-topped granny boots clicked on slick cobblestones as she picked her way to her minivan. Christened the Antiquemobile by Beth some years ago, more for its age than its utilitarian purpose, the brown van huddled in the cold like a fat, forlorn partridge. By the time Abby climbed inside, rain had drizzled down her neck and dampened the lace collar of her dress. Muttering dire imprecations against younger sisters in general and mercurial, impulsive ones in particular, she cranked the key. The engine coughed a few times, then caught. Clutching the wheel with both hands, she backed out of her parking space.

Or tried to.

The van's worn tires whirred alarmingly on slick pavement. Gulping, Abby let up on the foot pedal, then depressed it more slowly. To her relief, the van inched backward. She swung it around, shifted into drive and eased onto the street. Once into the stream of traffic heading south to the interstate, she jiggled the heater's switch. The air blower sputtered once or twice, then wheezed in defeat.

"Wonderful," she muttered as the damp chill whirled through the van. "Just wonderful!"

The tip of her nose tingling with cold, she headed for Atlanta's Hartsfield International Airport. On the way, she sorted through the long list of glowing adjectives Beth had used to describe her fiancé, Technical Sergeant Doug Jordan. It took some effort to turn Beth's ecstatic ramblings into a mental picture of the man she'd meet for the first time in a few minutes.

Tall. Broad-shouldered. Dark-haired and seriously handsome, with an angel's smile and a devilish gleam in his eyes. According to her sister, Jordy filled out his air force uniform like a Greek god and carried himself with an air of utter self-confidence that came with being a member of the air force's elite combat pararescue force—whatever that was. Abby just hoped Sergeant Jordan's self-confidence was up to being left at the proverbial altar.

She arrived at the airport an agonizing forty-five minutes later, wound as tight as a coil by the slippery roads and heavy traffic. Breathless, she dodged hordes of holiday travelers and reached the international gate area just moments after the announcement heralding the arrival of Delta's flight 73 from Heathrow.

No one in uniform, godlike or otherwise, lingered in the waiting room just outside the customs checkpoint. Chewing her lower lip, Abby searched the crowds. From the corner of one eye, she glimpsed the head and shoulders of a tall figure in a brown leather bomber jacket. Abby's first clue that this might be her man was the tight stretch of the leather across his broad shoulders. The second was the razor-short military cut of his dark brown hair. But it was his unmistakable air of authority that clinched the matter in her mind. Although he moved along with the stream of travelers, he seemed to hold himself aloof, apart, much as the leader of a pack would.

"Jordy?"

Abby's call got lost in the waves of noise filling

the thronged concourse. Flushed and still breathless from her mad dash through the airport, she hurried after the man. A few steps later, she caught hold of a patch of well-worn leather and tugged.

"Jordy?"

He swung around.

"I'm Abigail, Beth's sis—"

She broke off as eyes so dark a blue they appeared almost black ate into her. Involuntarily she retreated a step.

If this was Doug Jordan, Beth needed to work on her descriptive abilities. None of the adjectives she'd blithely tossed around fit this man. He sported a square, uncompromising jaw, a firm mouth, and a nose that had been broken once too often in the past. The rugged combination was arresting, but certainly didn't come close to handsome in Abby's book.

She had no idea whether his smile could be classified as angelic, since he wasn't wearing one, but the glint in his eyes could easily be considered devilish. He was older than Abby had assumed Doug Jordan would be. Well past thirty, she guessed, although the lines webbing the corners of his eyes could as well have been stamped there by experience as by age.

"You're Abby?" he responded with a lift of one dark brow. "Beth's sister?"

His deep, gravelly voice sent an unexpected shiver down her spine. No wonder Beth didn't have the nerve to face him, she thought. This wasn't the kind of man anyone shrugged off casually.

The midnight-blue eyes raked her from the top of her damp, wildly curling hair to the tips of her granny shoes. When he brought his gaze back to her face, it held a bold, masculine approval that sent an electrical shock skimming along Abby's nerves.

Her shock quickly gave way to a jolt of anger. An engaged man had no business giving anyone except his fiancée that particular look, she thought indignantly. Before she could tell him so, however, he shifted his leather carryall to his left hand. Then, to her utter amazement, he swept her up against his chest and covered her mouth with his own.

His lips were hard, as hard as the rest of the body pressed against hers. And warm. And altogether too seductive for a man about to be married.

Stunned, Abby registered the faint tang of a spicy after-shave. The smoky taste of Scotch. The feel of a big, callused hand cradling the back of her head. When his lips moved over hers, deepening the kiss, astonishment erupted into a hundred different emotions, not the least of which was fury.

Pete heard a muffled squeak, and felt the woman in his arms squirm. Firm breasts, discernible even through layers of wool cloak and leather jacket, pressed against his chest. Sudden, spine-stiffening awareness hammered through him, along with the realization that the brotherly kiss Doug Jordan had asked him to deliver to his new sister-in-law had slipped right past brotherly and was hovering somewhere around explosive.

It had started out innocently enough. Pete hadn't intended anything more than a good-natured exchange. A warm greeting. But her lips were sweeter than anything he'd tasted in a long, long time, and he discovered that he didn't want to release them.

Reluctantly he lifted his head and loosened the arm he'd wrapped around her waist. She jerked backward, leaving the scent of damp wool and flowery perfume behind. The glare she zinged at him packed twice the firepower of a Sidewinder missile.

"Are you crazy, or do prospective in-laws customarily assault each other where you come from?"

"Not customarily, but then, I'm not a prospective in-law."

Her eyes narrowed dangerously. "You're not Doug Jordan?"

"No, ma'am." He sketched a salute with the tips of two fingers. "Senior Master Sergeant Pete O'Brian, at your service. I'm Jordy's supervisor."

"His supervisor?"

"I'm afraid Jordy couldn't make it back to the States."

"Couldn't make it!" she echoed blankly. "Why not? Where is he?"

He thought for a moment. "About two thousand feet over a very cold, very hostile little country, about to jump into the middle of a civil war. Our unit got orders to deploy just an hour before Jordy was supposed to leave for home."

"Good grief! Didn't the fact that he was supposed to get married today make any difference?"

Pete lifted a brow at her faintly accusing look. "Not to me. Or to him, when the orders came down. Jordy's a professional."

While she digested that one, he glanced around the emptying terminal. "So where's the bride? I have a message for her."

A taut silence brought his gaze swinging back to the woman before him. She pursed her lips, then answered with obvious reluctance.

"About twenty thousand feet over the Atlantic. On her way to Singapore, by way of Paris and Cairo."

"No kidding?" Pete's mouth curled. "Well, what do you know? I bet Jordy she wouldn't show."

"What?"

The bet had just been a joke, although Pete hadn't really expected the ditzy flight attendant Doug Jordan had met during a weekend in London to go through with their hasty marriage plans. From the little he'd seen of Beth Davis, Pete could tell she lacked the depth to live up to her rash promises.

Jordy had fallen for her, though. Fallen hard, despite Pete's caustic suggestion that the young sergeant was just experiencing a healthy dose of male lechery. Which pretty well described the feeling

Beth Davis's older sister was stirring in Pete this very minute.

She stood ramrod-stiff before him, arms crossed, brown eyes flashing. She didn't come close to the gut-twisting, throat-closing physical perfection of her sister, of course, but few women did. Pete had been around long enough, however, to recognize that Abigail Davis occupied a class all by herself.

Her wildly curling hair was streaked with every color of the sun, from pale wheat to burnt umber, and her skin glistened with a dewy softness that reminded him of fresh-cut flowers and vanilla pudding. She stood a good six inches less than his own six-one, but that firm, tip-tilted chin warned Pete she didn't consider either his size or his presence particularly significant. Her creamy skin and soft, full mouth pulled at him, though, almost as much as the intelligence in her brown eyes. Obviously, Abby Davis possessed more than her younger sister's thimbleful of common sense.

And, just as obviously, she wasn't letting him off the hook. A delicately arched brow a few shades darker than her tawny hair lifted.

"You were about to explain this bet?"

"Considering the fact that the bride and groom had known each other less than thirty-six hours, it was a pretty safe bet. I know Jordy. When he makes up his mind, there's no changing it. But your sister didn't strike me as…"

"As what?"

The slight narrowing of her doe eyes should have alerted Pete. If he'd had any sleep at all in the past seventy-two hours, he probably wouldn't have missed the danger signal. But the bunged-up knee that had kept him from participating in the short-notice deployment hadn't prevented him from overseeing the preparations for it. After a marathon round-the-clock planning session, he'd put Jordy and the rest of his squad on a transport plane, just hours before he had to leave for the States himself. Then he'd spent most of the long flight home reworking the ops plan in his mind, trying to convince himself that he hadn't sent his men into a political and military quagmire with no escape route. Weariness now dragged at him like beggars in a back alley, and made him finish with more truth than diplomacy.

"She didn't strike me as the steady, reliable type," he said with a small shrug.

Abby bristled. Beth had her faults, which she'd have been the first to admit. Whatever she lacked in common sense or staying power, however, she more than made up for in spontaneity and warmth. Those she loved, she loved generously and unconditionally. Unfortunately, she tended to fall out of love as frequently as she fell into it.

As Abby knew better than anyone, that instability stemmed from their childhood. Beth had been so much younger when their parents died in a car accident. She'd learned to transfer her affections as easily as a puppy, first to the aunt who took the Davis girls in, then to the series of foster homes they were sent to when their widowed aunt proved emotionally incapable of raising two children. Over the years, the bond between the sisters had proven the only bedrock in their transient lives.

That bond had seen them through the difficult years, until Abby turned eighteen, got a full-time job, rented her first apartment and petitioned the court for custody of her younger sister. Ten years later, it still shaped Abby's life, and served as Beth's safety net in situations like this.

"I wouldn't be so quick to disparage my sister," she replied acidly. "After all, Doug Jordan didn't show up for his own wedding, either."

O'Brian's smirk faded. "The circumstances are entirely different. In Jordy's case, it was a matter of duty."

"I'm not sure I think very much of a man who puts duty before his wife."

"I wouldn't think very much of a man who didn't."

Their eyes locked, dark blue flint striking sparks off angry brown shale.

"What about you?" Abby retorted tartly. "Shouldn't you be off doing your duty?"

He didn't answer right away. When he did, a muscle twitched in his right cheek. "Yes, I should."

She watched the small movement with some surprise. Apparently she'd struck a nerve. He drew in a slow breath, and then a weariness seemed to settle over his face, etching deep lines in the tanned skin.

"Look, I had to come back to the States anyway. Jordy asked me to swing through Atlanta and explain his deployment to Beth. He also wanted me to tell her…" His jaw worked. "To tell her that he loves her."

The words came out with a rusty edge, as though it pained him to acknowledge anything as human as emotion.

Abby winced inwardly. In her irritation with O'Brian, she'd forgotten the other emotions involved in this little drama. Darn her sister, anyway.

"I'll give Beth the message."

O'Brian nodded, hefting his carryall. "Guess I'd better go find a cab and a hotel. It's been a long flight."

Thinking of the thousands of football fans and holiday travelers thronging the city, Abby hesitated.

"You don't have a hotel reservation?"

"No, I changed my flight at the last minute to get to Atlanta. I'll find something, though." He tipped her another salute. "Nice meeting you, Abigail."

She couldn't quite bring herself to return the polite sentiment. "Happy Thanksgiving…er…"

"Pete."

"Pete."

He was a good ten yards away before she noticed his uneven gait. Frowning, she shifted a few paces to one side and followed his progress down the concourse. It was more than just an uneven gait, she discovered. O'Brian walked with a decided limp. He held himself so erect and square-shouldered, it wasn't noticeable immediately, but now that she focused on it, she wondered how she could have missed it earlier.

As she watched him move away, embarrassment flooded through her. Oh, nice going, Abby! Nothing like deriding the man for not doing his so-called duty when he'd obviously been injured in some way, then sending him on his way, a stranger in an unfamiliar city.

Resolutely Abby quashed her guilt. Hey, he wasn't her responsibility. Having felt a few of his sharp edges, she'd be surprised if he was anyone's responsibility but his own.

Still, he had gone out of his way to do a favor for Jordy and Beth. He was going to have a heck of time finding anyplace to stay tonight…and she did happen to have a honeymoon cottage reserved.

She glanced at her watch and barely stifled a groan. There was no way she'd get back her hefty deposit on the cottage, not at this late hour. Nor would she recoup any of the sunk costs for the two-tiered chocolate-rum-raisin wedding cake Beth had requested. Or for the crown rib roast and delicate onion soufflé the Pines's chef was probably preparing at this very moment.

Her gaze swung to a disappearing patch of brown leather.

Darn Beth anyway!

Chapter 2

Abby caught up with O'Brian while he waited for the shuttle to the main terminal. He acknowledged her appearance at his side with a quirk of one dark brow.

"I don't know how long you plan to be in the Atlanta area...." she began hesitantly.

"A few days. When I changed my reservations, I had to take a layover I hadn't planned on."

"You might have trouble finding a place to stay. The big Georgia-Georgia Tech game is tomorrow. The city's under siege by sixty thousand or so avid fans."

A glimmer of something that might have been amusement stirred in his deep cobalt eyes. "I've slept on everything from a moving ice floe to a tree limb sixty feet above the jungle floor. If I have to, I can make myself comfortable on a park bench."

She would have written Mr. Macho off then and there, if his amusement hadn't evolved into a slow, crooked and totally unexpected grin.

"Thanks for the warning, though."

Abby blinked. Good grief! When he smiled, really smiled, those rugged features came dangerously close to handsome, after all.

She was still dealing with the impact of that devastating arrangement of his facial features when the shuttle whooshed to a halt at the edge of the platform. An impatient traveler jockeyed for position, inadvertently thumping her suitcase into his right leg. Before Abby's eyes, O'Brian's heart-thumping grin twisted into an involuntary grimace. His knee buckled, and he wobbled for an instant.

She caught his arm with both hands, concern lancing through her. Beth would have recognized the "mother" look on her face instantly.

"Are you all right?"

He righted himself. "Yes."

Her fingers curled into the soft leather sleeve. He didn't look all right. Not with those deep grooves slashing into the skin at the sides of his mouth and his eyes gone hard and flat.

"Are you sure?"

The tight, closed look on his face gave way to a

flicker of annoyance. He reversed their roles, tugging his arm free to take hers instead.

"I'm fine. Just feeling a little jet lag." He guided her across the platform. "Watch your step here."

She wedged herself into the shuttle car and snagged a few inches of hand space on a shiny metal pole. He followed, bracing a hand high above hers. His body bracketed hers. To Abby's consternation, his scent seemed to envelop her. She suspected she'd never again catch a whiff of fine-grained leather without thinking of this man. And his kiss.

As furious as that kiss had made her at the time, in retrospect she had to admit it ranked right up there among the top dozen or so she'd received. Well, maybe among the top three.

Come on! Who was she kidding? She'd never been kissed like that, not even by the man she'd thought she loved.

No nun, Abby had managed to squeeze in a semirespectable social life while struggling to get Beth through college and flight school, putting in long hours at work and studying for her licensing as an appraiser. Along the way, she'd experienced her share of male embraces. Some had left her breathless. A few had made her ache for more. One man's had made her think she'd found the permanency that had eluded her since her parents' death.

It wasn't anyone's fault that Derek's interest had swung from the older sister to the younger the day Beth breezed back into Atlanta after a four-month rotation in South America. She was so beautiful, so full of mischief and life, few men could resist her. Derek couldn't, anyway.

His handsome image drifted through Abby's mind, surprisingly hazy and indistinct. She was congratulating herself on the fact that thinking about him occasioned nothing more than a mild twinge of regret when the shuttle car jerked forward.

Her shoulder bumped Pete's chest.

His hips nudged hers.

Intimately.

For several long seconds, she felt the length of him against her back and bottom. A suffocating heat that had nothing to do with the warmth in the jammed car climbed up Abby's neck. Flustered, she pressed closer to the metal upright. The swaying, jostling crowd defeated her best efforts to preserve a modicum of airspace between her and the man behind her, however. By the time the underground train glided to a halt at the main terminal, she felt as stiff and compressed as corrugated cardboard.

A firm hold on her elbow steadied her against the buffeting streams of pedestrians pouring out of the shuttle. Abby felt his strength right through her layers of wool and mohair. Frowning slightly over her reaction to this stranger, she paced beside him. They were halfway through the main terminal before she recalled her reason for catching up with him in the first place.

"I booked a room—well, a cottage, actually—for

Jordy and Beth at the Pines Inn and Resort. You're welcome to use it."

He glanced down at her, polite refusal forming in his eyes. Shrewdly Abby guessed he didn't like accepting favors. From anyone. Then his dark blue gaze swept the jam-packed terminal.

"Maybe I'll take you up on the offer," he said slowly. "That's the Pines, right?"

"Right. I should warn you, though, it's about fifteen miles north of the city."

"No problem, as long as a taxi driver can find it." He slowed to a halt a few yards from the main exit and extended his hand. "Thanks, Abigail."

She put her palm in his, absorbing the heat and roughness of his skin against hers.

"You're welcome."

He hesitated, and then his mouth hitched in that crooked smile. "About that kiss a while ago. It was out of line. Way out of line."

"You're right. It was."

"I should apologize."

She arched a brow. "Yes, you should."

"The problem is, I'm not sorry."

Now that her anger had cooled, Abby wasn't all that sorry, either. But that wasn't something a woman admitted to a man she'd only met a few minutes ago. One she wasn't even sure she liked.

"Would you accept dinner instead of an apology?"

As soon as the words were out of his mouth, Pete

could have kicked himself. He needed sleep, about two or three days' worth. Even more important, he needed to nip this reluctant attraction he felt for Abigail Davis in the bud. One look at her had been enough to tell Pete she wasn't his type.

Although the lady certainly didn't pull any punches, she had that warm, delicious, *womanly* aura that spelled big trouble to any man with enough sense to recognize it. Unlike her fun-loving sister, Abby Davis no doubt expected more from a man than a weekend in Soho. Everything about her shouted quality. And respect. And permanence. The kind of permanence that came with long-term relationships, maybe even marriage.

Pete had learned the hard way that there wasn't anything permanent in a military marriage. Not in his, anyway. It had been plagued from the start by too many absences, too few joyful reunions. After the stormy breakup eight years ago, he'd sworn to avoid the kind of relationships that demanded more time and attention than he could give them while he wore a uniform. Which meant, he decided with a flicker of real regret, avoiding women like Abby Davis.

From the uncertainty chasing across her face, she didn't appear too thrilled with the prospect of having dinner with him, either. He couldn't blame her. Not after the way he'd manhandled her. Before he could think of a graceful way to withdraw his offer, however, she took him up on it. More or less.

"I'll tell you what. There's a nine-course wedding

dinner and a chocolate-rum-raisin wedding cake waiting for the missing bride and groom at the Pines. Why don't we share the dinner, so we can tell our respective sister and subordinate what they missed later?"

"You've got a deal."

Abby regretted the offer the moment she stepped outside the terminal. Icy sleet drummed down on the overhead canopy with a tinny staccato beat. Alarming little mounds of slush were piled up along the pavement. It splashed over her feet whenever a car whooshed by. What was more, the lowering gray sky gave every indication that the storm was only going to get worse.

Shoulders hunched against the piercing wind, she jammed her hands in her pockets and waited for the bus to the parking lot. As she shifted from foot to foot to keep the cold from seeping through her thin soles, she weighed the pros of dinner with Pete O'Brian against the cons of a thirty-mile round-trip in this mess.

She was careful by nature, and overly cautious as a result of years of acting as a foil for the high-strung, effervescent Beth. Her every instinct screamed at her to back out of the trip to the Pines. The sensible thing to do would be to inch her way home through the heavy traffic and curl up with a good book under the down-filled comforter that covered her iron bedstead.

She was framing the words to renege on her offer

when the parking-lot shuttle bus pulled up. Once inside, Pete settled his long frame on the seat beside her, stashed his carryall under his legs and reached down with a strong, blunt-fingered hand to massage his knee.

Abby frowned, then looked up and caught his glance. This time, she wasn't about to let him off with the excuse of jet lag.

"I made a bad jump a few weeks ago," he muttered, reading her expression. "Hit the ground a little harder than I'd intended to."

"A jump? You mean, like out of a plane?"

Nodding, he tucked his hand into his jacket pocket and eased his shoulders back against the seat. Abby found herself squeezed between his solid frame and a portly Georgia football fan in a red ball cap with an equally portly bulldog emblazoned on its bill.

"Do you do that often?" she asked, edging sideways to keep her hips and thighs from bumping O'Brian's. "Jump out of planes, I mean?"

"I guess that depends on your definition of *often*. Sometimes we go for months with nothing but our requal jumps. Other times, it seems like we're popping the chutes every week."

"Once would be too often for me," Abby admitted, shuddering. "For the life of me, I can't understand why anyone would want to jump out of an airplane that wasn't diving straight down."

He slanted her an amused glance. "If it was diving

straight down, your chances of jumping out would be pretty slim."

The sound of an audible gulp brought their heads around.

"I'm flying back to Schenectady after the game tomorrow," the portly football fan next to her said sheepishly. "Would you two mind talking about something other than planes going down?"

Pete laughed and obligingly changed the subject to the odds of the Bulldogs' awesome offense plowing right through Georgia Tech's injury-ridden defensive line. The others on the bus were quick to add their opinions, and the conversation soon degenerated into an unabashedly partisan debate. Although Abby had her own opinions about Georgia's so-called powerhouse offense, she let the lively discussion flow around her. She much preferred to watch Pete's face as he refereed the debate.

It was an intriguing one, she decided again, with character stamped in the lines fanning from the corners of his eyes and bracketing his mouth. Character and, she guessed, perhaps a residue of pain. Obviously he still hadn't recovered from that bad jump he mentioned, which no doubt explained why he hadn't accompanied Jordy and the rest of his unit on their unexpected deployment. Maybe he'd come back to the States on convalescent leave. Idly Abby wondered how long he'd be in the States…and who he might have left behind in England.

The thought jerked her out of her contemplation

of his strong, firm chin and bumpy nose. Startled, she realized she'd agreed to have dinner with a man she knew absolutely nothing about. He might very well have a wife and three kids waiting for him overseas.

She frowned, trying to remember whether the hands tucked in his jacket pockets sported any rings of the plain-gold-band variety. She didn't think so, but that didn't mean much these days. For safety reasons, a good number of men and women in hazardous professions didn't wear rings. Jumping out of airplanes ranked right up there among the most hazardous, in Abby's book.

Nor did that bone-melting kiss rule out the possibility that he was otherwise attached. Abby hadn't tangled with many married men on the prowl, but she'd come across one or two in her time. Her frown deepening, she stole another glance at Pete O'Brian's face. She didn't know why, but she couldn't bring herself to believe he was a member of that particular subspecies. She'd make it a point to find out, though, over dinner.

It wasn't until she was unlocking the door to the Antiquemobile that Abby realized she'd unconsciously decided to make the drive to the Pines after all. Well, she could only hope the weather didn't worsen and make her regret her decision.

Gripping the wheel with tight fists, she eased out of the parking lot and into the stream of traffic heading north on slick, slush-covered roads. She breathed a quiet sigh of relief when the slush splattered and disappeared under the churning tires. The stuff was ugly, but not icy.

"I'm sorry the heater doesn't work," she murmured, hunching her shoulders against the frigid air in the van. "It went out a few years ago, and I never bothered to get it fixed. We don't usually get this kind of weather in Atlanta."

She threw him a quick smile. "Although I suppose it doesn't faze a man who slept on an ice floe."

Pete smiled back, but his eyes held concern as he surveyed the gray drizzle on the windshield.

"Maybe driving to the Pines isn't such a good idea. I don't like taking you so far out of your way, especially on roads like this."

"They're not as bad as I was afraid they'd be. I don't think we'll have any problem."

Careful, cautious Abby mentally crossed all ten fingers, and those of her toes that weren't frozen from the cold and dampness. She would have worried herself to a quiet frazzle if Beth had been the one out driving in this kind of weather.

"Besides, I really need to speak to the manager. The chocolate-rum-raisin cake's already paid for, but maybe there's a chance I can recoup a few of the other costs of this unwedding."

"Are you saying your sister left you holding the bag *and* the bill when she backed out on Jordy?"

Abby dragged her gaze from the road and leveled him a look as frosty as the air in the van. "I think we'd better settle something right now, O'Brian. My sister isn't perfect, I admit, but I won't tolerate criticism of her, particularly from someone who doesn't even know her."

He didn't take offense at her blunt speaking. If anything, Abby thought she caught a glint of approval in his dark eyes. Military men, she supposed, appreciated the concepts of loyalty and brotherhood. Or, in this case, sisterhood.

"Fair enough," he replied. "For the record, though, I do know Beth. Or maybe I should say I've met her. I was with Jordy the weekend he bumped into her and—" his mouth curled downward "—went off the deep end."

"That's one way to put it," she agreed, relenting a little. Personally, she'd used a few stronger phrases during the nights she tossed and turned and fretted over Beth's rash decision to marry a near stranger.

"It's the only polite way to put it."

Abby shot him a quick glance. "I take it you don't subscribe to the theory of love at first sight?"

"No. Lust at first sight, maybe. The right mix of chemicals will always generate a spontaneous combustion, but that kind of fire flares hot, and usually burns out fast."

Abby suspected he spoke from personal experience. Given the way he'd ignited tiny flames in her blood within seconds of their meeting, he'd probably sparked his fair share of good-size conflagrations with other, more willing partners. Still, the cynicism in his reply bothered her.

"Is that what you think love is?" she asked curiously. "A purely chemical reaction?"

"What else?"

"I don't know," she murmured, more to herself than to him. "But I hope it's more. Much more."

Deciding that the conversation had drifted into far-too-personal channels, she steered it toward the soaring Atlanta skyline on their left. Tomorrow's big game. The unusual weather.

Pete followed her lead, his hands shoved into his pockets and his long legs stretched out as far as the van would allow. The fact that the lady didn't have any better definition than he did of the hazy, indefinable and, in his opinion, highly overrated emotion called love intrigued him. So she wasn't involved with someone she considered herself in love with.

The thought gave him a twist of pleasure at some deep, visceral level. He wrote off the sensation as a mindless male response to the knowledge that an attractive female was available. An attractive female who just happened to fit in his arms perfectly. One whose sexy, tantalizing mouth would no doubt drift through his dreams tonight.

Regret once again stirred beneath his layers of bone-deep tiredness. Regret, and the realization that one taste of Abby Davis wasn't quite enough to satisfy him. It was just as well that he wouldn't see Doug Jordan's almost-in-law again after tonight. Tasting her could fast become addictive.

Banishing an insidious image of a private feast that included Abby as the main course, Pete responded easily to her conversational gambits. After a few miles, however, he let the conversation die away altogether. The wet roads required her attention. Not wanting to distract her, he crossed his ankles and gave every appearance of being absorbed in the gray landscape outside.

He had plenty of time to absorb it. Rush-hour traffic, and the driving rain slowed the already sluggish pace around Atlanta's busy loop. When they finally exited onto a less busy state road, the traffic moved a little more quickly, but the air in the van grew progressively colder with every mile north they progressed. Gradually the weak afternoon light faded to a purplish gloom. Headlights flickered on. The windshield wipers worked steadily.

By the time they passed through a small village appropriately called Pineville and turned off at tall brick pillars announcing the Pines Inn and Golf Resort, Pete felt distinctly uncomfortable about taking Abby so far out of her way. He didn't say anything while she negotiated the narrow, winding access road that cut through timber-covered hills. But when she pulled up at the sprawling two-story artistry of weathered cedar, native stone and soaring glass that constituted the resort's main lodge, he stopped her before she got out of the van.

"Why don't we pass on dinner?" he suggested. "I don't like the idea of you tackling these roads after dark."

Abby didn't particularly like the idea herself, but she'd come this far. A hot meal—particularly one she'd already paid for—would go a long way toward dispelling the ice crystals in her blood and make the drive home a less daunting prospect.

"I'm here now," she replied with a small shrug. "I might as well indulge myself with a taste of that rum-raisin cake before heading home."

"You can take it with you. Or," he amended slowly, his eyes holding hers, "you could stay at the inn tonight. That way, I wouldn't have to worry about you driving home alone—and we could share an unwedding breakfast, in addition to dinner."

Abby stared at him, her jaw sagging. Then she gave herself a mental shake. For heaven's sake, the man wasn't suggesting she spend the night with him.

Was he?

She peered at him through the gloom. For the life of her, she couldn't tell. His face was in shadows, and his eyes were a deep, impenetrable black. She opted for a neutral response.

"I doubt if they'll have room. We only got the honeymoon cottage on such short notice because it's so isolated from the main lodge."

And so outrageously expensive, she added silently. "Let's get you checked in and track down our dinner.

Then I'll head home, and you can sleep off your jet lag in a bed you'll have to see to believe."

They walked through the tall, weathered oak doors of the inn and stepped into a scene of total chaos. A chartered busload of University of Georgia alumni, sporting heavily jowled bulldogs on everything from designer jackets to diamond-encrusted pendants, filled every square inch of the lobby. They laughed and chattered among themselves while harried desk clerks tried to sort out what appeared to be a major foul-up in reservations. Leaving Pete to work his way through the amorphous, free-flowing lines, Abby sought out the manager.

He'd left half an hour ago, she soon discovered. As had the special events coordinator. Unable to confirm exactly what charges had been incurred at this point, a distracted assistant manager promised Abby someone would call her tomorrow with concrete figures. He also assured her that he'd notify the justice of the peace who was supposed to perform the ceremony in less than an hour that the wedding was off.

Disappointed that her long trip hadn't produced more concrete results, Abby returned to the lobby. She found Pete a few paces closer to the front desk, still caught in the throng of alumni. At his insistence, she gave him the confirmation number, then slipped off her cloak and settled down to wait in a wingback chair done in rich burgundy fabric.

Palming her hands down the slim, calf-length skirt

of her black velveteen dress, she smoothed away the worst of the wrinkles. With its wide collar of delicate Brussels lace and its bone buttons, it would do well enough for dinner at a four-star restaurant. She just wished she could slip off her thin-soled granny boots and massage some warmth back into her frozen feet.

Pete made his way over to her some twenty minutes later, a rueful smile in his eyes and tired lines etched deep in his face.

"I'm checked in, but it's going to be a while yet before I can get to the cabin to clean up. Their shuttle service is overwhelmed at this point." He rasped a hand across a chin stubbled with dark shadows. "If you don't mind waiting another few minutes, I'll find a men's room and scrape off a few layers."

Abby pushed herself out of the chair, ignoring the instant protest from her still-numb toes. "Don't be silly. I'll drive you to the cottage. Besides, I'd like to see if it lives up to its extravagant advertising."

"At these prices, it better," Pete said wryly, shepherding her through the lobby with a hand at the small of her back. The casual touch was probably nothing more than an unconscious gesture on his part, but it sent a sudden dart of awareness through Abby.

"Which reminds me," he added casually. "You'll need to sign the credit slip when we come back."

"Credit slip?"

"For the deposit you put down to guarantee the

room. I had them credit your charge card and bill the room to mine."

"You didn't have to do that," she protested. "I offered you the use of the cottage tonight because it was already paid for. I didn't intend for you to get stuck with expensive accommodations you hadn't planned on."

He shrugged off her objections. "As you pointed out, I was lucky to get a room at all. There's no reason for you to foot the bill for me. Or for Jordy, for that matter," he tacked on, propelling her toward the door once more. "I'll talk to him when I get back about the fix this aborted wedding put you in."

"Wait a minute." Abby dug in her heels, a little indignant at his blithe assumption of authority in something that wasn't really any of his business. "You don't need to talk to anyone. The bride's family is responsible for the wedding arrangements, you know."

"I'm sure Jordy didn't realize his ditzy fiancée stuck you with—" He broke off and tried, unsuccessfully, to recover. "Sorry. What I meant is that I know Jordy. He's a solid troop, one of the best in my squad. He'll want to reimburse you for expenses incurred on his behalf."

Abby lifted her chin. Any desire she might have felt to share dinner with this hard-eyed cynical stranger faded in the face of a fierce protectiveness that was as natural to her as breathing.

"Back off, O'Brian. Any expenses I incurred on

my *sister's* behalf are no concern of yours. Or anyone else's."

His jaw squared. So did his shoulders.

Abby refused to be intimidated, although she eyed the muscle twitching in his left cheek with a touch of wary interest. The expression in his eyes confirmed the impression she'd formed at the airport that this wasn't a man to cross.

"Have it your way," he conceded, with a distinct lack of graciousness.

"I will."

She spun around and sailed through the crowded lobby. Pete followed, his carryall clenched in one fist. They both halted outside the inn, pinned under the awning by the cold, pelting rain.

"It's not letting up."

The deep voice at her shoulder was still a little clipped around the edges.

"No, it's not." She fished in her purse for her keys. "I think I'd better leave you to handle the rum-raisin cake by yourself, after all."

Abby knew darn well her decision to back out of dinner had more to do with Pete's careless comment about Beth than with the weather. She suspected he knew it, too.

Tough!

She dashed to the van, wondering just what it was about Pete O'Brian that got to her so easily. In the short time she'd known him, she'd run the gamut from astonishment to fury to reluctant awareness to simmering anger once more. Since she'd always considered herself the sober, steady sibling, she didn't understand or particularly like his unsettling affect on her.

It was just as well that she was heading home after she dropped him off at the cottage, Abby decided. The man bothered her, plain and simple. In ways she wasn't up to dealing with tonight.

Following the directions Pete culled from a map of the resort, she circled a huddle of buildings he identified as the golf pro shop and starter shack, then aimed the van up a steep, narrow path. The winding road corkscrewed past the Pines' famous cottages. Shingle-roofed structures the size of a house, they were tucked away amid stands of tall, dark firs. Gritting her teeth, Abby negotiating each switchback turn in the road at a pace a snail could have challenged. When she pulled up at the two-story cottage that sat in solitary splendor atop the crest, she shifted into park, but kept the motor running.

Pete reached for the carryall stashed under his feet, then slewed around in his seat to face her.

"I really think you should reconsider driving home tonight. Stay here. It looks like a big place," he added. "Two stories. We'd have one apiece."

Well, that settled the question of whether his earlier invitation to share the cottage cloaked some ulterior motive. She offered him her hand and a small smile.

"No, thanks. It's all yours."

"You sure?"

"I'm sure."

He searched her face for a moment, then opened the door and eased outside. "I appreciate the lift, Abby."

"It was the least I could do for Jordy's personal messenger."

She waited until Pete had unlocked the cottage door before she put the van in gear. He stood silhouetted in a spill of light from the interior as she drove off, telling herself it was ridiculous to feel this perverse niggle of disappointment at the way the evening had turned out.

Her disappointment quickly gave way to con_ sternation. Some law of physics that she apparently didn't understand made going down steep hills more treacherous than going up. She negotiated the first hairpin turn at a slow crawl, her muscles knotted with tension.

The common sense Abby prided herself on asserted itself before she reached the second turn. If she could have turned the van around on the narrow path, she might have swallowed both her pride and her irritation and taken O'Brian up on his offer. Since she couldn't, she decided she'd stop at the main lodge and wait till this drizzle let up before tackling the drive home.

She never made it to the second turn.

While she was still some yards away, the Antiquemobile hit a slick patch, slid off the road and slammed sideways into a tree.

Chapter 3

Pete should have been out by now.

He should have crashed twenty seconds after stepping out of the shower.

When the taillights on Abby's van had disappeared, he'd come inside the cottage and barely glanced at the soaring open-beamed oak ceilings and luxurious furnishings before heading for the loft bedroom. Dumping his gear bag, he'd hit the shower with a sigh of sheer pleasure. He'd returned to the bedroom scant moments later, fully intending to sink into oblivion in the half-acre bed that dominated the spacious loft.

Instead, he found himself standing beside the huge bed, ignoring the weariness that ate into his bones like a sad, sorry song. One corner of his tired mind admired the massive bed frame done in polished oak, metal scrollwork and gleaming brass. A less aesthetic part acknowledged that a bed like this was built to be shared.

With someone like Abby.

His body tightening, Pete gave in to the half-formed fantasy that hovered at the back of his consciousness. It began with the kiss at the airport and took wing. With unswerving male directness, it led to a vision of Abby sprawled across this ocean of royal blue spread, her arms outflung and her honey-streaked hair tumbling in wild abandon. Her brown eyes heavy-lidded. Her soft, full mouth curving in invitation.

Sure, O'Brian. Sure.

That soft, full mouth had chewed him up and spit him out in small, well-masticated pieces during their confrontation in the lobby. For all her refined appearance and warm smile, Abigail Davis could fire up hotter and faster than a phosphorous grenade in defense of that bubbleheaded sister of hers.

Shaking his head, Pete snagged his jeans from the foot of the bed. His bare feet sank into thick wheat-colored carpet as he headed back down the stairs. He was too tired to sleep, he acknowledged. And too irritated by the way his misguided, heavy-handed attempt to make sure Abby didn't get stuck with all the costs of this wedding had backfired on him. He wasn't exactly sure why he even cared, except that the long, cold ride in her decrepit van had convinced him she wasn't exactly rolling in cash.

That, and the fact that his stomach still tightened every time he let himself think about that damned kiss. The memory of her mouth under his pulled at him, as did the woman herself. Despite her prickliness every time her sister's name entered the conversation, or maybe because of it, she characterized everything he admired in a woman and wouldn't let himself respond to.

He liked the way she'd stood up to him. Respected her loyalty to her sister. The sensual appeal in her slender body and delicate, aristocratic features didn't exactly repulse him, either, he admitted with a wry twist of his lips. No wonder he'd felt that kick to the gut when he kissed her, a solid hit he termed lust, for lack of any better description.

Still, he couldn't believe he'd invited her to share this cottage tonight. Twice! Good thing she hadn't taken him up on either invitation. As bone-weary as he was, he wouldn't have gotten much sleep, thinking about Abby all alone in that big bed, and there wasn't much likelihood she'd have shared it with him.

He snapped on a low table lamp and crossed to the oak wall unit at one end of the vast sitting room, confident one of its paneled doors would yield a wet bar stocked with a classy brand of Scotch. He found it on the second try. Splashing a good three fingers into a heavy crystal glass, he took an appreciative sip.

Very classy, he decided as it burned a slow, satisfying line down his throat.

Like Abigail Davis.

He took the Scotch with him to the cavernous stone fireplace, which was conveniently equipped with a gas starter. Within moments, tiny pinpoints of blue flame licked along the stacked logs. Propping a foot on the low stone fender, Pete marveled at the tangled web of circumstance that had led him to an argument over personal finances with a woman he hardly knew.

If Beth hadn't gotten cold feet and skipped out on her wedding.

If Jordy hadn't deployed just hours before he was due to leave for the States.

If Pete hadn't made a downwind landing two weeks ago and torn his anterior cruciate ligament all to hell...

Unconsciously he massaged his knee with a steady, rhythmic motion. He stared into the fire, seeing vivid, pulse-tripping images of that last jump form and reform in the dancing flames.

The black hole of the open cargo door yawned before him. In his mind's eye, he saw his men go out, one after another. He heard the snick of the static-line clips. The sudden catch in the rhythm. The jumpmaster's frantic shout.

Again and again, he relived the nightmare of trying to retrieve Carrington's body.

With a vicious curse, Pete downed the rest of his

Scotch and shoved the glass onto the mantel. The doubts and questions that had plagued him since the accident pounded through his brain. He should have seen that Carrington was too nervous. Should have caught the way his fist had wrapped around the static line. Dammit, he should have…

A sudden banging dragged him from his private hell. He swung around, his muscles coiled, as if in anticipation of attack.

Another thump rattled the front door, and then a wavery voice carried through the solid wood.

"Pete? It's me, Abby. I've…I've had an accident."

He crossed the room in four long strides and wrenched the door open. It went crashing back against the wall. The shivering, bedraggled woman on the doorstep flinched at the violence, then lifted a shaky hand to gesture vaguely behind her.

"The van…in a ditch. I walked…"

Pete's training kicked in before the words were half out of his mouth. Raking her from head to toe with a swift, blade-sharp glance, he cut off her stumbling recital.

"Are you hurt?"

"I…I…"

Her teeth were chattering so hard she couldn't speak. Resisting the impulse to sweep her wet, trembling body into his arms and carry her inside, Pete took a firm grip on her arm instead. She'd walked this far. He wouldn't add to any trauma she might have sustained by jostling her unnecessarily now.

He got her inside, kicked the door shut and peeled her sodden cape from her shoulders. A swift visual showed no protruding bones or obvious hematomas.

"Tell me if you're hurting, Abby."

His voice soothed, calmed, demanded.

"No... I don't..."

He slid his hands under her wet hair and wrapped them around her neck. His skilled fingers found no step-offs, no deformities or abnormalities that might suggest the spinal injuries so common in vehicle accidents. Capturing her cheeks and chin in a firm, gentle vise, he tilted her face toward the light. Her eyes were wide and teary, but the pupils hadn't dilated with shock. Although clammy, the skin under his hands retained enough heat for him to rule out hypothermia.

"I'm not...hurt. Just wet and...cold."

"We'll fix that in a minute."

Holding back the relief that clamored in his veins, Pete swiftly attacked the buttons on the front of her black dress. She closed her hands over his, a startled question in her eyes.

"It's okay. I need to check your ribs."

Swallowing, she dropped her hands.

Pete worked swiftly. In his twenty-two years in rescue, he'd seen too many cases where crew members' minds had selectively shut down to pain while their bodies endured unbelievable trauma. Men had dodged the enemy for hours while carrying their own amputated limbs. Others had crawled incredible distances with the bones in both legs shattered. Abby might well have suffered internal injuries she didn't feel, couldn't acknowledge.

Easing her dress down to her hips, he ran exploring hands over ribs encased in wet black silk. Her heart thumped solidly against his palms. Every rib felt whole and in place. He released the relief he'd been holding back. It flowed through him, a hot, surging wave that made his fingers want to grip the wet silk.

"I don't think you broke anything."

"Yes, I did…." She got the words out through racking shivers. "My van…is all…dented."

Grinning, Pete scooped her up and headed for the stairs, leaving dress and cloak in wet heaps on the floor. "If that's the worst of the damages, I'd say you're in pretty good shape, Ms. Davis."

Very good shape, he amended as she curled into him, seeking warmth. High, firm breasts flattened against his bare chest. Nipples rigid with cold peaked under the wet silk and poked into his skin. Hanging on to his professional detachment with some effort, Pete forced himself to ignore the sensations she caused in the upper portion of his body. He wasn't quite as successful with the lower portion. Each step up the stairs brought her nicely rounded bottom bumping into his groin.

He carried her into the bathroom that took up half of the loft. Relief edged with regret lanced through him when she pulled together a shaky smile.

"I...can man...age."

He lowered her feet to the thick carpet, but kept an arm around her waist while he reached into the freestanding glass-and-brass shower cubicle to twist the knobs. When steam filled the stall, he disengaged himself.

"I'll round up some dry clothes while you defrost. Call me when you're through."

Abby didn't think she'd ever be through. In fact, she seriously considered taking up permanent residence in the glass shower stall. Blessed heat swirled around it, and around her. Hot water streamed down her body to pool at her feet. For the first time since leaving the shop this morning, her toes felt as though they were still attached to the rest of her. She propped her shoulders against the sturdy glass wall, fighting the urge to just slide down and puddle on the royal blue tile for the rest of the night, if not the rest of her life.

Gradually the few seconds of stark terror she'd experienced when the van slid sideways across the icy road faded from her consciousness. So did the sickening crunch when its back end had slammed into the tree. She had no idea how much damage the Antiquemobile had sustained. At this moment, she didn't really care. She knew she could increase the amount of the small-business loan she planned to take out, just enough to cover the cost of a new van to complement her new shop. She'd think about that later, though. Right now, more important matters concerned her.

Like where she was going to find the energy to turn off the taps and step out of the shower. Pete provided the motivation some moments later by rapping on the bathroom door.

"Abby? If you're going under for the third time, I'm pretty good at mouth-to-mouth."

She smiled ruefully. Good? Judging by his kiss, she'd say he was a whole lot better than good. If she had to rate Pete O'Brian's mouth-to-mouth technique on a scale ranging from shattering to mind-bending, she'd give him one-hundred-percent erotic.

What a shame that same incredibly skilled mouth had a tendency to voice rather unflattering opinions of Beth. Sighing, she lifted her face to the pulsing stream.

Abby wasn't blind to her sister's faults, as many people seemed to think—Marissa, particularly. She just weighed them against the uncritical, unrestrained love Beth gave her. A love that had buoyed her during the bleak years after their parents' deaths. A fierce love that had kept them together every time the nameless, faceless "system" tried to separate the Davis girls.

"Abby?"

"I'll be out in a minute."

"I didn't bring much except my uniform and some exercise gear back to the States with me. I left some sweats on the bed for you. While you dress, I'll go downstairs and fix you something hot to drink."

Reaching for the white ceramic faucets, Abby cut off the life-giving warmth and stepped out of the stall. Luckily, the bathroom came equipped with a thick terry robe, a blow-dryer, and an assortment of luxurious lotions and creams. Feeling almost human again, she dried her hair, then went into the bedroom.

Two of her could have fit into the faded maroon sweats and thick socks Pete had left on the bed. The sweatshirt was emblazoned with USAF PARARESCUE in big silver letters on the back, and it hung to her knees. She rolled the maroon sweatpants up at the waist and cuffs, then pulled the warm socks on gratefully over her perennially cold feet.

Pete met her at the bottom of the staircase and handed her a steaming mug. Wrapping both palms around the footed mug, Abby sniffed at the chocolate-scented swirls rising above its rim.

"Mmm…this smells wonderful."

"You might try a test sip before you…"

His warning came too late. Abby had already blown the steam away and taken a big gulp.

Her eyes widened in shock, then filled with instant tears. She tried without success to work her paralyzed throat muscles. At her frantic, gurgling appeal, Pete thumped her on the back. Swallow by fiery swallow, the explosive brew scorched its way down her windpipe. By the time it reached her stomach, every nerve in her body was sending out distress signals.

"Wh-what's in this?"

"Hot chocolate. A little rum. The finest cognac money can buy. And several other ingredients from the well-stocked bar that you probably don't want to know about."

"Good Lord!" Tears trickling down her cheeks, Abby gaped at the innocuous-looking mug.

"The PJs have a name for this particular pick-me-up," Pete told her, grinning. "But we don't use it in mixed company."

"I'm not surprised!" She swiped the back of her hand across her eyes. "Is that what you call yourselves, you and Jordy? PJs?"

"It's an old abbreviation, for parajumpers. We're assigned to pararescue or special tactics now, but the original initials still follow us around." He gestured with his own mug. "Why don't you sit down by the fire and recover?"

"I don't think I'll ever recover."

She crossed the oak floor and sank into a love seat done in a rich blue-green-and-gold plaid. Pete took the facing love seat, his long legs angled toward the fire and a lazy smile tugging at his mouth. He'd pulled on a blue cotton shirt, she saw, and well-used running shoes that undoubtedly saw duty with the warm sweats she was now wearing. His beaver-brown hair glistened with dark lights, telling Abby that he'd taken advantage of the shower stall upstairs sometime prior to her extended occupancy.

He looked loose, and more relaxed than she'd yet seen him. And very much at home amid the luxury of oak paneling, rich fabrics and the fine handcrafted furnishings that filled the cottage. Strange, Abby mused, taking another, far more cautious sip from the steaming mug. With his rugged, uncompromising features and tough exterior, she wouldn't have imagined that he could appear so... so approachable.

And so incredibly sexy.

"I'll go down and take a look at the van in the morning," he said, breaking into her disturbing thoughts. "Maybe I can get it out of the ditch."

"Maybe. But you'll have to unwrap the back end from around a pine tree first."

"That bad, huh?"

"That bad. Oh, well, Beth's been urging me to retire the Antiquemobile for ages. I guess it's time to think about a replacement."

"That's one thing your sister and I can agree on, anyway."

Abby threw him a warning look. Wisely, he retreated to safer ground.

"Are you hungry? I started to call the kitchen and ask them to deliver that cake you promised me, but I thought I'd better wait and see if you were still up to it."

"Rum-soaked raisins on top of the PJs' special

concoction? I don't think so. But I wouldn't mind a taste of the standing rib roast and Vidalia-onion soufflé I ordered for the wedding supper."

"Onion soufflé?"

The doubtful note in his voice won a chuckle from her. "Trust me. It's the chef's specialty. People come from all over the South just to experience it."

"If you say so. Hang tight. I'll call room service."

He went across the room to consult the resort directory on the desk angled beside a curtained floor-to-ceiling window. A few moments later he returned, a crease between his dark brows.

"They promised to do their best, but it'll take a while. The overflow of football fans and a number of strategic personnel absences due to the weather have taxed their resources to the limit."

Abby tucked her toes under her on the well-cushioned couch, not altogether unhappy about the delay. So she hadn't eaten anything since breakfast? So her stomach had performed a joyous leap at the mere mention of food? She wouldn't mind some time before the fire to savor her potent drink, and the even more potent male opposite her.

"In case my teeth were chattering too loudly for you to hear it before, I want to thank you again for taking me in. And for the, ah, physical exam."

His eyes glinted at her delicate reference to the way he'd stripped her of everything but her underwear and her granny boots, then run his hands over her body.

Even in her wet, shaking state, Abby had seen that he knew what he was doing.

"You're welcome."

"Is that part of your job? Giving first aid, I mean."

"We can do a little better than first aid. Every PJ qualifies for national level certification as an EMT before graduating from our academy. We're also trained in arctic and jungle survival, aircrew operations and underwater egress."

"And jumping out of airplanes," she added with a grimace.

A shadow rippled across his face. Or it might have been the flickering firelight. It was gone so swiftly, she wasn't sure.

"That's part of the job," he replied evenly. "Not my favorite part, I'll admit."

"Which is?"

His shoulders relaxed under their covering of blue cotton. "Putting our chopper down beside a smoking pile of wreckage and watching a crew member run toward us, a grin plastered across his face. Or her face," he amended, with a smile at Abby. "A growing number of our air force aircrew members are women."

"Good for them!"

His smile broadened. "Right now, women are barred from participating in direct combat, which includes combat rescue. But I don't think it'll be long before the first female PJ reports for duty."

Abby knew little about the military, and nothing at all about combat rescue, but she'd heard enough about Tailhook and other scandals in the news to suspect that not all military men welcomed females in their ranks. Curious about where Pete stood on the matter, she probed further.

"Will you have a problem accepting a female PJ?"

"I've been in rescue twenty-two years. It's my life. I'll accept anyone or anything that improves our ability to perform our mission."

The quiet dignity of his reply gave Abby her first glimpse behind Pete O'Brian's impenetrable exterior. This man was a far more complex creature than his tough-guy image suggested.

"What about you, Abigail? How long have you been into antiques?"

"How did you know I'm in the antique business?"

"Jordy told me. He also gave me your phone numbers at home and at work, in case there was a foul-up at the airport and Beth and I missed each other."

They both left unsaid just how big a foul-up occurred at the airport.

"I was going to call you tomorrow, you know," he added slowly, almost reluctantly.

Surprise and pleasure percolated through her. "No, I didn't know."

"I wanted to make sure you got home okay. Besides, I owed you a dinner, remember?"

Abby remembered. She also remembered that she'd intended to find out a bit more about him during that dinner…like his exact marital status. She nibbled on her lower lip, searching for a subtle way to find out what she wanted to know. There wasn't one, she decided, so she opted for a direct approach.

"I don't usually accept dinner invitations from men I don't know. Is there someone waiting for you in England who might object to us dining together?"

"No, I'm divorced. My wife got tired of a husband who spent more time in the air than on the ground."

Even though that was the answer she'd been looking for, Abby felt uncomfortable at having pried it out of him.

"Oh, I'm sorry."

"It happened a long time ago. Almost eight years, and I still spend more time in the air than on the ground. Too much to form the kind of relationship where anyone would be waiting for me when I got down, anyway. How about you?" he asked, neatly turning the tables. "Anyone waiting for you at home?"

His frank response deserved an equally honest answer.

"No, no one. I've been too busy with work and getting Beth through school. And with studying for my appraiser's license." She couldn't resist adding a pleased little footnote. "I got it last year."

"Okay, I admit my ignorance. What does a person do with an appraiser's license?"

"Detailed descriptions of antiques for insurance purposes, mostly. Also, I value the contents of homes and conduct sales when families need to dispose of an estate. Right now I'm working out of shop called Things Past, but I plan to open my own business."

"Your own antique business? I'm impressed."

Abby took another sip of the chocolate neutron bomb, then set it aside. Once a person knew what to expect, the drink was actually pretty palatable. Welcome warmth curled in her tummy as she drew up her legs and propped her chin on her knees.

"I've been saving every penny since Beth finished college," she confided. "And spending every weekend scouring the countryside for stock. I've got things stashed in rental storage facilities all around Atlanta."

"What kind of things?"

"*All* kinds of things. Primitives. Glassware. Jewelry. Beautiful pieces of period furniture."

"Good stuff, huh?"

Warmed by the chocolate and his interest, Abby opened up far more than she usually did. Beth didn't share her passion for all things old and well loved. Marissa did, of course, but for obvious reasons, Abby hadn't told her boss about her careful acquisitions.

"You should see the George IV four-poster bed I

found in an old barn outside Macon." Her eyes lit up as she described her treasure. "It's solid mahogany. Crafted by one of the premier cabinetmakers in England. I've traced it to a bill of lading written in 1838. It was shipped to Twelve Oaks Plantation as a birthday gift for Mrs. Burgess Clement, of the Macon Clements."

"Pretty fancy pedigree."

The fervent light in Abby's cinnamon-brown eyes fascinated Pete. This was an aspect of her he hadn't yet seen. Vibrant. Glowing. Lost in the pleasure of her profession.

His fingers tightened on the ceramic mug. What would it take, he wondered, to nudge that pleasure one step further? To make it less professional? More personal?

"The bed was on Twelve Oaks' property inventory until well after the War between the States," she continued. "Mrs. Clements passed it to one of her granddaughters, who in turn passed it to one of the great-great-granddaughters. Can you imagine all the Clement women who must have slept in that bed? Birthed their babies there? Welcomed their men home there?"

Her soft, dreamy query evoked a juxtaposition of Abby and beds that took Pete by the throat. He swallowed, hard, and set his mug aside. No more of the PJs' special concoction for him. He had enough trouble reining in his galloping fantasies as it was.

His abrupt movement drew her out of her reverie.

Smiling, she brought him into the conversation. "I'll bet you've seen the inside of some beautiful manor houses in England, filled with all kinds of treasures."

Pete had seen the inside of more pubs than manor houses, but he responded to the deep-seated need in her eyes.

"I've been to Windsor a few times. And to Stonecross Keep, which isn't far from Mildenhall, where we're stationed."

"Really? What period is it?"

"Stonecross? Norman, I think. It's pretty solid, all square towers and stone battlements."

"What about the inside? How is it furnished?"

Pete's mouth curved. If one of his troops had told him he'd be spending an evening discussing castle furniture with a woman who triggered some very fundamental instincts in him, he would have sent the man for a psych eval. Hoping that none of this would get ever back to Jordy, he searched his memory for details of medieval furnishings.

Either his account of black-beamed ceilings and big, square trestle tables was more boring than even he thought it would be, or the PJs' brew was more potent than Abby was used to. Halfway through his rambling discourse, her lids fluttered down. Once. Twice. The third time, they didn't quite make it back up.

Pete droned on, inventing details when his sketchy memory failed. After the shock of the accident, she could probably use a short nap until dinner arrived. He wouldn't mind resting his sandpapery eyelids for a few minutes, either.

Her jaw waggled on its perch atop her knees, then slid off. She jerked awake, embarrassment staining her cheeks. Moments later, she sagged against the couch. She was out for the count.

Moving with a stealth unaffected by his stiff knee, Pete mounted the stairs and pulled a couple of blankets from the closet at the rear of the loft. When he tucked the downy royal blue cover around Abby's shoulders, she gave a little mewl of delight and burrowed into its warmth. Her chin caught Pete's hand. Sighing, she dug a nest for it in his palm.

Smiling, he gave in to temptation and stroked the side of her jaw with his thumb. Her skin felt as silky as it looked, reminding him of the rippling, sun-warmed stream he used to fish in as a boy. Her scent drifted up to him, a mixture of shower soap and chocolate. Pete detected her soft, steady pulse under his thumb pad. His tripped into double time.

The lust he felt for Abby expanded, deepened, took on different shapes and colors. Like those in a kaleidoscope, the shapes had no meaning. The colors tumbled and changed too swiftly to have any substance. Pete felt the subtle shift, and it was all he could do not to gather her in his arms and join her on the plaid love seat.

Exercising a discretion he suspected he'd regret later, he retreated to the opposite sofa. Then he rested his head against the high back, propped his feet on the oak coffee table and gave himself up to the pleasure of watching the firelight play on Abby's face.

Minutes, or maybe hours, later, a muffled thump jerked him from a deep, exhausted sleep.

Groggy, he decided that dinner must have finally arrived. Only after he pushed himself upright did he realize that someone had turned off the heat. And the lights. An inky blackness pierced only by a dim red glow from the dying fire blanketed the entire cottage. Cold air knifed into his lungs with each breath.

Instant, instinctive wariness wiped away his grogginess. Something was wrong. Very wrong.

His gaze narrowed on the empty love seat opposite his. As swift and silent as a jungle cat, he rose to his feet. The tension that had become second nature to him in the past few weeks coiled in his gut. Like a predator seeking its prey, he searched the darkness.

She was down on one knee beside his leather carryall. Undershirts spilled onto the floor, forming vague white blurs. In the meager glow from the fire, the object she held in her hand was unmistakable. Its twisted, tortured shape had been burned into Pete's soul.

He crossed the floor in three noiseless strides. Wrapping a hard hand around her upper arm, he yanked her to her feet. She gave a startled squeak and dropped the piece of metal. It clattered on the oak flooring and lay between them like a small, lethal bomb.

Pete's fingers dug into her soft flesh. "What the hell were you doing with that?"

Chapter 4

Speechless with surprise, Abby stared at the man who gripped her. His face was a shadowed mask in the dim red glow of the fire, but she couldn't mistake the anger in his dark eyes.

When she didn't respond immediately, he bent, dragging her down with him, and scooped up the bit of metal.

"Answer me, dammit. What did you want with this?"

Abby found her voice, and a healthy surge of anger, as well.

"I didn't want *anything* with it. It fell out on the floor when I was digging through your underwear, and I picked it up."

"You want to tell me why you were digging through my gear?"

"You want to let go of my arm?"

They faced each other, his eyes cold and flat, hers narrowed to daggers behind a shield of thick lashes. Abby stood her ground, unflinching. The silence stretched between them like a challenge.

At last he uncurled his fingers, one by one. The apology, when it came, sounded like the scrape of broken glass.

"I'm sorry."

"You should be," she shot back, giving him a look that should have sliced six inches off him then and there. "You scared me half to death. Just what is that thing, anyway?"

His jaw squared. "A static-line retriever support."

"Oh, that tells me a lot!"

Imperceptibly the stark lines in his face eased. He rolled his shoulders, as if shifting a mountainous weight, and sidestepped her sarcastic retort.

"What were you doing in my carryall?"

"If you must know, I was looking for another pair of socks."

She was more exasperated than angry now, and a little embarrassed at having been caught rooting around in his underwear, although she wasn't about to admit it.

"My feet were cold. They *are* cold. They're freezing, as a matter of fact. Along with the rest of me. I didn't think you'd mind if I borrowed another pair of socks, since everything else I'm wearing at this moment happens to be yours. Obviously, I was wrong."

"You're welcome to the socks."

"Thank you very much. Now, would you mind telling what the heck this little scene is all about? And then turn up the heat in this place," Abby added, rubbing her arms as a series of shivers racked her. "You may enjoy sleeping on glaciers and ice packs. I don't."

"I didn't turn off the heat," he replied, his voice almost back to its normal rumble. "Or the lights, for that matter. We must have blown a fuse. I'll go find the circuit box."

He slipped the shard of metal into his pocket and started to turn away. This time it was Abby who latched on to an arm with a tight grip.

"Oh, no, you don't. I want an answer, O'Brian. I think I deserve one, after that little display of overdone machoism. What the heck just happened here? What is that bit of metal, anyway?"

A tight almost-smile cranked up one corner of his mouth. "Machoism? Is that a word?"

"If it isn't, it should be. It's the only way to describe your behavior." She folded her arms across her sweatshirt-clad chest. "I'm waiting."

"You're also freezing," he pointed out.

His gaze skimmed down to her feet, crossed one over the other in a futile attempt to warm her ice-cold digits. As he took in her awkward, pigeon-toed stance, the remaining tension drained from his face.

"Let me get the heat and lights back on. Then I'll tell you what I can."

He'd tell her what he could? She frowned, skeptical, and now curious, as well.

When she didn't budge, he gave a faint, tired smile. "I promise."

Brows furrowed, Abby headed back to the love seat she'd vacated just moments before. Grabbing one of the blankets, she draped it around her shoulders and knelt to stir the glowing embers with the poker while Pete shrugged into his leather jacket. As she watched him head for the front door, it occurred to her that there might be more to his return to the States than the simple desire to do Jordy a favor.

She had no idea what, although she guessed it was linked to the strange object she'd found while rooting around for an extra pair of socks. Frowning, she extracted a log from the neat stack on the hearth and laid it in the grate before adding kindling to the glowing embers to rebuild a flame.

Pete returned almost immediately. Bolting the door behind him, he crossed the darkened room in his swift stride.

"It's not a blown fuse. The whole resort's dark. There isn't light showing anywhere, not even at the main lodge below us."

"You're kidding!" She peered at his shadowed face and groaned. "You're not kidding."

"'Fraid not. A main transformer must have blown. Or maybe the weather took down some power lines."

He reached for the phone on the end table. Frowning, he listened for a few seconds, then replaced the receiver.

"The phones are gone, too. I'm not surprised. It's really nasty out there. Everything's coated with ice and slick as spit."

"Oh, no! I suppose that means we won't get our dinner."

Tilting his wrist to the firelight, Pete squinted at his watch. "We didn't get our dinner four hours ago. Guess we were both too exhausted to notice."

"I'm not exhausted now," she mumbled, poking at the fire. "Just hungry."

Pete hunkered down beside her and warmed his hands at the growing blaze. "After seeing what it's like out there, my guess is we'll be lucky to get breakfast."

Until that moment, Abby had been feeling a hollow sort of emptiness. At the thought of missing out on tomorrow's breakfast, as well as tonight's onion soufflé, she went from empty to positively starving.

She rose, gathering the folds of her blanket. They both needed sustenance, and she wanted an explanation. Deciding food came first, she headed for the kitchenette tucked below the loft.

"This place has to come equipped with a stash of munchies. It's got everything else. You tend the cook fire, and I'll go hunt for food."

She found a cache in the kitchen, and another in the wet bar. Arms laden with an assortment of packages, bottles and cans, she returned to the sitting room. Welcome heat now radiated from the fire Pete had restored to full strength.

"How do cashews, Eagle brand sour-cream potato chips, red caviar and cocktail olives sound?"

"Except for the caviar, pretty darn good."

"We'll leave that for the next stranded guests, then." She dumped the packages on the coffee table and placed the cans and bottles in a neat row. "You have a choice. Imported wine, imported beer, imported mineral water or Georgia's own orange cream soda."

"I'll have whatever you're having."

Pete added another log to the now blazing fire, then rose and dusted his hands on his thighs. While Abby went back to the kitchen to search for a bottle opener, he shoved one of the facing love seats aside and swung the other around to face the fire, crowding it and the coffee table as close to the heat source as was safe.

Abby's steps slowed when she saw the new arrangement. It made more sense, of course, to share the small love seat and catch all the heat they could from the fire. But did she really want to huddle close to a man who had all but attacked her a few moments ago?

No, *attacked* was the wrong word. He'd startled her, certainly. The intensity of his third degree had jolted her, just as his grip on her arm had angered her. Still, she hadn't felt physically threatened. Not for a moment.

It came as a slight shock to Abby to realize that she trusted Pete. She'd met him only a few hours ago, yet some deep-seated feminine instinct told her he wouldn't harm her. Not intentionally, and not physically.

Emotionally, however, Senior Master Sergeant Pete O'Brian constituted a serious threat to her inner peace. Honesty compelled Abby to admit that she still hadn't quite recovered from his kiss. Or from the feel of his hands, gentle and sure on her ribs, when he'd searched for possible injuries. Yet every time she came close to liking the blasted man, he said or did something that put up her hackles—like accusing her of rifling his carryall to find a twisted scrap of metal!

Curiosity about that small, unidentifiable object overcame the doubts she harbored about Pete O'Brian's impact on her emotions. She wanted to know more about it. More about him.

She waited until they'd settled on the love seat, one blanket draped across their laps, another over their shoulders. The blazing fire sent the frosty chill in the cottage retreating to the shadows. Pete attacked the junk-food feast with hungry gusto. Abby matched him munch for munch. After they tossed a pile of empty packages aside, she dusted the potato-chip crumbs from her lap and hunched her knees under the blanket.

"I'm still waiting," she reminded him.

He didn't pretend to misunderstand. Resting his orange pop bottle on his stomach, he gave her a long, considering look.

"It's not exactly a bedtime story, Abby."

The warning raised a ripple of gooseflesh that had nothing to do with the cold. Tucking her arms under the blanket, she shifted a bit to face him.

"Tell me."

His gaze drifted to the fire. Abby sensed that he was sifting. Sorting. Deciding what he "could" tell her. He was quiet for so long, she almost prompted him again.

Something held her back. The taut cast to his face, maybe, bronzed by the firelight. Or the midnight-blue eyes that saw things she didn't in the dancing flames.

"It was a training jump," he said at last, his voice flat. "A night requal. I didn't need the canopy time, but I wanted to test our new free-fall rig."

Abby waited for him to continue, unconsciously massaging her ever-cold toes under the blanket. The small movement distracted him. He glanced down, then turned to set aside his soft drink. To her surprise, he slipped his arms under the cover and lifted her feet into his lap. His hands took up where hers had left off. Through a double layer of heavy cotton socks, Abby felt his strength. And warmth. And gentleness.

The story he told her wasn't gentle, though. It came out slowly. In measured bits. As though the horror were more manageable in small pieces.

"The others were doing static-line jumps. It was a clear night for a change, but windy. The team went out, one by one. All except Carrington. Our rookie."

His hands stilled, then resumed their slow stroking.

"The kid was nervous, despite his bravado. He checked his static line. Rechecked it. Held it in his left hand as he went out the door."

His fingers dug into her arch. Abby held her breath.

"I was right behind him."

Pete stared into the fire, seeing again the black hole of the open hatch. Feeling the cold wind slice into him. Hearing the rattle of the metal hook on the static line as Carrington went out.

"The kid didn't let go in time. His arm tangled in the line, hung him up. Then the slipstream caught him. Slammed him against the plane's belly. Hard. Then he hit again."

It was a parachutist's second-worst nightmare. A hung jumper, tethered by a thin, tensile umbilical to a plane plowing through the night skies at a hundred and thirty knots.

"He was unconscious, so we couldn't cut his static line loose. The pilot banked, trying to angle the plane so the jumpmaster could winch him in."

He's hooked! The jumpmaster's frantic shouts pounded in Pete's head. *Dammit, he's hooked on something! I can't reel him in!*

They'd worked together, he and the young sergeant. Cursing and wrenching at the static-line retriever, while Carrington slammed into the undercarriage time and again.

"Then the retriever support gave."

Pete's voice gave no hint of the panic that had sliced through him when the metal support snapped and Carrington's tether whipped out the open hatch. Pete had followed less than a second later, diving into blackness, searching for the rookie's chem lights and flashing strobe in a vast, empty hell.

"I went out after him."

He'd caught the spinning, tumbling Carrington seconds before it would have been too late for both of them.

"I yanked the cord on his reserve. It's smaller than the free-fall chute, faster. He hit the ground before me, hard. Then the wind caught him. I followed his strobe, flew into his canopy. It wasn't a pretty landing, but I stopped his drag."

The soft, indrawn hiss beside him dragged Pete back from a dark, deserted hayfield.

"Was…was he all right?"

"He survived, but he'll never fly again."

The doctors weren't sure he'd ever walk again, either, but the kid was determined to prove them wrong.

"The accident board examined everything. Our jump procedures. The kid's training records. They sent the static-line retriever back for stress and fatigue analysis. The findings are confidential…."

His words trailed off. He shouldn't be telling her this much. Pete knew it. A military man to his bone, he believed in discipline, in rules and regulations, in making the system work.

Then his eyes locked with hers. He saw sympathy in their brown depths, and a strength that Beth must have turned to continually. Against his better judgment, Pete felt himself drawn to that same, steady strength.

"The board determined it was a freak accident, compounded by simple human error. The support shouldn't have failed, but it did. Carrington should have released his static line sooner, but he didn't. I should have seen how he gripped the line, but I didn't."

He didn't realize his fingers had frozen around Abby's foot until she tried to tug it free. He frowned down at his lap, trying to remember just how the heck her feet had ended up there in the first place. Belatedly he loosened his grip. She surged up onto her knees, dragging the blankets with her.

"Surely they don't blame you for the accident!" she exclaimed. "No one could blame you. My God, you brought him down!"

Pete blinked at the avenging goddess who knelt beside him, her hair a wild halo of disheveled curls, her brown eyes fired with indignation on his behalf. Her passion pushed the black, bleak night back into the small chamber of his mind where it would always reside.

"No, they don't blame me," he replied quietly. "I blame myself."

Shocked, she sank back on her heels. "Why?"

"I should have seen how nervous the kid was. He was still a rookie, and too damn cocky for his own good." He let out a long, slow breath. "That's why I pried that scrap of metal off the plane. Why I keep it as a reminder of what can go wrong every time I send my men on a training mission or out on an operation."

He slanted her an apologetic glance.

"I guess that's why I overreacted a while ago, too. I'm sorry."

"Apology accepted."

The reply was low, hardly more than a whisper. Pete closed the door in his mind. He wasn't looking for sympathy, and didn't want it. Abby wasn't quite ready to let go of that night, though.

"Is that what brought you back to the States?" she asked. "The accident?"

Nodding, he reached for her foot. "I bunged up

my knee and am off jump status for a while. I'm scheduled to meet a medical evaluation board in San Antonio next week."

She gave a tiny sigh of pleasure when he began to knead her toes once more. "So what does a medical evaluation board do?"

"Poke and probe and run more tests."

Abby suspected there was more to this medical board than his deliberately offhand reply indicated. Surely there were doctors in England who could poke and probe and run tests. The fact that Pete had been sent back to the States held a significance she didn't understand. But before she could ask, he dragged her foot out from under the blanket and lifted it to eye level.

"Good Lord, woman, you're the first person I've ever met with Popsicles attached to her ankles."

"Now you know why I wanted those socks!"

"What do you do, put your shoes in the freezer at night to slow the circulation in your feet?"

"I've always been, er, cold-toed."

"Here, scoot over this way and put your feet to the fire."

Somehow, Abby ended up more in his lap than out of it. Some way, his arm slipped from the back of the love seat to the circle of her waist. Strangely uninclined to rectify the situation, she wiggled a bit to make herself more comfortable.

It occurred to her that they fit together perfectly. He was taller than she, and far more solid. Yet hip matched hip, and thigh nestled against thigh. Her shoulder tucked under his at just the right angle. His formed the perfect support for her head. She felt the fine hair at her temple stir with each slow, steady breath he took.

She wouldn't mind at all if the electricity stayed off awhile. A good while.

When she realized the dangerous path her thoughts were taking, Abby tried to cut them off. She and Pete would only be together for a few more hours, she reminded herself sternly. Just until the sun came up and warmed the icy roads. Then she'd go back to an apartment filled with floor plans and sketches for her new shop, and he'd go back to the military that was his life.

Their chosen lifestyles couldn't be more different, Abby mused. Hers centered around the need for an anchor, for stability, for the roots she craved. His involved constant movement, and the danger he'd touched on so briefly tonight.

For these few hours, though, their separate paths had merged, a tiny voice argued. For these few hours, they were together.

The small, insistent voice came from someplace deep inside Abby. Someplace she hadn't explored in a long time. Not since Derek. No, not even during Derek. She couldn't remember ever feeling this slow, insidious pleasure the first time he'd taken her in his arms.

Not that Pete had taken her in his arms, exactly.

He was just…sharing her warmth. As she was sharing his.

Sure. Of course. Uh-huh. Even Beth hadn't resorted to that lame excuse during her rather tumultuous postadolescent years. Sighing at the confused, half-formed jumble of needs Pete stirred in her, Abby snuggled against his side.

His voice rumbled against her ear. "Toes warm enough now?"

Smiling, she angled her head back. "I'm warm all over."

She hadn't intended any sort of double entendre, but of course the hidden meaning jumped out at her the moment the words were out. Embarrassment eddied through Abby, and a glint appeared in Pete's indigo eyes. For the life of her, she couldn't tell whether it was amusement, interest or regret.

"Me too," he admitted. "All over."

Abby's pulse tripped, skipped, then took off at triple speed. She might not have meant to convey a sensual message. Pete certainly did. She saw it in the way his gaze moved over her face and snagged on her mouth. Heard it in the husky note in his voice.

Abby held her breath, sure that he would follow up on that interesting remark. All he had to do was bend his head. Just an inch or two. When he didn't, disappointment prickled the surface of her skin.

"Abby?"

"Mmmm?"

"About that kiss at the airport…"

"Yes?"

"I told you I wasn't sorry."

"Yes."

"If I kiss you again, I'm afraid I might be. Very sorry. Because a kiss won't be enough this time."

He was right. The mouth hovering just inches from her own set off alarms all over her body. One kiss wouldn't be enough, she acknowledged. For either of them. Taking it any further would be crazy, though. And stupid. *Not* something that sober, sensible Abby should even contemplate, let alone indulge in.

A lifetime of caution, of shielding herself and Beth from the unintentional hurt too often caused by the strangers who passed through their lives, pulled Abby back from the brink.

"Then we'd better forgo the kiss and just enjoy the fire." She infused her reply with a deliberately light note. "We don't want you to regret what we both know would be a mistake."

His breath came out in a long, slow release. Then he nodded and settled himself more comfortably against the sofa. A slight adjustment brought Abby against his warmth.

"Too late," he murmured against her hair. "I already do."

Chapter 5

Abby woke to a world of piercing white light. It filled the cottage with dazzling brightness, and made the cold seem even sharper and more cutting.

She curled in a tight ball under the mounded blue covers, testing the air with the tip of her nose. Obviously, the electricity hadn't been restored during the night. Nor had the phone service. The receiver was off the hook on the end table, she saw, but no shrill beep sounded to advise her of that fact.

"Great," she muttered, tucking her nose back under the covers. So much for the Pines' exalted reputation. No heat. No phone service. Probably no hot water. No hot breakfast. No hot anything, except the fire blazing cheerfully in the grate.

And the memory of a night spent in Pete's arms.

That alone was enough to suffuse Abby's entire being with a wash of delicious warmth. She closed her eyes, recalling each shift of their bodies as they'd drifted into sleep. The times Pete had gotten up to feed the fire, then returned to gather her against him. His rather sonorous breathing a couple of times during the night. Her deplorable tendency to drape herself around him like plastic wrap in her sleep.

Common sense had motivated her to draw back from Pete's kiss. Her body had reacted to him on a more instinctive level, seeking warmth and comfort and a closeness that was all too physical.

His body had reacted, too.

Abby's face burned as she remembered how she'd dozed off and somehow hitched a leg up his hip. She'd come awake with a start when he gave a little grunt and tried to ease her knee from his groin. They'd both pretended not to notice the rigid protrusion her knee bumped against as it resumed its rightful place.

"Are you finally awake?"

She responded to the amused query by hunching the blankets up over her ears.

"No."

"Not ready to face the winter wonderland yet?"

She wasn't ready to face *him,* not while the memory of what her knee had encountered during its inadvertent explorations remained so vivid.

"I thought you might want to know the cottage has

a gas water heater. There's enough left in the tank for a quick shower, if you want one."

Abby poked her head out of the blankets. Suddenly her layers of T-shirts and sweats and socks and blankets felt a little gamy.

"I want one."

He grinned, and the thought rocketed through Abby that any woman who wasn't severely hormonally challenged would enjoy waking up to that particular arrangement of facial features. If only it came packaged with one or two of her more basic requirements for a mate, like a cheerful acceptance of Beth, with all her exasperating faults. Or a desire to build a nest, and occasionally occupy it.

From what Pete had told her last night, the military was far more than a profession to him. It was part of his being. An essential core of training and experience that had sent him plunging through a night sky to snatch a tumbling body back from certain death. Abby couldn't see a man like Pete O'Brian needing roots, especially not the comfortable Sunday-morning-pancake-breakfast kind she craved.

"I saw more wood stacked in a shed a little way down the road," he told her. "I'll go retrieve some while you hit the showers. Then we'll decide what to do about breakfast."

The mere thought of something other than sour-cream potato chips was enough to get Abby off the love seat and up the stairs. She enjoyed roughly three and a half minutes of hot water before the pulsing stream started to run tepid. When she stepped out of the glass cubicle, instant goose bumps danced all over her skin.

Unfortunately, her black velveteen dress hadn't dried before the electricity went out last night. It was still draped over the edge of the tub where Abby had wrung it out, frozen into position. Tiny bits of ice fell off the white lace collar when she fingered it. Pete's maroon sweats, slept-in though they were, would have to do for a little while longer yet.

With the speed of an actor changing between onstage scenes, Abby ripped off the terry robe and dived into the sweats. Sitting on the edge of the bed, she pulled on one pair of socks, then reached for another. A blur of movement outside caught her attention. Socks in hand, she rose to peer through the sliding glass doors that gave onto the balcony.

Pete was making his way down a steep slope to a shed set midway between the honeymoon cottage and its nearest neighbor, some hundred or so yards away. Traversing that sharp incline wasn't an easy task. The ground beneath his feet glittered with a layer of bright, shining crystal. Thick sleeves of glistening ice bowed the pines' branches, many of which had broken off under the crushing weight. The road leading away from the cottage gleamed like a ribbon of black coal in the sunlight. Its slick surface was no doubt why Pete had abandoned the road to work his way down the stubbled hillside.

He appeared to constitute the only living thing

in this frozen, fantastic tableau. With his dark hair, brown bomber jacket and blue jeans, he stood out against the glittering background. Clutching the socks, Abby stood by the windows, watching as he slipped and slid on the treacherous slope.

Her heart jumped to her throat when he went down on one knee. His bad knee, she saw at once. Even from her elevated perspective, she couldn't miss the grimace that twisted his face. He gripped his leg just above the kneecap and pushed himself up.

"Oh, Pete!"

Her heartfelt murmur of sympathy hung on the cold air. Biting her lip, she watched him struggle to rise. Absorbed in the drama, she didn't notice the shadow coming out of the trees beside him right away. When she did, she couldn't figure out just what it was that had snared her attention.

Her first thought was that it was some kind of an animal. Something big and furry and bent over. Whatever it was, it came close to the size of a man.

Good God! Were there bears in this part of Georgia?

She jerked forward, driven by an instinctive urge to yank open the windows and alert Pete to possible danger. She had both hands on the window latch when a flash of bright color snagged her eye. Her heart pounding, she squinted through the searing glare. Then she sagged against the glass doors, feeling weak with relief and slightly idiotic.

This particular variety of Georgia bear shaved

its legs and wore red ankle boots. It also appeared to be friendly. *Very* friendly, judging by the way it slipped an arm around Pete's waist and clung to him for support.

While Abby watched from above, Pete and the… creature started up the slope toward the cottage. Slowly. Carefully. Picking their way around pines and fallen branches. As they neared, Abby saw that the fur was reddish in color, more foxlike than bearish. From the length and stylish drape of the covering, she was willing to bet it wasn't the fake fun fur advocated by the politically correct.

Abby pulled on the second pair of socks and made her way to the front door to greet them. When she stepped onto the small porch, dazzling brightness blinded her. Flinging up a arm to shield her eyes from the glittering array of color and light, she squinted through the glare. Icy air knifed into her lungs with every breath.

Pete caught sight of her from twenty yards away and waved. It was *not* the wave of a man locked in a mortal struggle with a wild creature, Abby noted wryly.

"We've got company," he called, his breath frosting on the air. "This is Cherry. She and her husband are in the next cottage."

Abby peered at the black silk scarf wrapped around the woman's head. It covered her forehead, her nose, her mouth. It covered everything but a pair of sultry green eyes framed by impossibly long black lashes.

"Their phone and electricity are out, too," Pete reported, still panting from the climb. "Cherry saw me outside and came to see if ours was working."

The woman lifted a hand to push back her scarf. Flaming red hair spilled out, as vibrant and eye-catching as a flashing hazard signal.

"Poor Pete." She gave a husky, contralto laugh. "I practically fell into his arms when I got to him. He wasn't sure whether I was introducing myself or attacking him."

"Really?"

Abby declined to mention that she hadn't been all that sure, either. She didn't want to admit that she'd been on the verge of charging out of the cottage to rescue Pete from the clutches of a...Cherry.

The unwitting victim frowned as he took in her attire. "What are you doing outside without any shoes?"

"They weren't dry enough to put on yet."

"Well, you'd better get inside, before those ice cubes you call toes fall off. You and Cherry both. We decided we'd better combine forces to conserve firewood," he explained. "There's no telling how long it will take for the power to come back on."

"Oh. Good thinking."

"I'm going to go back down and tell..." He arched a question at the woman next to him.

"Irvin."

"I'll tell Irvin, and bring him back with me."

"Have him bring the rest of the party tray that's in the fridge," Cherry called as Pete started back down the slope, step by cautious step. "And the baguettes. Oh, and the Grey Poupon. I can't eat Danish ham without it."

Abby gave a joyous gasp. The strange feeling she'd experienced at the sight of this gorgeous, fox-furred female nestled against Pete's side evaporated.

"You have food? Real food?"

"Tons of it," Cherry replied with a friendly smile as she followed Abby inside. "You wouldn't guess it to see Irv, he's such a pipsqueak, but he chows down like a team of Clydesdales. He called ahead and made sure our cottage was well stocked before we checked in yesterday. Hey, this place is something!"

The statuesque redhead stood in the center of the room and spun in a slow circle. Her viridescent eyes gleamed as they took in the majestic proportions of the main sitting room, the soaring, beamed ceiling, the blues and greens and golds that gave richness and warmth to the oak furnishings.

"It's the honeymoon suite," Abby explained as she scooped a blanket from the love seat and draped it around her shoulders. Lifting a foot, she propped it on the hearth to toast.

"The honeymoon suite! Oh, sweetie, I'm sorry! Pete didn't tell me you were on your honeymoon." Hitching up the collar of her coat, Cherry headed for the door. "You two don't want Irv and me around while you invent new ways to keep warm."

"No, wait! We're not married. I mean, we're not on our honeymoon. That is, I'm not..."

When she stumbled to a halt, the other woman laughed and gave her a knowing wink.

"That's okay. Irvin and I aren't married, either. Well, he is. Sort of. He should have signed the divorce papers ages ago, but now he's decided he wants the Lincoln."

Abby lifted her other foot to the blaze, both amused and a bit daunted by the other woman's forthright disclosures. Shaking her fiery mane in disgust, Cherry strolled over to the hearth.

"I mean, why go to court over a four-year-old Lincoln? If they were fighting over her Jag, or the Maserati Irv bought me last year, I could see it. But a Lincoln? I ask you, does that make sense?"

Pouty red lips demanded an answer.

"Maybe it has sentimental value," Abby offered weakly.

The other woman huffed, then suddenly stilled. An arrested expression came into her vivid green eyes.

"You know," she said slowly, "you might just have something there. Irv and I almost wore out the shocks when we got caught in traffic after a Cowboys night game last year. For a little guy, he sure can..."

"The Cowboys?" Abby interjected hastily. "Are you from Dallas?"

"Irv has his practice there, although he was born

right here in Georgia, which is why we come back for this silly game every year. I'm from nowhere in particular. What about you, sweet— Say, what's your name, anyway?"

"I'm Abby. Abby Davis."

The visitor slid her hand from her coat pocket and extended it. A chunk of amethyst the size of Rhode Island caught the morning light, sending purple lasers all through the sitting room.

"I'm Cheryl Pryoskovich, but I go by my stage name, Cherry Delight."

Abby tried. She really tried. But she couldn't quite hold back a little choke as she shook Ms. Delight's hand.

At her helpless gurgle, Cherry's infectious laughter sprang loose. "I know, I know...."

Lifting her hands, she cascaded her thick mane through her fingers. In the process, she also let her coat drape open. Abby caught a glimpse of a minuscule fire-hydrant-red skirt, and a matching sweater stretched tight across a bust that could only be termed magnificent.

"With this orange hair, it was either Cherry Delight or Tomato Toots. I never would've broken out of skin flicks with that one following me around."

While Abby digested that interesting bit of information, her guest tucked her hands back in her pockets and glanced around the cottage once more.

"So you and Pete aren't married, huh? He must

have it really bad for you to put you up in style like this. What does he do, anyway?"

"He's in the air force, and he doesn't have it bad for me. We're just…acquaintances."

"Sure you are, sweetie," Cherry teased. "I suppose that's why you're wearing his sweatshirt? And why he was so worried about your little toesies?"

Abby had a feeling she wasn't going to win this one, but she gave it another try.

"Actually, I reserved this cottage for my sister and her fiancé. They were supposed to get married yesterday, but Beth chickened out. Then Pete showed up at the airport with the news that the groom had shipped out on a no-notice deployment."

"So you decided to stand in for the bride, and Pete played groom." Cherry waggled her auburn brows. "You lucky thing. If I didn't have Irv to play with, I wouldn't mind a few parlor games with a hunk of masculine maleness like Petie-kins, myself."

Abby gave up. She cast around in her mind for a polite topic of conversation, and had just decided there wasn't one when she heard the stomp of booted feet outside. Relief coursed through her, and curiosity about the man who held this stunning woman's affections.

Pete opened the door and stood aside. A balding, stoop-shouldered man in wire-rim glasses rushed in.

"Has it come on?" he demanded. He swiped at his glasses with a gloved hand to clear the frost and answered himself immediately. "No, I can feel it hasn't. It's freezing in here. Damn!"

Cherry had said that her...friend...was a little guy, but Abby had assumed she'd exaggerated somewhat.

She hadn't.

The top of Irv's shiny head couldn't reach the buxom redhead's chin. Padded as he was in a blue ski jacket and what looked like five or six layers of sweaters and shirts, he appeared almost as round as he was tall.

"Irv, sweetie, come meet Abby."

"In a minute. Let me try one of these outlets first. Just in case."

Her eyes widening, Abby watched him get down on hands and knees and stab a plug at a wall socket. He sat back, fumbling inside his jacket for a moment, then pulled out a five-inch TV set and held it a few inches away from his nose.

"Nothing! Damn!"

"Irv..."

"Hang on a minute. I want to try another plug."

Scrambling along the oak floor on all fours, he tried the next outlet. Then the next.

Abby swung her incredulous gaze back to Pete. Grinning, he deposited a bulging pillowcase on the coffee table.

"Irv was hoping we might have juice coming in from a separate line. Just enough to get the game."

Good Lord! Abby had forgotten all about the

game. The big Thanksgiving shoot-out. This was also the day a good part of the nation would sit down to a mouth-watering feast of turkey and dressing. Sweet-potato pie topped with pecans and little marshmallows. Green peas and rolls dripping with butter.

She eyed the bulging pillowcase on the coffee table with a combination of hope and resignation.

"It's bad enough the Pines didn't sand the roads so we could get out of here and make it to the stadium," Irv complained as he got to his feet. "There's no excuse for this extended power outage. Anderson's going to hear about it, that's for sure."

"Walt Anderson's chairman of the corporation that owns the Pines," Cherry explained in an aside to Abby. "Along with a string of other resorts. Irv does his gums, you know."

"Uh, no, I didn't."

Cherry beamed with pride. "Irvin's the best periodontist in Dallas."

Her proud smile folded into a sigh as she observed her companion's glum face.

"Poor baby. He's been calling a local radio station every half hour on his cellular phone to check on the roads. Now he's conserving the battery, so he can get updates on the score when the game starts. Assuming it starts at all, of course."

Irv shoved his glasses up the bridge of his nose with a stubby finger. "Of course it will. With millions in advertising riding on every minute of airtime, it has to. But we won't be there to see it." His pale blue eyes filled with despair. "I'm sorry, Cherub."

Cherub?

Once more Abby's startled gaze flew to Pete's. The laughter in them warmed her all the way down to her chilled toes. Cherry must have shared some of her artless confidences with him during their walk up the slope. Either that, or he'd figured out all by himself that angels didn't customarily robe themselves in cardinal-colored ankle boots, thigh-skimming skirts and tight sweaters. Nor did they tuck their… friends'…heads against their bosoms and plant wet little kisses all over their shiny crowns.

"Forget about the game, honey. If we miss it, we miss it. Now come meet Abby."

While Cherry performed the introductions, Pete restored the love seats to their original facing positions before the fire. The guests claimed one, leaving the other for Pete and Abby. The thought of once again sharing that yard or so of soft, well-cushioned space with the man now hunkered down before the fire, his muscled thighs straining against his jeans as he fed the blaze, sent anticipation singing through Abby's blood. With some effort, she repressed the unexpected sensation.

"Shall we eat here, close to the fire?"

"Oooh, let's!" Cherry exclaimed. "We'll have a picnic."

While Abby rooted around in the kitchenette for silverware and plates, Cherry found a linen tablecloth in a drawer and spread it over the coffee table. She then dug into the pillowcase, removing all kinds of goodies. At her suggestion, Pete unbent a hanger and used it to toast the baguettes. Irv spent his time jiggling the batteries in his TV, in the futile hope they might yet yield some power.

When the impromptu brunch was all laid out, Abby had to admit that, while it wasn't quite the elegant Thanksgiving feast the Pines had promised its guests, it would do. It would do nicely. Silver utensils gleamed. Crystal bar glasses sparkled. And the variety of delights arrayed on the snowy linen tablecloth made her wrap an arm across her stomach to keep it from yowling.

In addition to smoked Danish ham, Irv's party tray had yielded generous helpings of sliced turkey breast and cold roast beef. It also provided crunchy carrot sticks, celery stalks, smoked oysters, and an assortment of cheeses to complement the toasted French bread. Abby had added their contribution, which included what was left of the cashews, another full jar of olives, cocktail onions, the untouched caviar, orange cream soda and a bottle of champagne.

Cherry shuddered and passed on the soda, but declared the champagne "primo." Smiling, Pete topped off her glass and filled one for Irv. Then he draped a casual arm along the back of the love seat and offered a toast with the orange soda he and Abby had opted to share.

"Here's to old traditions, and new friends."

"To *good* friends," Cherry amended with her raspy laugh, lifting her champagne flute. She nudged Irv, who sighed and raised his, as well.

"Here's to the Bulldogs, who we won't be able to watch."

Their glances swung to Abby. She hesitated, all too conscious of Pete's arm behind her and the strangers across from her. She thought of her sister, somewhere between Paris and Cairo, and felt a tiny, familiar ache.

Holidays didn't tug at Beth's emotions as deeply as they did Abby's. She'd been so much younger when their parents died. Now, she barely remembered them. She didn't seem to miss being part of a family unit as much as her older sister did…especially during the holiday season.

In contrast, Abby felt their lack of roots most keenly at this particular time of year. Over time, Thanksgiving had evolved into her least favorite celebration. Even more than Christmas, it centered around hearth and home and family, the family she and Beth didn't have. Yet as she lifted her crystal goblet of cream soda and looked into Pete's dark blue eyes, she knew that this particular Thanksgiving would hold a special place in her memories. Memories she could bring out and savor long after he'd returned to England.

Her gaze shifted to Cherry, who'd good-naturedly shared more of herself in a half hour of acquaintance than many would in a lifetime. And to Irv, his eyes glum behind the glasses, a distracted smile sketched across his face.

As families gatherings went, this one didn't quite match the picture she always carried in her heart. But, like the makeshift feast, it would do. It would do nicely.

Smiling, Abby offered a toast.

"To us."

Chapter 6

Pete tipped his glass to Abby's, then brought it to his lips. To his surprise and vague disgust, he couldn't swallow. His throat had closed with the thunderous urge to kiss the mouth so close to his own.

He'd been fighting the same damn urge since the moment he'd drifted out of sleep early this morning and found Abby sprawled across his chest. The erotic, unconscious massage her knee had given him during the night had been torture enough. Waking up to the feel of her breasts flattened against him, her chin hooked in his collarbone and her breath moist on his neck had almost sent him over the edge.

The smile in her eyes at this moment had exactly the same effect on him. Heat rose under his skin. His hands curled with the need to reach for her. His body hardened. Painfully.

Sweating under his leather jacket, Pete set his glass aside. While the others chattered and filled their plates, he tried to deal with the intensity of the desire that built in him with every hour he spent in Abby's company. This growing, gut-tightening attraction was one of the reasons he'd invited the other couple to join them. He knew he wouldn't lose control and jump Abby's unsuspecting bones in a fit of passion, but a little distraction sure as hell wouldn't hurt.

Only he wasn't distracted. If anything, the presence of the others gave him a freedom to sit back and participate lazily in the free-flowing conversation, while he drank in the sight and the scent of the woman next to him.

Still fresh from her shower, she glowed with a natural beauty that Cherry, for all her stunning presence, didn't come close to. Her hair flowed over Pete's arm, a warm, living mass of tumbled curls. When she laughed at one of Cherry's more provocative attempts to distract Irv from his unhappiness about the game, the sound sent a spear of pleasure arrowing into Pete.

Careful, O'Brian. Go real careful here.

The warning came swift and silent and almost too late. Pete recognized that fact, and slowly withdrew his arm.

Dammit, he shouldn't be sitting here wondering how he could convince Abby to extend her stay at the Pines for the rest of the holiday weekend. He shouldn't be thinking up ways to get another shot at the kiss they'd both yanked back from last night. A woman with a yearning for a bed that could be passed to her great-great-granddaughter deserved more than Pete could give her.

More than he could give her right now, anyway.

Not for the first time since the accident, Pete found himself thinking about what came after his career. When he hung up his uniform for the last time, where would he be? What would he do with the rest of his life?

The questions lay, hazy and unanswered, at the back of his mind as brunch gave way to the kind of idle conversation that turns strangers into acquaintances, then to the shared laughter that leads to friendship. Abby's charm and Cherry's earthy, irrepressible humor more than made up for Irv's distraction and repeated calls to a local radio station on his cellular phone to check the progress on the roads and the power.

"The ice storm didn't do as much damage in the city as it did here," he relayed gloomily. "Atlanta's roads are already clearing. The game's supposed to start on schedule."

"Oh, sweetie, I'm sorry." Cherry slid her hand inside his jacket and bent down to nibble on his ear. "I'll make it up to you later, I promise."

Pete felt a stirring at his side. Glancing down, he saw Abby shift and look away from the other couple. She studied the dazzling white light outside the windows. The beams high overhead. The logs stacked beside the fire. When her roving gaze came full circle and snared Pete's, the dancing laughter in her eyes almost did him in.

The laughter yanked at him like a harness strap. That, and the complete lack of condemnation or censure. For all her refined air and ladylike manners, Abby was no prude. It hadn't taken Pete more than a few moments to recognize that Cherry was a graduate of the kinds of clubs the military authorities often declared off-limits. Abby couldn't have failed to recognize it, either. Yet she'd welcomed their unexpected guests with a cheerful smile and an unfeigned warmth.

Even now, with Cherry's hand drifting toward dangerous territory and Irv about to melt into a bald puddle on the opposite love seat, Abby displayed no embarrassment or disgust. Only that warm, gleaming laughter that drew Pete in over his head. Way over his head.

At that moment, his mental composite of Abigail Davis blurred, changed focus, reshaped itself. What emerged was a portrait of a woman. Not his admittedly male stereotype of a lady. A generous, vital woman. One he wanted with a hunger that hit him like a fist to the solar plexus.

He came within a breath of suggesting that Cherry and Irv retire to their own cottage and leave him free to nibble on Abby's ear…and her neck…and all parts south.

Luckily—or unluckily—Cherry chose that moment to plant a smacking kiss on Irv's cheek and pick up the conversation where it had been interrupted.

"So what are you going to call this shop of yours, Abby?"

"The Painted Door. I've found a wonderful old house in a part of Atlanta that's just coming back to its full glory. The house needs some work, not the least of which is sanding and refinishing the magnificent old pier-glass doors. I'm going to do that myself. I know just the color of antique green I want."

She wrapped her arms around her knees. The glowing animation that had fascinated Pete last night crept back.

"I plan to use the downstairs as a showcase for the antiques I've collected over the years. I'll live upstairs, until I get the place up and running, at least."

"Hey, maybe Irv and I can come for your grand opening. We're in Atlanta a lot. He's a guest lecturer at the university's school of dentistry." Cherry knuckled his shining scalp affectionately. "Tell them about that talk you gave on gingivitis, sweetie."

Under her good-natured prodding, Irv shucked some of his despondency over the game. It soon became apparent that a dry wit and a self-deprecating sense of humor lurked under the dentist's unprepossessing exterior. To Pete's surprise, he actually managed to hold his audience's interest in the unlikely subject. Neither Pete nor Abby objected, however, when the conversation once again ranged onto more general topics.

It had reached the lazy, wandering stage when a knock sounded on the door some time later. Pete answered it, with Irv crowding at his heels.

A weary-looking man in blue coveralls embroidered with the Pines' logo leaned a forearm against the doorframe. "Mr. O'Brian?"

"Yes."

"I'm Orlie Taggert, chief of maintenance here at the Pines. We're doing a check of the cottages. Everyone okay here?"

"We're fine. Dr. Mitchell and his party are here with us."

Relief creased Taggert's tired face. "Good. We stopped by their cottage and were worried when we didn't get an answer."

Irv nudged Pete aside, his face alight with hope. "Are the roads clear?"

"Not all of them. The county just isn't prepared to handle freak weather like this. I expect this is one of those storms folk will be talking 'bout ten, twenty years from now."

"But you made it up here."

"Had a time doing it, I'll tell you. We took a ton or so of sand out of the traps on the golf course and layered it heavy over the ice. Without that, we wouldn't have made it. The county folks are doin' their best, though. Shouldn't be too long now."

Irv's face fell. "Any idea how long it'll be before we get electricity, at least?"

Taggert hooked a thumb toward the golf cart on the pathway outside the cottage.

"I've got a crew from the power company with me. They say the lines from the substation that feeds the resort are down. We're going up there now to check it out. It's on the ridge, right behind this cottage. Can't say as I can estimate how long it'll take to fix whatever's wrong, but we'll do our best."

The prospect of restored power and sanded roads destroyed Irv's ability to concentrate on anything except his chances of making it to the game. He checked his watch repeatedly, and squinted out the window at the crew working their way on foot up the slope behind the cottage. When the climbers reached the crest of the ridge, Irv reported on their progress with glee.

"I'm going to get a report on the roads," he announced, flipping open his cellular phone. "I bet the situation's not as bad as ol' Orlie thought."

While he paced the floor, the phone glued to his ear, Cherry rose and reached for the plates.

"Guess we could clean up a bit." Her mouth curved in a mischievous grin. "Looks like Irv and I will be able to leave you two to your honeymooning soon."

"Sooner than you think," Irv crowed before Pete could come up with an answer. "The announcer says the sheriff's department reported some traffic movement on the state road."

Abby slid her toes out of Pete's hold and got up to help Cherry.

He should be relieved, Pete told himself. He shouldn't feel this ridiculous sense of impending loss. Dammit, if he spent much longer in this enforced intimacy with Abby, he wouldn't be able to keep his hands on just her feet.

Frowning, he began stacking the crystal glasses and carried them to the kitchenette. For some time, the only sound in the cottage was the chink of plates and glasses. Then the lamp beside the coffee table flickered on, and Irv gave a whoop of joy.

"They did it! Hot damn, they did it! Come on, Cherry. Let's get back to our cottage and get ready to leave for the game. With luck, we can still make the second half."

He tucked his mobile phone into his pocket and snatched up Cherry's coat.

"It was nice meeting you both," he got out in a rush, dumping the fox fur over her shoulders. "If you're ever in Dallas, give me a call. Or if you need some periodontal work, I can recommend a good gum specialist in your area. Come on, honey. Let's hustle."

"Irv! At least let me say goodbye." Smiling, Cherry offered Abby her hand. "The Painted Door, right? I'll come by next time we're in Atlanta. I don't know anything about antiques, but I do know my condo could use some classing up."

Abby returned her warm smile. "It'll be nice to see you again."

"Come on, baby. Let's move."

After a hurried goodbye to Pete, the Junoesque redhead let Irv drag her out the front door. With their departure, silence settled over the cottage, an empty silence that slowly took on a charged tension.

Abby glanced around the room, then back at Pete. He saw in her eyes the awareness that she would leave soon, too. With the restoration of electrical power, it probably wouldn't be long until phone service followed. She could make arrangements with her road service for the van and be on her way.

Pete almost asked her to stay.

He might have, if the lights hadn't flickered and gone off. A second later, they came on again, barely noticeable in the bright sunlight streaming through the windows. A faint hum sounded. The heating unit, he guessed. The sound tore at him.

Dammit, he wanted her to stay. Correction—he wanted *her*.

More than he could remember wanting anything in a long time. He searched her eyes for some clue that she wanted him, too.

He found it an instant before the explosion rattled the windows and rocked the cottage on its foundations.

Screeching, Abby flew into his hold.

Without thinking, Pete convulsed his arms around her, protecting her body with his. Percussion waves rolled through the air, hammering at his eardrums.

They were still reverberating when the front door burst open. A white-faced Irv rushed in, Cherry a half pace behind.

"Did you hear that?" he shrilled. "We saw it! The explosion, I mean. Up on the hill behind your cottage. There was a big flash, and now blue sparks are jumping all over the place."

Pushing Abby out of his arms, Pete flowed into action.

"It must be the maintenance crew. Irv, give Cherry your cellular phone, grab some blankets and come with me. Cherry, call 911 and tell them about the explosion. We'll apprise them of the exact situation as soon as we arrive on scene. Abby, find whatever you can in the way of first aid supplies, then you both follow us up the hill. Move, people, move!"

Abby had once heard that disasters caused people to suspend emotion and act on pure instinct. She soon discovered the truth of that statement.

Before she had time to fully grasp what had happened, Pete and Irv had disappeared out the door. Moments later, she and Cherry tore out after them and started up the hill. Panting and scrabbling for purchase on the icy stubble, they half pushed, half pulled each other up the slope.

As they neared the crest, Abby's heart pounded

with fear, and a growing dread of what they might find at the top. She could hear a snapping, sizzling sound, like sparks hitting water. A moan carried down to her, audible above her own rasping breath.

Her stomach clenched into a tight, quivering knot when she stumbled into a flat clearing atop the ridge. Just yards away was the entrance to a fenced enclosure housing several gray electrical boxes. The boxes huddled under a tall cranelike structure that trailed several loose wires. One thick wire undulated wildly, spitting traces of blue fire.

Horrified, Abby saw two men lying on the ground beside the boxes. Another stumbled around outside the enclosure, dazed, his clothing smoldering.

"Stay back!" Pete shouted. "Don't touch the fence or get near that wire!"

Dumping the blankets on the ground, Irv started toward the injured man. Pete yanked him back.

"If he's walking, he's alive."

"But—"

"In an electrical situation, the rules of triage are reversed. Ignore the wounded. Go for the dead. A little CPR can bring them back."

Irv swallowed, his face now ashen. "I haven't done CPR since dental school."

"I just took a refresher course at the Y," Abby panted. "I can help."

Pete eyed the snapping, dancing line. "Okay, when the wire whips up and away, I'll go in low and drag one out. You two start on him while I go after the other. Cherry, tell 911 we have two down, one walking. Tell them we'll need burn kits and—"

He broke off and darted into the enclosure, bent almost double. Abby didn't move, didn't breathe, didn't feel her nails gouging into her palms. Even with his bad knee, Pete moved fast, so fast the lump of terror lodged in her throat didn't have time to burst out.

He was back seconds later, dragging the victim with him. Abby went down on her knees and tilted the man's head back to clear his airways.

"Oh, God!" Irv exclaimed. "It's Orlie!"

The dentist dropped to his side and ripped open the maintenance man's jacket, using two fingers to find the exact spot under his sternum to apply pressure. Crossing one fist on top of the other, he hunched his shoulders and applied pressure.

Abby counted every push. "Fifteen one, fifteen two…"

After the fifth push, she bent and breathed into Orlie's open mouth. Then she rocked back out of Irv's way, dragged air into her lungs and started counting again.

"Fifteen-one, fifteen-two…"

Afterward, Abby could never believe that she'd counted and breathed and counted and breathed for only eight or ten minutes. It seemed like hours. Weeks. Years.

She saw Pete bring the second man out and start CPR on him. She heard Cherry call in a report over the cellular phone, then take off after the dazed, stumbling third victim. Draping her fur around his shivering form, Cherry guided him over to the makeshift triage center.

Pete spared him a glance, never ceasing his steady pumping rhythm. "Keep him warm, but...don't touch the burns...on his hands or face."

By the time Abby heard the distant sound of a helicopter, she'd lost all track of time, of space, of everything but the man on the ground. The violent wash of rotor blades as the chopper skimmed the treetops just above the clearing barely penetrated her fierce concentration. She counted aloud. And breathed. And counted aloud. And breathed.

Once she thought she felt a tremor in the flaccid throat muscles under her hand. Irv must have felt something, too.

"Come on, Orlie!" he shouted, pumping on the man's chest. "Breathe, damn it! Breathe!"

Abby was so absorbed in the life-and-death drama that she gave a little scream when hands closed around her shoulder and yanked her back.

"We've got him, ma'am. We've got him."

A hulking figure took her place beside the downed man. A warm coat dropped over her shoulders. A shaking Irv came to stand beside her. Cherry joined them moments later. They huddled together, watching, praying.

Relieved by a team of rescue personnel, Pete dragged himself to his feet. Unlike the others, though, he stayed at the center of the operation. The crew recognized his expertise, Abby saw. Responded to his authority.

Another helicopter landed in the road beside their cottage. Several helmeted men appeared in the clearing soon afterward. A siren wailed in the distance. The screen of rescuers surrounding the downed men shifted, allowing Abby a glimpse of the man Pete had worked on.

"He's sitting up!" Cherry gasped.

Abby's heart gave a thump of joy so great it hurt. The exhilaration lasted all of two or three seconds. Just long enough to recognize that Orlie still lay flat on his back, unmoving.

Radios cackled. More equipment appeared. Someone shouted that they had the power company's chief engineer on the line. Pete took the radio, gave a terse description of the disaster. Moments later, the snapping, whipping line jerked upward, then suddenly went dead.

The sizzling had barely ceased when a rawboned woman in a plaid hunting jacket and a yellow helmet came panting up the slope. The senior fireman on-scene turned to greet her.

"You got here fast, Mayor. You and the rest of the disaster response team. But the situation's under control, thanks to O'Brian here."

"What about the injured?"

Abby clutched Irv's arm with tight fists as she waited for the fireman's response.

"They're all right. They got a little crisped around the edges, though, so we're going to take 'em to County General."

"Thank God."

Silently Abby echoed the mayor's heartfelt prayer.

The fireman glanced at the stretchers being loaded onto the chopper. "I don't mind tellin' you, though, two of those boys wouldn't have made it if Mr. O'Brian here hadn't known what the hell he was about."

Tipping a finger to his hat, he went off to supervise the evacuation. The mayor tucked a whisp of iron-gray hair behind her ear and tilted Pete a sharp look.

"Where'd you get your training, Mr. O'Brian?"

"In the air force. It's what I do."

"From what I can see, you do it damn well. If you ever decide you want to turn civilian, you come see me, you hear? Pineville's not much more than a village, but we sure could use someone with your kind of background on the county staff."

"I wasn't the only one who responded," Pete replied, his smile encompassing the group still huddled together a few paces away. "You should be thanking Miss Davis and Dr.—"

"Miss Davis?" The mayor jerked around, her lively black eyes snapping from Abby to Cherry. "Is one of you the Miss Davis that's staying at the Pines?"

Abby nodded. "I am."

"I'm Doretta Calvin."

At Abby's blank look, the older woman smiled. "I'm the local JP, as well as the mayor of Pineville. I was supposed to preside over your marriage ceremony last night, but the cold burst the damn pipes in the town hall. I tried to get here after that little disaster, but by then the roads had iced over."

"Oh, no! The assistant manager didn't call you?"

"No, nobody called me." She peered at Abby, then at Irv. "Hey, it's not too late, you two. If you've got the license, I'd be happy to say the words while I'm here."

Belatedly Abby realized she still had both hands dug into Irv's arm. He tugged free of her hold, his eyes widening.

"No, no…" he stuttered. "You've got the wrong groom."

"I'll say," Cherry murmured with a low, throaty chuckle.

"And the wrong bride," Abby added.

"You didn't request the services of a JP?"

"Yes, I did, but not for me. For my sister."

"Your sister?" The mayor glanced around the still-crowded site. "Is she here?"

"No, she, ah…didn't make it to the Pines this weekend."

"Didn't make it to her own wedding?" The mayor's gray brows arched, and then her sharp gaze shifted to Pete. "Are you the groom, O'Brian?"

"No, he didn't make it, either."

Mayor Calvin rocked back on her heels, her weathered face creasing into a grin. "Not much of a wedding, was it? No bride, no groom, no justice of the peace."

Abby's accumulated tension eased into a smile. "No wedding supper. No electricity or heat in what was supposed to be the honeymoon cottage."

"And no game," Irv put in glumly.

Chapter 7

An hour later, Abby stood on the porch of the cottage beside Pete. A single thought drummed through her.

She should leave.

She should go inside, gather her things and leave.

Her common sense told her it was time to return to Atlanta and to her nice, quiet life. The past twenty-four hours had provided enough drama and nerve-twisting tension to last her a long, long time. Yet sober, sensible Abby lingered long after she should have left.

She'd waited at the accident site while a police officer took statements and another crew worked to restore power. A short while later, she'd bidden goodbye to the mayor and her team, then forced a smile at Irv's jubilant announcement that the state roads were open. When the heat and lights came back on throughout the resort, she'd cleaned up and changed out of the faithful maroon sweats.

Now she stood beside Pete, waving goodbye to Cherry and a beaming Irv as they drove off in the resort's limousine. A wrecker followed a short distance behind the limo, towing a sadly dented Antiquemobile. The Pines' grateful manager saw both vehicles off, then walked back to the porch.

"We'll take care of your van, Miss Davis," he assured her once more.

Shoulders hunched against the cold, the aristocratic-looking innkeeper wore the marks of worry and relief on his face, but he still carried himself with the dignity of his position.

"Please, keep the rental car until your van is repaired. We'll deliver it to you in Atlanta as soon as it's ready. Are you sure we can't do anything else for you?"

"No, thank you. You've been most generous."

More than generous, in fact. He'd already told her there'd be no charge for any of the costs associated with the canceled wedding. What was more, he'd invited her and Pete to stay at the resort as guests of the management for as long as they wished, separately or together.

It was the *together* part that held Abby at the Pines.

The word triggered a fierce need within her, one she only half understood. An urgent demand that went beyond the physical. Beyond sexual. It hummed in her veins and kept her fingers clenched around the keys to the rental car the manager had presented to her. The man beside her remained silent, but Abby felt him with every tingling sense as she tried to focus on the manager's face.

"It's the least we can do," he told her. "Orlie Taggert has been with the Pines for twenty-seven years. Thanks to you, he'll be with us another twenty-seven, God willing."

"Not just me."

"No, no, of course not. Dr. Mitchell and Miss, er, Delight will always be welcome here. And Sergeant O'Brian…"

He held out his hand to Pete.

"I hope you consider the Pines your home whenever you're in this part of the country."

The utterly sincere comment spiked the strange feelings inside Abby. They leapt in her chest. Grabbed at her heart. Neither she nor the manager had any idea when Pete might be back in this part of the country. She fisted her hand around the keys. Their sharp edges cut into her palm.

She was still clutching them when the manager drove off in one of the Pines' distinctive golf carts.

Unfolding her fist, she slipped the keys into the pocket of her cloak and went inside.

Pete followed, then leaned his shoulders against the door. His stance was easy, but questions shimmered in his dark blue eyes. The same questions she kept asking herself.

What was she doing?

Why had she stayed?

What did she want of him?

Abby didn't have any answers, either for herself or for him. She couldn't describe what held her. She only knew she didn't want to leave. Not now. Not yet.

She wet her lips. "You were spectacular up there, on the ridge."

"You were pretty spectacular yourself. When did you learn CPR?"

"I took a course at the Y years ago, when I got legal custody of Beth. I go for refresher training every couple of years."

"Smart lady."

They were dancing around the strange tension that gripped them. Abby knew it, but Pete was the one who acknowledged it.

Pushing his shoulders off the door, he closed the short distance between them and brought his hand up to cup her chin. A thumb traced along her cheek.

"It's okay, Abby. I understand what you're feeling."

"You do?"

"I feel it, too. A sort of high. A fierce satisfaction that won't go away."

That was true...to an extent. In those tense moments on the ridge, she'd shared some of the drama that routinely characterized Pete's life. Now she was experiencing some of the aftereffects of that adrenaline surge. She did feel the fierce satisfaction he'd described. A high she didn't want to let go of.

As she absorbed the feather-light stroke of Pete's thumb against her cheek, however, Abby acknowledged that the tremors running through her were more than just aftershocks. Far more. They went deeper, took on a more personal slant.

Unlike Pete, however, she didn't claim to understand her hazy, whirling emotions. Understanding could come later, she decided. Thinking would come later. Right now, she wanted more than the touch of his hand on her cheek.

His mouth curved in an understanding smile. "After a successful mission, we always feel the need to celebrate. To reaffirm life, I guess."

Her heart thudding, she took her courage in hand.

"How do you think we should celebrate?"

His smile moved from his lips to his eyes. "I can think of all kinds of ways to celebrate with you, Abigail, but none we wouldn't regret even more than the kiss we passed on last night."

He wasn't making this easy on her, she thought with an inner groan.

"I've been thinking about that kiss," she told him.

"Me too. A lot."

"I'm not so sure now it would have been a mistake."

His thumb stilled. Abby's blood began to pulse with a heat that had nothing to do with the restored electrical power or the mohair lining of her cloak.

"I don't want either of us to leave here with regrets, Abby."

She saw the hunger in his eyes, and felt a thrill of response deep in her belly.

"My only regret," she replied on a puff of need, "is that we're talking about it so much."

Turning her head, she brought her mouth against his palm. Her lashes fluttered down as she savored the contact with his flesh. It warmed under the wash of her breath, and bathed her face in heat. She pressed a soft kiss into the center of his palm, then another against the mound of his thumb. Her mouth moved to his fingers, her lips dragging against the pull of his skin. Her hand came up and folded over his, trapping it while she explored the rough hills and shallow valleys.

Pete didn't move. Hardly breathed. He'd never felt anything so erotic in his life as the whisper of heat from Abby's lips...until her tongue dipped into the hollow of his palm.

At the touch of her tongue on his skin, every nerve in his arm jumped. He knew he should pull his hand away. He told himself he should call a halt to this loveplay before it stopped being play.

He understood what was driving her. The same exultation sang in his veins, all mixed up with the physical attraction that had been building inside him from the moment he first laid eyes on her. It was a dangerous, combustible combination, and it fast carried him to the flash point.

"Abby. Sweetheart."

The words were a plea, and a warning.

"It's okay," she murmured against his palm. "I don't bite. Not very hard, anyway."

As if to prove her point, she nipped the mound of flesh at the base of his thumb. Then she soothed the sting with a slow, wet stroke of her tongue.

He wanted her. Pete had never wanted anything in his life as much as he wanted to bury himself in this woman's soft, slick flesh.

She wanted him, as well. He'd seen it in her eyes just before the explosion. He felt it now in the slow, seductive movement of her mouth and the velvety rasp of her tongue against his hand.

He looked down at her, imprinting the sweep of her dark lashes against her cheek in his memory bank. His hungry gaze detailed the curve of her neck. The unruly, gold-streaked hair she'd tamed into some kind of a loose braid. The prim white lace collar on her dress peeking out of the loose cloak.

This was the Abby he'd first met at the airport. This delicate, elegant creature. Then she'd struck him as the kind of woman who would expect more from a man than a fun weekend. Now, Pete realized with a tight ache, he wanted to give her more.

He couldn't give her the permanence she craved, though, and that stark, undeniable fact held him rigidly in check. He didn't know where he'd be next month, let alone next year. He'd lost one woman to the demands of his career. He didn't want to lose another.

She wasn't asking for evermores, a voice within him snarled. She wasn't asking for anything. Instead, she was giving him a slow, hot pleasure that drove everything else out of his mind.

Suddenly, without warning, the touch of her lips on his hand wasn't enough. For either of them.

Pete couldn't tell whether he jerked his hand away first or Abby lifted her head. However the shift occurred, it freed her mouth for his.

She arched into his kiss, fitting herself against him eagerly. Her arms slid free of her cloak and wrapped around his neck. Her hunger slammed into him with the force of a canopy snapping open after a long, spiraling free-fall. He dug his hands through her hair, framing her face, taking everything her mouth offered.

He had no idea how long he held her mouth captive, or when his hands left her hair. He only knew that the tight ache in his groin had expanded to a fierce, driving demand when he stripped off her voluminous cape and went to work on the buttons on the front of her dress. Moments later, it puddled at her feet.

"That's the second time you've peeled off my clothes in the middle of the sitting room," Abby said, a little breathlessly. "At least this time the heat's on."

Pete grinned. "That it is, sweetheart."

Her choke of laughter shattered his restraint. He yanked at the zipper on his jacket. Seconds later, it joined the pile on the floor. His hands speared around her waist. Curling his fingers into her black silk teddy, he pulled her against him.

"You have no idea how crazy this thing you're wearing made me the first time I saw it."

"Really?"

His hands slid up her back, then around to her front. "Really."

Lips parted, she quivered under his touch. Tight nipples budded against the black covering, and Pete sucked in a swift, stabbing breath.

"I know it isn't a George III four-poster that came over on the *Mayflower*," he growled, sweeping her into his arms, "but I've been fantasizing about you in the bed upstairs since the moment I saw it."

"George IV," Abby panted, hooking her arms around his neck. "It's George IV. And I had a few fantasies myself."

Pete attacked the stairs, not sure he could make it all the way to the loft with her breath hot in his ear and her teeth nipping at his lobe.

He did. Barely.

They tumbled to the bed together. Panting, laughing, tugging, they stripped each other of all but her panties and one of his socks. Bodies pressed together at every possible pressure point, they rolled across the bed. Greedily, he took what her mouth offered. Eagerly, she explored him with her hands and teeth and tongue. Rock-hard and hungry, Pete hooked his hands around her waist and lifted her up. His mouth closed over the tantalizing flesh of her breast.

Abby propped her hands on his shoulders, gasping when he took the aching nipple in his teeth. She'd expected her need to erupt with cataclysmic force as he nipped and teased and suckled, but she'd underestimated by several seismic degrees the total impact on her system. Fiery, volcanic heat rushed from her breast to her belly, and liquid pleasure flowed like lava from there to every nerve center in her body.

She writhed on top of him and under him, groping, stroking, returning the pleasure he gave her. Their bodies slicked, inside and out. Her hips rocked into his. A rough-haired leg scraped against her inner thigh. Somehow, in the melee of searching hands and tangled limbs, she lost her panties and he lost his other sock.

His fingers probed her wet center to prepare her. Then, without warning, he levered himself up and rolled off the bed.

"Pete... What?"

"We need protection."

It took a moment for Abby to grasp his meaning. "I...I don't have any."

"I don't, either..."

"Oh, noooo!"

His eyes danced at her anguished wail. "But I know where I can get some. Hang tight."

As if she could do anything else!

He trotted to the bathroom, and Abby pushed herself up on one elbow. Her heavy-lidded eyes cataloged a well-muscled back, a trim waist, and a world-class set of buns. She was still dealing with the impact of his tight, neat buttocks on her overheated respiratory system when he returned, a selection of brightly colored packets fanned out in his fist like a deck of cards.

"When the Pines advertises a honeymoon cottage equipped with all the amenities, they mean *all* the amenities."

The reminder that they occupied the honeymoon suite stirred a small, stray longing in one corner of Abby's heart. Resolutely she banished it. She hadn't asked Pete for any promises, and certainly didn't expect any. Ever practical, always realistic, she knew that tomorrow would take care of itself. Tonight, all she asked for was the feel of his arms around her and the thrust of his body into hers.

Lifting a brow, she nodded to the colorful array.

"You don't really think we'll need all those, do you?"

"A man can only hope."

Laughing, Abby opened her arms to him. Only later, much later, did she realize that she'd opened her heart, as well.

The sound of the shower dragged her from a deep, exhausted sleep. She lay facedown, sprawled sideways across a sea of rumpled sheets. Too boneless to do more than lift an eyelid, she tried to determine what time it was.

Shadows lurked in the corners of the loft. Chill air prickled her shoulders and bare backside. It had to be late afternoon, she decided, or early evening.

It took some effort, but she managed to roll over, dragging a handful of the bedspread with her. Cocooned in its warmth, she stared at the massive beams overhead and estimated the time that had passed since she'd yanked on a leather sleeve at the airport yesterday afternoon.

Twenty-six hours, she guessed. Twenty-eight at most.

It seemed longer. Half a lifetime, at least. So much had happened in those hours, not the least of which was the energetic contortions, helpless laughter and soaring, shattering climaxes that had left a scattering of foil packets on the floor beside the bed.

Her thoughts shifted gears, moving from backward to forward. How long had Pete said he'd be in Atlanta?

A few days, she thought. Next week, he had to meet that medical board in San Antonio. They had the rest of the holiday weekend before the real world intervened.

Once more she counted. Three days. Another seventy-two hours. A quick smile curved her mouth. The idea of seventy-two more hours with Pete sent joyful anticipation spinning through her limp body.

The very intensity of her joy startled Abby out of her haze of pleasure. Her smile fading, she thought of all the warnings, all the sage advice, she'd ever given Beth. Her words came back to haunt her now.

It wasn't wise to feel so deeply, or so fast.

Rushing into a relationship only opened your heart all the more quickly to the possibility of loss.

Beth hadn't ever heeded her advice, of course. She tumbled into love with all the exuberance of her warm, generous nature, and fell out of it just as quickly. Abby, on the other hand, had never been in love. She realized that now, with cutting clarity. Derek had never generated anything close to the tumultuous pleasure she'd just experienced.

No, not pleasure. With shattering honesty, Abby admitted that she'd found more in Pete's arms than physical pleasure. More than the celebration of life he'd described. It wasn't love…exactly. She couldn't be in love with a man she'd only met yesterday. But this came far too close to that undefinable emotion for her to take lightly.

She was trying to deal with that sobering

realization when Pete walked out of the bathroom. His jeans rode low on his hips, and damp sheened his chest. At the sight of the hair curling across his bare skin, Abby's breasts tingled. Swallowing, she pushed the memory of that soft, springy hair abrading her nipples out of her mind. She wasn't quite as successful at dodging the impact of the amusement in his dark eyes, however. That went straight to her heart.

Slinging his towel around his neck, he surveyed her nest of covers. "Are you settled in for the night?"

"I don't know," she answered truthfully.

"Since we're all out of cashews and cocktail olives, I thought you might want to go down to the main lodge for dinner."

When she hesitated, he dipped a knee on the mattress and planted his hands beside her head, caging her in.

"They might have some of that chocolate-rum-raisin cake left," he said temptingly, dropping a kiss on her nose.

Abby grabbed at the excuse. She couldn't think with Pete bending over her like this, let alone sort through the tiny, stinging nuclear reactions his mere proximity set off in her bloodstream.

"That sounds good. Very good!"

She wiggled out from under him, taking the covers with her. Trailing bedspread and sheet, she headed for the bathroom.

"Maybe we can ask the chef to whip up another onion soufflé for us, too."

She closed the door on Pete's comical grimace, then leaned against it. Shutting her eyes, she drew in a deep breath and waited for her heart to stop pinging against her ribs.

Not smart, Abby. Staying here was not smart. She knew that now. She also knew she'd make exactly the same decision, given the same choice.

She had a different choice facing her now, though. One she couldn't put off for seventy-two hours, as much as she wanted to.

Pete was waiting when she came downstairs, a gleam of quiet satisfaction in his eyes.

"I called the hospital while you were dressing. One of the men has already gone home. The other two are being treated for superficial burns, but should be discharged tomorrow."

"Oh, thank goodness!"

He picked up her cloak and settled it on her shoulders. His hands lingered, squeezing gently. "I talked to Orlie. He said to say hello. And thanks."

Abby basked in the glow of their shared triumph during the drive down to the inn. With Pete behind the wheel of the rental car and the tires crunching deep into the gravel, this trip wasn't nearly as nerve-racking as her last attempt to navigate the twisting corkscrew road.

Pete had called ahead for a table, seriously underestimating the pomp and circumstance that simple request would generate. The night manager met them at the front door and ushered them inside. As he escorted them through the lobby, heads turned and guests stopped them to shake hands. Abby's glow quickly gave way to embarrassment. She wasn't used to being the center of attention.

With some relief, she took the seat the manager held out for her at a table set in a paneled alcove. Soft flames flickered in the gas wall fixtures. A candle floated in a cut-crystal rose bowl on the table. The headwaiter beamed at them both and bowed.

"Please, if you'll trust us, the Pines would like to offer you a special menu, prepared in your honor."

Pete deferred to Abby, who nodded.

When the wine steward poured a pale, bubbling aperitif, she fiddled with the stem of her glass, unsure how to broach the subject of what came after dinner. She soon discovered that the presence of a hovering wait staff precluded the kind of conversation she wanted to have with Pete. After dinner, Abby promised herself. They'd talk after dinner. For now, she'd simply enjoy the incredible array of dishes set before her.

The Pines' chef had prepared a sumptuous feast for the eye, as well as the stomach. Course followed course, each more delicious than the last. Melon soup with lobster and mint. Watercress-and-walnut salad.

Turkey breast in shallot-and-brown-butter sauce, served with tomato coulis. And, to Abby's delight, the specialty of the house. The chef himself came to their table to present his golden, puff-crowned masterpiece...along with the thanks of the entire kitchen staff.

After working his way through the feast with the healthy appetite of a good-size man, Pete graciously admitted that the Vidalia onion concoction exceeded even Abby's advance PR work. So much so that he ruefully shook his head at the mention of dessert.

"I don't think I can force any more down tonight. How do scrambled eggs and rum-raisin pancakes for breakfast sound?"

Abby drew in a deep breath and waited to respond until the server had poured a fragrant stream of coffee into their cups and moved away.

"I won't be here for breakfast," she said slowly, forcing herself to meet Pete's eyes. "I'm going home after dinner."

He tilted back in his chair, studying her face in the candlelight. When he didn't respond right away, the small, tight ache in her chest told her she'd made the right decision.

"Regrets already, Abby?"

The soft question stabbed at her heart.

"No! None! But...I think you were right. What happened between us this afternoon was something

I've never experienced. That celebration of life you talked about. It was…special, and I want to keep it that way."

Another silence stretched across the table.

"So do I."

Chapter 8

Pete climbed out of the cab and stood on the sidewalk outside the upscale antique and gift shop. The bright Georgia sunshine that had been so noticeably absent the past few days warmed his shoulders. He shifted them under the layer of leather and told himself for the dozenth time that he had no business tracking Abby down at her place of work.

She'd called the shots exactly right the night before last. With brutal honesty, she'd recognized that their afternoon of passion had sprung from an explosive combination of simmering attraction, enforced intimacy and shared danger.

Pete had recognized it, too. He'd always known that the right mix of elements could generate that kind of spontaneous combustion, causing a fire that flared hot and burned fast. Sure enough, it had. When Abby melted into his arms, they'd certainly combusted, then flared so hot that Pete broke out in a sweat whenever he let himself think about those hours with her.

The problem was, the fire inside him hadn't burned out yet.

Against his better judgment, he'd decided to see Abby again before he left for San Antonio tomorrow. Just once more. To see if he could douse this steady, burning need.

Right, O'Brian. Sure.

He knew damn well he didn't want to douse it. He wanted to fan the flame until they were both consumed by it. What he wanted to do and what he would let himself do were two different matters, however. Still, he couldn't leave without seeing her once more. Squaring his shoulders, Pete pushed on the old-fashioned brass latch and walked into another world.

Instantly, a heavy, nose-twitching scent of dried rose petals assaulted him. They were everywhere, in crystal bowls and little trays and baskets scattered across every level surface. Fighting both a grimace and a sneeze, Pete followed the narrow path that led through the crowded shop.

If Things Past specialized in anything in particular, he couldn't decide what it was. His haphazard route took him around arrangements of embroidered pillows, scented candles, dried flowers, ticking grandfather clocks, furniture groupings and carved sideboards so massive they could have graced the great hall of Stonecross Keep. Framed pictures occupied every inch of wall, and glass-fronted cabinets displayed collections of china, crystal, jewelry and dolls.

Things Past wasn't a man kind of place, he decided. It was too elegant and overscented...much like the woman who glided forward to greet him. Her musky perfume reached Pete long before she did.

"May I help you?"

"I hope so. I'm looking for Abby Davis."

"Abigail? Is she expecting you?"

"No."

The woman's heavily mascaraed eyes drifted down his throat, measured his chest, then returned to his face.

"I'm Marissa DeVries, Abigail's employer. Perhaps if you tell me what you need, I can take care of it for you."

Pete had never felt particularly inclined to discuss his business with strangers. He felt even less inclined to discuss it with a woman who made him want to check his zipper to see if it was all the way up.

"I don't think so." A hint of steel edged into his voice. "Is Abby here?"

Thin, penciled brows arched. "She's in the storeroom. You can go through there."

Pete followed the wave of her hand, dismissing the

woman instantly from his mind as the anticipation of seeing Abby crawled all over his skin.

He found her kneeling beside an open crate, surrounded by mounds of air-puffed packing nuggets. Urn-shaped vases, flowered plates and china figurines were lined up in a neat row behind her. Pete paused just outside the door and watched while she lovingly ran a finger tip around the rim of a pink vase. He didn't want to startle her and make her drop the thing. For all he knew, it was a priceless treasure from the court of a Russian czar.

While Abby examined the vase, Pete examined Abby. The sunlight streaming through the back window painted her in shades of blue and gold. She wore a jumpsuit in a deep royal blue that flattered her slender figure and did serious damage to Pete's self-control. Gold filigree buttons decorated the front, and a gold belt emphasized her slim waist. She'd clasped her hair at the back of her neck with an ornamental clip, but, as usual, unruly strands escaped to frame her face.

As enticing as she looked, however, it was the expression in her eyes that tugged at Pete. They glowed with pleasure as she tipped the vase to examine the markings on its bottom. She loved what she did. It was obvious in the careful, loving way she handled the vase, and in the joy it gave her.

He must have made some movement, because she looked up then. Her pleasure yielded to surprise, then to pleasure again. But this was a different kind of pleasure. A polite kind. The kind a woman plastered on her face when a casual acquaintance unexpectedly showed up at her door.

"Pete! What are you doing here?"

He couldn't very well admit he'd been asking himself that exact question since the moment he'd set foot inside the shop.

"I brought you something."

Moving forward, he held out a hand to help her up. She hesitated, then put her fingers in his. He kept his hold loose, but not without effort. Once up, she gave her bottom a quick dusting, then tilted her head.

"Did I forget something at the Pines?"

"No." He dug in his jacket pocket. "I had some time to kill this morning, and came into the city. I was browsing the bookstores, looking for the latest Tom Clancy, when I found this."

Brown paper crackled as she took the package he held out. When she slid the small volume out of the bag and saw its title, she gave a little gasp. Pete decided that small sound of joy more than made up for the long trip downtown.

"Once upon a Mattress," she read aloud, her eyes dancing. *"A History of Bed-Making through the Ages."*

"I flipped through it," Pete offered. "There's a picture and description of a four-poster they say is George IV."

"You're kidding!" She fanned the pages. "Where is it?"

"Page 92. I'm not sure it's your George," he cautioned, angling around to peer over her shoulder as she thumbed the pages.

"Oh, it's not." Disappointment colored her voice, but then she turned and beamed him a smile. "But it's close enough to give me a better idea of its value. Thank you."

It was all he could do not to kiss her. She was standing so close he could see the small golden flecks in her brown eyes and catch her scent, a lighter floral than the overpowering dried roses. Shoving his hands into his pockets to keep from wrapping them around her shoulders, he stepped back.

"You're welcome."

She folded the book against her chest. Tilting her head, she chewed on her lower lip a moment before breaking the small silence that lay between them like a question.

"Would you like to see it? My George, I mean? I took it out of storage yesterday and set it up in the house on Peabody Street."

"Are you moving in already?"

"Not officially, but my offer's been accepted and the Realtor gave me a key." She hugged the book to her chest, smiling happily. "We have to wait for the final appraisal to come back before we close, but the owner didn't mind if I took one piece in."

Pete started to refuse. He'd already stretched his self-discipline about as far as it would stretch. But he couldn't bring himself to squelch Abby's pleasure.

"How could I pass up the chance to see the bed old Mrs. Clement…"

"Of the Macon Clements," she interjected, lifting a brow.

He grinned. "…of the Macon Clements…passed to her great-great-granddaughter? Let's go."

As she dug her purse out of the desk drawer and reached for the lightweight wool coat she'd left hanging on a hook behind the door, sensible, responsible Abby couldn't think of anything more foolish than spending another few hours with Pete.

Hadn't she learned her lesson? Hadn't she spent the past two nights working hard not to regret those stolen hours at the Pines? Over and over, she'd told herself that she'd made the right decision when she declined to stay for rum-raisin pancakes. After two sleepless nights, she'd almost convinced herself.

Well, she'd have plenty of nights to work on not regretting her time with Pete. He'd be gone soon, and she'd be up to her ears in the business she'd sunk most of her savings and all of her dreams into. A few more hours was all they'd have.

Abby decided to snatch at them.

First, however, she had to get past the roadblock she knew Marissa would throw in her path. As if on cue, the raven-haired store owner appeared from one of the alcoves. Her thin brows sliced downward when she saw Abby's purse and coat.

"Are you going somewhere?"

"I'm taking an early lunch."

The older woman's glance strayed from her employee to Pete, then back. From the arch look of inquiry in Marissa's face, Abby gathered that she wanted an introduction and an explanation. Having minimized Pete's involvement in her abbreviated account of her unplanned stay at the Pines, Abby wasn't quite up to explaining him to her inquisitive employer now.

"I'll be back in an hour or so," she assured Marissa, dodging the issue.

Clearly annoyed, the shop owner tapped a high-heeled foot on the *faux* marble tiles.

"Really, Abigail, I would appreciate a bit more notice before you juggle the work schedule like this. I have a customer coming in at two for a consultation. I'll need you on the floor then."

Abby headed for the back door, throwing a reassuring smile over her shoulder. "I'll be back."

"Maybe," Pete tossed in.

He shut the door on the shop owner's indignant glare and followed Abby outside.

"Whew! What's the politically correct term for *witch* these days?"

"I wish I knew. Marissa's become…a bit more difficult than usual since I gave notice."

She led the way to the rental car furnished by the Pines and unlocked the passenger door for Pete. As she walked around to the driver's side, the bright sunshine put a spring in her step. After the drizzle of the past days, the sky was an impossible blue. The cool, clean November breeze carried more zip than nip. Abby breathed the crisp air, felt it bubble in her veins.

She paused with her hand halfway to the door handle. As it had at the inn, the intensity of her sensory perceptions startled her. She felt as though she'd suddenly wakened after a heavy sleep.

Sobering, she recognized that this singing in her veins had little to do with the sunshine. Careful, she cautioned herself as she slid behind the wheel. Tread lightly here, Abigail. You have only a few hours.

It took half of one of those hours to reach their destination. Peabody Street wound through a once-fashionable part of Atlanta that had succumbed to age and abandonment and was now fighting its way back. Many of the deteriorating mansions on either side of the wide street still bore the scars of subdivision and graffiti, but a good number had been restored in loving detail with grants from the Georgia Historical Places Preservation Society. The peppering of For Sale and Sold signs planted in the front yards was a sure indication of the resurgence of interest in the area. Abby had staked her future on that renaissance.

Her house stood on a corner, a white two-story Palladian-style home with a columned front porch that was perfect for the wicker furniture and ferns she planned to set out. The entire front facade was skirted by green rhododendrons and azaleas that would blaze with color in the spring. A huge magnolia shaded half the front yard. On the other side, a latticework arch in dire need of a coat of white paint framed a weed-clogged fountain.

Cleaning the fountain would be one of Abby's first priorities. She could almost hear the soft trickle of water from the imp's stone urn as she led Pete up the brick sidewalk. Eagerly she gestured to the three-sided two-story window embrasures on either side of the front door.

"Those bay windows will make perfect display areas. When the shutters are thrown back, you can see right through the house."

Abby fiddled with the touchy lock on the weathered, peeling doors. "I'm going to paint these...."

"I know." His mouth crooked up in the grin that did such funny things to her respiratory system. "Green."

She nodded and pushed the double doors open. She was surprised and pleased that Pete would remember such a small detail.

He did a slow turn in the center of the wide hall that ran from the front to the back of the house, taking in the tall-ceilinged rooms on either side. Abby's gaze followed his, skimming over peeling wallpaper and chunks of plaster missing from the ceiling. She wasn't sure why his opinion mattered so much, but she waited for it anxiously. When he brought his gaze back to hers, it held a touch of doubt.

"You've got your work cut out here."

She chewed on her lower lip. "I know."

"But I can see why you're excited about this place." His doubt folded into a smile. "That crown molding must be eight inches all the way around."

"Ten," Abby said, her breath coming out in a little rush. "It's solid oak, too, not pine. So is the wainscoting in the dining room. Wait until you see it!"

Pete followed her through the downstairs rooms, his initial doubts easing with closer inspection. From what he could see, the basic structure of the house was sound. The fixtures and walls and wiring needed work, though. A lot of work.

Abby didn't minimize the challenge ahead of her. Instead, she seemed to relish it.

"I'm going to do a room at a time," she told him happily. "I'll start with the downstairs, since that will be my main display area, and work my way upstairs. Eventually, I may open some of the upstairs rooms, as well. I'll have to see how it goes, and how much privacy I want to maintain."

Pete followed her up the wide, curving staircase. "You don't anticipate any problems with living and working in the same location?"

"No! I want to showcase my pieces in a home, not cram them into a cluttered, overcrowded rabbit warren like Things Past. My clients will see them as they should be seen, well-used and well-loved."

She stopped outside the room at the front of the upstairs landing, a rueful smile on her face.

"Of course, there is a small problem with that plan. I have a tendency to get too attached to some of my acquisitions...like old George here."

Throwing open the double doors to the master suite, she stepped aside. Pete whistled, low and long. The massive four-poster bed stood in solitary splendor in the center of the room. Without mattresses or draperies, it still presented a majestic air, as though it had reclaimed its rightful place in the world.

"So this is Mrs. Clement's legacy."

Strolling into the room, Pete ran a hand over the intricately carved footboard. A pineapple motif was carved into the polished mahogany, matching the knobs that topped the four tall posts.

"How in the world did the movers get it up those stairs?"

"The movers didn't. I did."

"What?"

"It comes apart," Abby told him eagerly. "The posts have several sections that unscrew on wooden dowels. The frame just hooks together. Even the headboard and footboards are made of grooved wooden panels that come apart easily. Furniture used to be crafted that way so it could be transported overland by wagon."

She gripped one of the tall posts and swung in a small arch.

"Yet it's so solid when it's put together. So…so enduring."

Pete didn't realize he'd stepped too close until her swing brought her in his direction. Without thinking, he caught her in his arms, surprising himself as much as he did Abby. Her smiling exuberance slipped away, like the sun going behind a cloud. She looked up at him, confusion and wariness creeping into her eyes.

The confusion Pete could understand. He felt it, too. In spades. The wariness made him ache.

He didn't try to deny any longer the need that had brought him into the city this morning to see Abby. He recognized that it wasn't lust, wasn't simply a dangerous mix of chemicals. It went deeper, spread farther through his mind and his heart. If he hadn't seen her face as she showed him her house and her bed, he might have risked asking her to…

To what, O'Brian? Move with him every eighteen or twenty-four months? Keep her treasures in storage and put her dreams on hold for another eight, ten years? Grow more and more bitter with each remote assignment, less tolerant with every short-notice deployment?

Fighting the need to tighten his arms and bring her warmth into his, he tried to make her…and himself… understand.

"I have to leave tomorrow."

"I know."

"I don't want to."

Christ, he hadn't meant to say that! He didn't know why he had, except that it was the truth. Only this particular truth complicated matters far more than he'd intended when he climbed out of that cab.

She swallowed, then managed a shaky smile. "I didn't know that."

That small, trembling curve of her mouth pierced through his shield like a Teflon-coated spear point. He combed his hands through her hair, allowing himself one last touch.

"I could love you, Abby. So easily."

She searched his eyes. Then her smile softened into a gentle acknowledgment that tore at his soul.

"You did love me," she replied. "So wonder-fully."

"I can't stop thinking about those hours we spent together."

"I've thought about them once or twice myself."

Pete forced himself to go on. He didn't want any shadows or unanswered questions between them when he left.

"Sweetheart, if I could, and if you'd let me, I'd curl up with you in that bed and spend the rest of my life there."

Her lips parted, closed, then parted again, as if the words she wanted wouldn't come.

"But you can't," she got out at last.

"No."

"And I wouldn't let you. I've seen you in action, remember? I know how good you are. Despite that twisted piece of metal you carry around like a hair shirt—or maybe because of it—I suspect you're one of the best."

She tried for light and easy, but Pete saw the hurt in her eyes. Dammit! He'd sworn he'd never cause another woman that kind of hurt.

"I won't ask you to put aside all your dreams and come with me, and I can't ask you to wait for me. Aside from the fact that I don't have the right, it wouldn't be fair to you."

"Maybe…" She wet her lips. "Maybe I'm a better judge of what's fair for me."

"I've been down this road once, Abby. I've seen what happens when there are too many goodbyes between a man and a woman. I don't want that to happen to us."

Abby pulled out of his arms and turned away, refusing to let him see the piercing ache his words gave her. And the anger. She'd discovered that she didn't like being compared to Pete's former wife. Any more than she liked his assumptions about what would and wouldn't be fair to her.

Shoving her hurt into a small corner of her heart to be examined later, she drew her dignity around her. As with Derek, she wouldn't try to bind a man who wasn't sure he wanted her.

"Look, I appreciate your concern over what would or wouldn't be fair for me, but I'm a big girl. I make my own decisions. I have for a long time. That's why I chose to leave the inn when I did, before we both—" she gave a helpless shrug "—before we started worrying about goodbyes."

Pete raked a hand through his hair. Abby saw frustration in the abrupt gesture and in the wire-tight lines of his body. She might have sympathized with him, but she was feeling more than a little wired herself right now. There was no point in prolonging the agony, for either of them.

"I'd better get back to the shop."

He studied her face for long moments, then nodded. "Yeah, I guess you'd better."

Abby left the bedroom first. Trailing a hand along the smooth, well-worn banister, she started down the stairs. From the corner of her eye, she saw Pete give the bed a last long look, then firmly shut the bedroom doors.

They made the drive back downtown in uneasy silence. They really didn't have anything more to say to each other, Abby realized as she negotiated the traffic. They'd said it all. All that could be said between them, anyway. Except those damnable goodbyes.

They made them quickly—Abby first, then Pete.

She hoped that his medical board went well.

He wished her success with her new home.

Then they shared a brief kiss that satisfied neither of them.

Abby stood beside the rental car while he slipped

on a pair of aviator sunglasses, shoved his hands in his jacket pockets and turned to leave.

She made it to the back door of the shop before she swung around, her hand on the brass knob and her heart in her throat.

"Pete?"

He turned, his eyes shielded behind the mirrored lenses. "Yes?"

"Just for the record, I could love you, too. Easily."

Chapter 9

The white-coated surgeon dropped a thick manila folder on his desk and swiveled to face his patient. "It's the classic good-news-bad-news scenario, Sergeant O'Brian. Which do you want first?"

Pete tugged on his uniform coat to square it over his shoulders. After five days of tests and more tests at Wilford Hall, the huge medical complex located on Lackland Air Force Base, just south of San Antonio, he was ready for the final verdict.

"Give it to me the way that makes most sense, Doc."

The surgeon drummed his fingers on the sheaf of X rays and lab reports, marshaling his thoughts. A lieutenant colonel with two rows of framed degrees behind his desk and a blunt, no-nonsense air of authority, Dr. McMillin took his job seriously. So seriously he'd requested that Pete meet him in his office on Saturday morning, instead of waiting for his scheduled appointment on Monday.

"Your right anterior cruciate ligament is shot to hell. Your last jump shredded what little was left of it after twenty-plus years of hitting the ground harder than a body is supposed to."

Pete's mouth curved. "Is that the bad news or the good news?"

"The bad. And it gets worse." The surgeon's gray eyes met Pete's steadily. "Our initial tests indicated there might be enough ligament tissue left for us to weave in a synthetic fiber and restructure the ACL, but it appears there isn't."

Although the second series of tests he'd gone through had given Pete the suspicion that the damage was more extensive than he'd thought, the verdict hit him square in the chest. With more than twenty-two years in the jump business, he accepted bad knees and spinal compression as a risk of his profession. But there were bad knees, and then there were bad knees. Most could be repaired enough for a man to return to jump status. From what the colonel was saying, it seemed his couldn't.

He leveled the doc a straight look. "I hope you're not going to suggest that the good news is a total knee replacement?"

They both knew that an artificial knee would take him off jump status permanently.

"No, I know that's the last option you'd consider," Colonel McMillin replied, passing a hand over his buzz-cut gray hair. "What I want to talk to you about is a new procedure we're testing. It involves fitting a plastic cap over your own bone. We attach the muscle to that with artificial ligaments."

"I've heard of the procedure," Pete replied. "I've also heard it hasn't been all that successful to date."

"It's had mixed results," McMillin admitted. "A civilian surgeon who specializes in sports-related injuries reports some success. We've tried it twice here, once on a teenager who took a body block during football practice and once on another PJ."

Pete knew the man the doc was referring to, a shoe-leather-tough Vietnam vet, a good troop and a damn fine PJ. He now served behind a desk.

"Let me be sure I've got it straight, Doc." He leaned forward, wanting his options laid clear. "If this plastic cap works, I go back on jump status. If it doesn't, I don't."

"It's not quite that cut-and-dried, O'Brian. This is still an experimental procedure. We haven't had a good take with it yet. If it works, then we'll evaluate whether you should start hitting the chutes again."

Pete nodded, his eyes hooded. "Fair enough."

"Think about it over the weekend. If you decide

you want to be our third guinea pig, call my secretary Monday morning and we'll set you up for surgery."

Pete walked out of the multistory medical center, his highly glossed jump boots sounding a steady beat on the concrete sidewalk. Bright Texas sunlight glinted on the silver *US*s pinned to his lapels and on the shiny wings positioned above the rows of ribbons on his chest. With the unconscious arrogance that came with being a PJ, he squared his maroon beret on his head, then tugged it to precisely the right angle over his brow.

As he made his way toward his rental car, a distant drumbeat carried on the morning air. He stopped, cocking his head as the sound took on a familiar rhythm. He hadn't marched to that beat in years, but he identified it immediately. The basic trainees were marching onto the parade field adjacent to the hospital complex in preparation for their graduation ceremony.

As the center for all air force basic military training, Lackland conducted a formal parade every six weeks or so to mark the recruits' graduation from boot camp. Since the base was also the site of the ten-week PJ indoctrination course that followed immediately after basic training, Pete had attended a good number of these parades prior to interviewing the candidates for the PJ career field. He always enjoyed the ceremony. The color and pageantry of the event stirred something deep within him.

The beat of that distant drum now drew him like a siren's call. After his session with the doc this morning and too many long nights of thinking about Abby, he needed to focus on something outside himself. Something simple. Something basic.

Something he could enjoy, then walk away from without a sense of having left a part of himself behind.

Dropping his car keys into his pocket, he headed for the broad, grassy field a half mile or so away. He stood down field, well away from the bleachers filled with proud parents and spouses, excited children, invited guests and the uniformed training instructors who'd worked twenty hours a day for the past six weeks to turn raw recruits into disciplined airmen.

The troops were massed across the field from the bleachers and the reviewing stand, with the colors in the center. The Stars and Stripes waved in the breeze. Several foreign flags ranged next to it, in recognition of the students from other nations sent to Lackland for basic training. Behind them flew the service flags, heavy with battle streamers earned during bloody engagements on land, on sea and in hostile skies.

Pete's eyes fixed on the blue air force flag. Even from this distance, he could pick out several of the distinctive streamers. They matched the campaign ribbons he wore on his chest. He'd served in his share of distant battles, and flown through a few hostile skies.

Pulling his gaze from the flags, he let it drift down

squadron after squadron of short-sheared, blue-suited troops standing at parade rest, legs spread, hands clasped loosely behind their backs.

Christ, they looked so young! And so damned eager. He felt a tug of envy for the future that stretched so limitlessly before them. What honor would they bring to the just-issued uniforms they wore so proudly? How many battle streamers would they add to the flags waving in the breeze? How many of them would end their careers too soon, like Carrington?

Pete slipped his hand into his pants pocket, searching through the keys and pocket change for a twisted scrap of metal. His eyes on the field, he fingered the constant reminder of his heavy responsibilities to those young, eager rookies.

He shoved those responsibilities to the back of his mind when an officer quickstepped to the center of the field and faced the massed squadrons.

"Sooooooound adjutant's call!"

The military band belted out a few short chords, alerting the troops and the visitors to the start of the ceremonies.

"Bring your groups to at-tennnn-shun!"

One after another, group and squadron commanders echoed the adjutant's bellowed order. The air reverberated with the bellowed commands. Five hundred chins lifted. A thousand heels clicked. Shoulders squared. Chests puffed. Guidons whipped up, and blue-and-gold squadron pennants snapped in the breeze.

Unconsciously Pete pulled back his shoulders and dropped his hands in loose fists at his side. His pulse accelerating in a quick, steady beat, he listened to the ritual announcements that signaled the start of the ceremonies.

When the reviewing party arrived and the colors marched forward, Pete came to rigid, square-shouldered attention. At the first note of the national anthem, his right arm sliced up in sync with all the others on the field. Palm blade-straight, fingertips just touching his brow, he stood tall. The emotions that comrades-in-arms rarely, if ever, admitted to pounded through his veins…the same emotions that drove men and women to leave their homes and their families and don a uniform that made them targets for hostile forces.

Pride. Patriotism. A sense of belonging to a larger community. A need to return some measure of service to the nation that nourished them.

Throughout the ceremonies, he stood at the end of the field. He barely heard the introduction of the reviewing party. Watched with abstracted interest when the officers massed at the center and marched forward, then returned to lead their troops. Listened with only a part of himself to the stirring remarks by the commanding general. His thoughts stayed focused entirely on the troops.

The future belonged to them. To these men and

women who stepped out in massed squadrons, then columned right and hit their stride to the stirring beat of the air force anthem. Arms whipping up, they saluted the reviewing officer as they marched past. From where he stood, alone and proud, Senior Master Sergeant O'Brian saluted them.

As they passed, one squadron after another, Pete remembered how he'd stepped out some twenty-two years ago. Like these eager men and women, he'd marched off this field, straight into two decades of excitement and routine, incredible challenges and occasional frustrations. He'd made decisions during those two decades that he regretted, certainly. There had been moments he'd sell his soul to relive. But for twenty-two years, he'd given everything in him he had to give.

Now he might have a chance to march another few years into that future.

Or into a different future.

I could love you, too. Easily.

The words echoed faintly over the tromp of marching feet. They wove through the chords of stirring, martial music.

He could see Abby standing with one hand on the door to the shop. The sunlight had made a fuzzy halo of her hair and dusted her skin. Lord, she had the most beautiful skin. Pete's fists bunched tighter.

Of all the goodbyes he'd ever said, that one had hurt the most. It still hurt. This time, though, he suspected that neither time nor distance would ease the ache.

I could love you, too.

Pete waited until after the last squadron had passed in review. He stood silent while the airmen tossed their caps in the air in exuberant glee. Then he walked back to the hospital parking lot, searched out his rental car and drove to the visiting senior NCO quarters.

Tossing the car keys and his maroon beret on the coffee table, he unbuttoned his blue coat and loosened his tie. Hands shoved into his pockets, he stood at the window. He had some hard thinking to do before he reached for the phone sitting on the desk.

When the phone shrilled, Abby was literally up to her ears in boxes.

She'd decided to take advantage of her Saturday afternoon off to start packing her personal things. The professionals would move the large pieces, but she wanted to sort through and wrap the smaller items herself. Given her penchant for collecting treasures, it was a laborious task. Thank goodness Beth had called from L.A. and promised to come over and help when her flight landed in Atlanta later this afternoon. Her sister always needed time for her internal clock to reset itself after an international run. Packing would be as good a way as any to work off her body's confusion over abrupt time zone changes, she'd insisted.

Abby lifted a stack of books from the bookshelf and tucked them into a box, mulling over the brief call. Beth had asked how her fiancé had taken her nonappearance at the wedding, of course. The news of Jordy's unexpected deployment to the world's current hot spot had shocked Beth into a long, tense silence. She'd hung up shortly afterward, but not before she told Abby that she needed her sage advice and counsel when she got into Atlanta.

Sighing, Abby reached for another stack of books. She didn't feel up to dishing out advice to Beth, or to anyone else, for that matter. In fact, she heartily wished there was someone she could turn to for a little counseling herself. She hadn't felt this…this empty in years.

She should be simmering with excitement right now. She should be tucking her things into boxes with the joyous expectation of unpacking them in the old, well-loved home she'd always longed for. The house on Peabody Street was all but hers.

True, the appraisal had returned with an estimated value some four thousand dollars lower than expected. Her Realtor had gone back to renegotiate the price with the owners, but Abby had already privately decided to eat the difference if they proved recalcitrant, since she'd budgeted for the original amount anyway.

So where was the thrill of excitement that usually rippled through her when she thought about her house? What had happened to the pleasure she felt each time she stopped by the place after work and wandered through its rooms? Why didn't her heart jump at the thought of sleeping in her four-poster bed?

There was only one answer to all the questions that now plagued her, and he hadn't called. Not once since he'd left Atlanta.

Damn O'Brian, anyway. How could he have walked into her life, cut a swath through her dreams and walked out again, just like that?

Even more to the point, how could she have let him?

Abby sat back on her heels, the books clutched in her hands. He was probably on his way back to England by now. To the air base located close to… Where was it? Stonecross Keep. Vague descriptions of square stone towers, black-beamed ceilings and trestle tables drifted through her mind, followed by an image of Pete sprawled in the love seat opposite hers, his long legs stretched toward the fire as he'd dug through his memory for the details she demanded.

Almost immediately, another image crowded that one aside. Of her and Pete sharing the same love seat. Of his hands massaging her frigid toes with a gentleness that made her ache almost as much as the memory of their passionate hours in the loft.

The shrill of the phone ripped through her fragile memories and laid her wide open for a rush of hope. Dumping the books in a heap on the floor, she shoved aside a stack of boxes and snatched up the receiver.

"Hello."

"Abby?"

The sound of a woman's husky voice sent disappointment lancing into her heart. It was all she could do to force out a reply.

"Yes?"

"It's me, Cherry."

Abby summoned a smile and a warm greeting. As soon as the polite preliminaries were over, Cherry plunged right into the reason for her call.

"Listen, sweetie, I have a big favor to ask you. I know it's an imposition, but you're the only other woman I know in Atlanta, and even if you weren't, I feel like we're friends. Please say you'll do it."

Abby smiled at the breathless, excited rush. "Sure, if I can."

"Would you be my maid of honor? Tonight? At the Pines?"

"What?"

"Irv pushed his divorce through as soon as we got back to Dallas," Cherry reported, happiness bubbling like a fountain in her voice. "He signed the papers last night, and we flew back to Atlanta this morning to get the blood test and the license. Georgia's still his legal residence for tax purposes, you know."

"Er, no, I didn't know."

"It is, and we are. Getting married tonight, I mean! Can you believe it it?"

Abby grinned. "I believe it! Just out of curiosity, though, what happened to the Lincoln?"

Cherry's infectious gurgle of laughter came over the line. "Irv gave it to his ex…after I reminded him that we'd pretty well worn out the shocks, anyway."

"Good for both of you!"

Cherry sobered. "Irv says he realized something up there on that ridge, when he was working on Orlie with you. Life's too uncertain to take anything for granted. He says sometimes you just gotta go for it. You know, take that leap…like you're doing, sinking all your savings into your new shop."

Before Abby could respond to that, she rushed on. "So he called the mayor. Remember her? The one who tried to marry you and Irv?"

"I remember."

"She's going to perform the ceremony, and Orlie's going to give me away, and I'd really love it if you'd be my maid of honor."

"I…"

"I know this is awfully short notice. I would have called you earlier, but we weren't sure we could get the blood tests and the license done, and then we were rushing around so much I didn't have time to call. But say you'll do it!"

"Of course I will. I'd be honored."

"Oh, Abby, thank you! We'll send a car for you. Is an hour from now okay? The ceremony's at six."

"You don't need to send a car. I got my van back yesterday, in better condition than when I bought it. I'll drive up."

"No, you won't. We're doing this right. Tell

me your address and we'll send a limo. Oh, and Abby?"

"Yes?"

"You'd better wear something white, for tradition's sake, because I'm wearing red!"

"Now why doesn't that surprise me?"

Laughing, Abby hung up. Cherry's contagious happiness kept her smiling as she weaved her way through her scattered possessions. She'd have to shuck her jeans and grubby t-shirt and grab a quick shower if she was going to be ready by the time the limo arrived.

She walked into the bedroom thinking how strange it was that she'd never been to the Pines before, and now she'd been asked to participate in her second wedding there in less than a week. Hopefully, this wedding would come off better than the last one. With any luck, Cherry and Irv wouldn't have to bundle under layers and layers of blankets to keep warm when they shared that sybaritic bed in the honeymoon cottage.

At the memory of the hours she'd spent with Pete in that huge bed, she froze with her jeans peeled halfway down her hips. Breath suspended, she waited for the ache to pass.

It didn't. It pooled in a spot just under her heart and stayed there, a heavy, constant hurt.

Shoving her jeans off, Abby shook her head. Sweet heavens, how could she have been such a fool? After all those years of giving Beth advice, of trying to keep her from tumbling in and out of love, she'd done exactly the same thing. Or almost the same thing. She'd tumbled into love, apparently, but she hadn't quite reached the "out of it" stage yet. She was beginning to suspect she never would.

Unlike Beth, though, she hadn't had the courage to reach out and grab at that love. Steady, cautious Abby had retreated into her safe world and watched Pete walk away, just as she'd watched Derek What's-his-name walk out of her arms into her sister's charmed circle.

She hadn't even tried to hold on to Pete, she thought in disgust. Or find the middle ground between her dreams and his duty. She'd let him go back to his life, and she'd stayed in hers. So here she was, surrounded by cardboard boxes and about to act as maid of honor at another woman's wedding.

Some life, Abigail. Some dreams!

She sank down on the edge of the bed, her mind churning. Gradually her hurt became anger at herself, then slowly tipped into something else. Something less painful. More positive. Determination gathered, bit by bit, at the outer corners of her heart. Then it folded in on itself, until it became an insistent, demanding force.

Dammit, Irv was right. More or less. Sometimes a person just had to go for it—only in this case, Abby had gone for the wrong thing. For a supposedly intelligent woman, she'd taken far too long to realize that a home was so much more than just a house. It was shared laughter, and sour-cream potato chips before the fire, and someone warming your toes for you on a cold night.

That kind of home you could make anywhere, she told herself fiercely. It didn't have to be on Peabody Street, or even in Atlanta.

Pete's highly mobile career didn't have to mean only goodbyes. So he spent a lot of time in the air! He had to come down sometime, didn't he? And when he did, she'd be there. She'd welcome him home, just as Mrs. Clement's descendants had welcomed their men for generation after generation. She'd take her heart and her hopes and her portable George IV wherever Pete went.

Her determination flowered into a fierce, pounding joy, tempered by just a touch of reality.

Okay, so he hadn't said he wanted her with him wherever he went. He hadn't even said that he loved her, exactly. Only that he *could* love her. Well, any woman worth her salt ought to be able to turn that *could* into *does*.

And if she didn't? The voice of caution that she could never quite shake struggled to be heard over the pounding of her heart. If she failed to convince Pete? What then?

Then she'd pick up the pieces and go on. But at least she would have tried. For once in her life, she would have thrown aside all caution and common sense and followed her heart, not her head.

She sat absolutely still on the bed for several long

moments, then reached out and yanked the phone off the nightstand. Her hands trembling, she started dialing.

Chapter 10

Pete strode out of Atlanta's airport with more adrenaline coursing through his veins than he'd pumped before his very first jump.

He hadn't taken time to change out of his uniform. After placing a quick call to the hospital and another to his overseas unit, he'd barely taken time to throw his things in his carryall before checking out of the visiting NCO quarters. He'd arrived at the San Antonio airport just as a flight to Atlanta was boarding. It had taken some fast ticketing and a first-class seat, but he'd made the flight.

Moments after the plane touched down at its destination, he was out the door and heading for the airport exit. This time, no flushed, curly-haired creature in a black cloak tugged at his sleeve to stop him. This time, he couldn't shift his carryall into his left hand and sweep her against him with his right, as he ached to do. But he would. Dammit, he would. Before he boarded the plane that would take him back to England, he was going to hold her and kiss her and try to convince her that they'd already said all their goodbyes.

He probably should call ahead, he thought as he hailed a cab. Abby might not want to see him. Hell, she might not even want to talk to him after their last session, but what he had to say couldn't be said over the phone.

Slinging his bag and himself into the cab, he gave the driver directions to Things Past. The trip into the city seemed to take twice as long as it had the last time. Curbing his simmering impatience with some effort, he used the time to marshal his arguments.

When they pulled up at the shop, Pete was half out of the cab before he saw the Closed sign on the door. His colorful curse raised the cabbie's brows.

"Got a problem, Sarge?"

"Yeah, I do."

Pete eyed the sign in disgust. He hadn't counted on the shop closing early on Saturday afternoons. He had no idea where Abby lived. Where she *planned* to live, yes. But where she currently resided, no. He climbed back into the cab and slammed the door.

"Pull over at the next phone booth you see. I have to check an address."

With the taxi idling behind him, he flipped through the fat phone directory. As he'd expected, he found no listing for Abigail Davis. When he saw the multiple A. Davises in the directory, he muttered another curse and pulled out the piece of paper Jordy had given him containing both Beth's and Abby's phone numbers. The paper unfolded easily along well-worn crease lines. He'd taken it out more times than he could count this past week and stared at the number scrawled across it.

Eyes narrowed, he checked the scribbled phone numbers against those listed in the directory. Moments later, he climbed back in the cab and slammed the door.

"Ten-sixteen Philmont, and hurry."

The cabbie grinned. "Fasten your seat belt. This baby moves about as fast as the F-4s I used to work on."

Reining in his impatience, Pete met his gaze in the mirror. "How long were you in?"

"Only one hitch. Vietnam was enough for me. Though I hafta tell you, I never took the flak at Tan Son Nhut that I take when I drive through some parts of this city."

Pete listened with half an ear to the vet's rambling and occasionally raunchy stories of his days in the service. With each turn of the tires, he felt his control slipping closer and closer to the edge of its restraint.

When they pulled up in front of a mellow brick-fronted apartment complex, the sight of Abby's brown van kicked his pulse into overdrive. His heart slamming against his ribs, Pete paid off the cabbie, wished him luck, then leaned on the doorbell of 1016.

He'd anticipated surprise.

He'd hoped for at least a cool welcome.

What he hadn't counted on was that the woman who opened the door would take one astonished look at him, turn deathly pale and crumple in a faint.

"Christ!"

Pete caught her before she hit the tiled floor of the foyer. Scooping her into his arms, he kicked the door shut and carried her into an apartment that in ordinary circumstances might have been spacious and airy. Right now, it looked as though a Scud missile had zeroed in on it.

Boxes were scattered everywhere, some empty, some sealed, others half packed. Pete couldn't find a chair or sofa that didn't have books or linens or knick-knacks stacked on it. He stood in the middle of the room, his burden a dead weight in his arms, and tried to find someplace to lay her. Finally he lifted a boot and nudged a stack of linens off a plush Victorian armchair.

She gave a little groan when he eased her into the chair. Pete stared down at her for a moment, then carved a path into the kitchen and rummaged through more boxes until he found a saucepan. Deciding it would have to do, he half filled it with water and returned to the living room.

"Beth! Beth, wake up!"

He loosened the dark blue tie of her airline uniform, slid a hand under her neck to raise her head and held the pot to her lips.

"Here, take some water."

When the liquid trickled into her mouth, Beth sputtered and choked and came awake. Before Pete could remove the pot, she lunged up and knocked it aside. Cold water hit him squarely in the face. He jerked back, only to have Beth grab his lapels and follow him.

"It's Jordy, isn't it? Oh, God, I know it's Jordy."

"No…"

"Tell me!" She clung to him like a burr, sobbing. "Tell me, Pete! Is he dead?"

He closed his hands over hers, trying to ease her frantic grip. "No, he's not dead!"

She moaned. "He's wounded. Isn't he? He's wounded and calling for me." Tears poured down her cheeks. "It's all my fault. If I hadn't run out on him…"

"Beth…"

"Where is he, Pete? Tell me. I'll go to him. I can—"

"Beth, calm down! Jordy's not injured. Or he wasn't when I called back to the unit a few hours ago."

His words finally penetrated her hiccuping sobs.

"He's okay? Really?"

Pete's voice gentled. "Really."

She sagged against him in relief.

Pete patted her awkwardly on the back, waiting for her sobs to cease. His patience ran out before her sniffles.

Easing her away, he looked down into the face that he, like Jordy, had once thought perfect. Her features were finer than her sister's, and her hair was a paler, silkier blond. But she didn't have Abby's firm chin or her wide, full mouth. Nor, Pete remembered belatedly, did she have her incisive intelligence.

"Why are you wearing all your ribbons and stuff?" she asked through watery sniffs. At his blank look, she waved a hand distractedly. "That's...that's what frightened me so much."

Pete couldn't help himself. He had to ask. "My ribbons scared you?"

"I thought—" She gulped. "You know, like in the movies. Men in full dress uniform show up at the front door to...to notify the next of kin."

Pete was forced to point out the obvious. "Beth, you're not Jordy's next of kin."

It was a mistake. Her eyes teared up again.

"I know. But I want to be. I think."

Pete let that one pass. He had more important things on his mind than Beth's mercurial relationship with her almost-groom. Tugging her hands free of his lapels, he did a quick scan of the cluttered room.

"Where's Abby?"

"Abby?"

"Your sister?"

She sniffed. "Why do you want to see Abby?"

"I need to talk to her about a personal matter. Where is she?"

Her tears drying, she looked up at Pete in surprise. "A personal matter? With Abby?"

"Beth…"

The low, strangled snarl sent her back a pace. "She's…she's at the Pines."

"The Pines?"

"She went to a wedding. Another wedding."

Her chin wobbled for a moment, and Pete braced himself for more tears. Bravely Beth fought them back.

"She left the strangest note. It's in the kitchen. Evidently her dentist is getting married to a woman named…Peaches, I think it was."

It took Pete only a second or two to connect the dentist with Irv, and Irv with Peaches, a.k.a. Cherry. Evidently the periodontist had finally decided to claim his woman. Good for him!

Beth's flawless face clouded with confusion. "I don't know why Abby didn't mention going to this wedding when I called her earlier."

Pete didn't know, either, and didn't particularly care. He didn't intend to wait any longer to stake his own claim.

"Did you drive here?" he asked Beth.

"No, I took a cab from the airport."

"Do you know where Abby keeps the keys to the van?"

His curt question triggered another confused frown.

"That's something else I don't understand. The Antiquemobile got a complete face-lift while I was gone, and Abby never said a word about it. Although I suppose she had to get it in good working order before she goes on this trip."

"What trip?"

"Her note said she was going on a trip tomorrow. To Stone Keep." Beth's brow knit. "Maybe she meant Stone Mountain. That's only a few miles from here, though why she'd have the van—"

She gave a startled squeak as Pete gripped her arms.

"Stonecross Keep? Did Abby say she was going to Stonecross Keep?"

"That…that might have been it. I'll have to check the note."

Pete felt as though a flare had just been set off inside him. A burst of white-hot fire spiraled through his chest, then burned with a searing heat. He stood rock-still for several moments, waiting for the flame to subside. Seconds later, he realized this was one conflagration that wasn't going to burn itself out.

The fact that Abby had decided to go to England told him that she might be feeling the same steady flame.

While Pete tried to steady his rocketing emotions,

Beth worried her lower lip with perfect white teeth and put her own interpretation on her sister's cryptic note.

"It isn't like Abby to just take off like this. I hope she's not sick or something."

"She's something," Pete said under his breath. "I sure hope she's something."

Abby tried not to grin as she matched her step to the recorded sounds of the wedding march and glided down the aisle formed by rows of chairs. Despite her best efforts, the astounded expressions on the faces of the handful of guests who'd hastily assembled for the wedding had her mouth curving. Quickly she buried her nose in her lavish bouquet to hide her laughter.

With her face bathed in the heady scent of long-stemmed red roses, she traveled the length of the banquet room toward the small party waiting in front of the massive stone fireplace. Cherry followed, on Orlie Taggert's arm. If Irv saw anything amiss in his bride's attire, Abby couldn't tell it from his beaming face. Mayor Calvin, on the other hand, gaped when she caught her first sight of the bridal party.

True to her word, Cherry had chosen to wear red. Bright, traffic-light red. Eye-popping red, accented with thousands of sequins. They shimmered on the bride's formfitting dress and shaped her magnificent bosom. More sequins dotted the short veil pinned to her upswept flaming red hair. Even the streamers trailing from her huge bouquet of crimson roses glittered with spangles. The only nonred article on her person was the antique sterling-silver pin studded with blue topaz that she'd borrowed from Abby.

Abby herself was dressed more like a bride than the bride. Following Cherry's instructions, she'd worn off-white, an ankle-length skirt in a creamy ivory wool and a matching hand-knit tunic studded with tiny drop pearls. Thank goodness she had. Any other color would have clashed horribly with the Cherry's dazzling fire-engine-red dress.

Still fighting a grin, she nodded to Irv and the mayor, then stepped to the side. The bride placed a kiss on Orlie's leathery cheek, released his arm, then moved into position. Cherry stood a good six inches taller than her groom, and anyone who saw the look they exchanged at that moment knew height didn't make a whisker of difference to either one of them. Gripping hands, they faced each other.

The mayor cleared her throat. Her weathered face creasing, she looked from Cherry to Abby. Then she winked at Irv.

"You sure you've got the right bride this time?"

He grinned. "I'm sure."

"Well, let's get you two—"

She broke off as the doors at the back of the banquet room rattled. Irv threw a look over his shoulder, then gave Cherry a quick grin.

"Hey, my office manager must have finally tracked Pete down. He made it!"

Abby swung around, her nails digging into the

stems of her rose bouquet. Disbelieving, she watched a tall, broad-shouldered figure stand aside while Beth rushed into the banquet room. For probably the first time in her adult life, Abby didn't spare a thought for her sister. She barely gave her a glance. Her entire being was focused on the man who followed Beth in.

Seeing him in uniform for the first time, Abby knew that the agonizing decision she'd made an hour ago was the right one. He wore his uniform easily, but she saw the pride that went into its tailored fit, the boots polished to a mirror gloss, and the precise alignment of his silver wings above his ribbons. He belonged in air force blue.

And she belonged with him.

He closed the doors behind him and leaned against them, his mouth curving in the crooked grin that made Abby's lungs forget to pump. Across the length of the banquet room, their eyes locked.

At that moment, her last doubts vanished. Wherever they went, they'd go together. Whatever bed they slept in, they'd sleep together. Tears prickled her lids, and she had to bury her nose in her bouquet once more to keep from crying during Cherry's and Irv's exchange of vows.

Any hope she might have harbored that she'd get Pete alone after the brief ceremony vanished as soon as a laughing, radiant Cherry released Irv from a passionate embrace. Hooking one arm through Irv's, she used the other to signal to Pete to join the small group milling around the wedding party.

When he approached, Irv thumped him on the back in a hearty greeting. "I'm glad you got my message. Thanks for coming, buddy."

"I didn't get your message, but you're welcome." Smiling, Pete bent and gave Cherry a kiss on one cheek. "You make a stunning bride."

She laughed up at him. "I do, don't I?"

Over Irv's shining bald crown, Pete caught Abby's smile. She looked so vibrant, so joyous, so…welcoming, that everything he'd planned to say to her got lost in the need to hold her.

He'd taken exactly half a step toward her when the mayor's sturdy form planted itself in front of him.

"Nice to see you in these parts again, O'Brian." She shook his hand, her shrewd gaze assessing his rows of ribbons. "I suppose it's too much to hope that you're thinking 'bout staying. I wasn't just pushing air around when I said we could use a man like you."

Pete flashed Abby another look.

"As a matter of fact," he said slowly, "I have been thinking about staying. Permanently."

Abby's eyes rounded in surprise. Edging around the mayor and Irv, Pete moved swiftly to her side.

"I didn't plan to tell you like this."

She swallowed. "Tell me what?"

Before he could answer, Beth wedged her way through the crowd and joined them.

"Abby, are you all right?"

"I'm fine. Tell me what, Pete?"

"Are you sure?" The younger woman peered into her sister's face anxiously. "You look a little pale."

Abby ignored her sister. "Tell me what, Pete?"

He glanced at the faces surrounding them. Their avid interest told Pete his chances of getting Abby alone right now were nonexistent. Resigning himself to saying what he had to say before the curious audience, he reached for her hand.

"I've put in my papers, sweetheart. I called my commander this morning to let him know. I'm getting out of the service as soon as I get back to England and process the retirement."

Dismay flooded her brown eyes. "Oh, Pete, why?"

His stomach lurched at her stricken expression. Dismay wasn't quite the reaction he'd been hoping for.

"Because I gave the air force my future once," he said quietly, his fingers gripping hers. "It was all I wanted then, all I thought I needed. Now I know I need more. I need you."

"But you didn't have to give it up. I—"

He cut her off, his hold on her hand tight and hard.

"I don't want any more goodbyes between us, Abby. I want to stay with you always. I want to curl up with you in Mrs. Clement's bed, and help you turn the house on Peabody Street into a home."

Her dismay gave way to an almost comical chagrin.

Pete didn't care for that reaction much more than he had the last.

"If you'll let me, Abby, I want to share your dreams."

His gut twisting, he waited for her reply. To his profound relief, her mouth lifted in a tremulous smile.

"You can curl up with me anywhere. For as long as you want."

He loosened his death grip on her hand and reached for her.

"But…"

The small caveat froze him in place. "But?"

"But I think you should know, I withdrew my offer on the house on Peabody Street."

"What?"

His exclamation got lost in Beth's startled gasp.

"Abby! You gave up your house?"

The stunned expressions on the faces of the two people she loved most in the world made Abby take a deep breath. She'd sort out Beth's feelings later. Right now, all that mattered to her was Pete's.

"The appraisal came in too low, which gave me a legal out. So I called the Realtor and told her I didn't want the house." Her tentative smile widened, then spilled into a grin. "I also mentioned that I was leaving for an extended stay in England."

"England!" Beth squeaked.

Cherry gave a low, throaty chuckle and gripped

Irv's arm with red-polished nails. "Good for you, sweetie! Go for it!"

Even Mayor Calvin got into the act. Her face folding into crags and valleys, she glanced from Abby to Pete.

"Well, well… Looks like we've got another bride, and the right groom, this time."

Abby ignored them all. Her whole being was centered on the man standing before her.

Her heart gave a painful thump of joy as Pete's blue eyes lit with laughter…and with a love that warmed her all the way to her toes.

"So you gave up your house, and I gave up the air force." He opened his arms to her. "I sure glad we've still got George III."

"George IV."

With a strangled sound that hovered somewhere between a sob and a laugh, she fell into his welcoming arms. His mouth was warm and hard and demanding. Hers asked for more, much more.

When he scooped her up in his arms, her stomach tightened in joyous anticipation. Whatever she asked for, he would give her.

"We'll call you as soon as we get the license and the blood tests," Pete told the grinning mayor. "It may be a few days."

"Anytime, O'Brian."

They were halfway to the back of the banquet room when Abby realized she was still clutching her bouquet.

"Pete! Wait a moment!"

Twisting in his arms, she tossed the roses in a long arc. Beth caught them, her face a study in confusion and doubtful happiness for her sister.

"Hold these for me, Sissy. And call Gulliver's Travels, would you? Tell them I need to change my reservation to London. I want to go on flight…?" She arched an inquiry at Pete.

"You don't have to go all that way with me," he told her softly. "I'll be back within a few weeks. I promise."

She wrapped her arms around his neck. "Oh, no, my darling. No more goodbyes, remember? Whither thou goest, I'm going, too. When we get back from England, we'll figure out whither we go next."

"Where we're going next," he murmured, "is to the closest available cottage."

It wasn't the honeymoon suite.

There was no freestanding glass-and-brass shower stall in the loft bathroom. The stone fireplace wasn't quite as massive as the one that had warmed them before.

But the Pines' management had provided a bottle of champagne with a dusty label that made Pete's brows arch, and the bed was as wide and as sinfully inviting as the one they'd shared.

Abby lay awake long after the fire had dimmed to a glow and the little bit of champagne in the green bottle had gone flat. Pete's head was heavy on her breasts, and his breath was warm against her skin.

She smiled, knowing she was home.

Epilogue

Distracted by the excited chatter in the outer office, Lucy Falco glanced away from her busy computer screen.

She caught a glimpse of Tiffany's silver curls, nodding emphatically, and the flutter of a gray reservation form in her hand. Tucking a stray strand of her dark brown hair behind her ear, she rose and joined the travel agents clustered around the older woman.

"*And* I have them booked into a medieval manor house for an entire week," Tiffany told the assembled group, lifting a finely penciled brow. "It's only open to a select clientele. Veddy veddy posh, you know."

"Who do you have booked into a manor house?"

Lucy asked, smiling at her subordinate's somewhat less than successful attempt at an English accent.

"Abby Davis. Or I guess I should say Abby O'Brian. She and her husband are leaving tomorrow for London. I had to scramble to get her reservation changed to the same flight he was booked on, I'll tell you. Then I had to track down some information on this manor house she wants to stay in on her honeymoon."

"What manor house?"

Tiffany handed Lucy the gray confirmation sheet. "It's called Stonecross Keep. It isn't on any of our regular tour listings. I had to fax our contacts in London for a description of the facilities and a price quote."

"After the disaster at the Pines, I'm surprised Abby trusts us to take care of her honeymoon arrangements," one of the other agents put in.

"The ice storm of the century was hardly the fault of Gulliver's Travels," Tiffany declared loftily. Then she abandoned her dignity and gave an earthy chuckle. "Besides, who needs heat or hot water on a honeymoon?"

Lucy's lips curved in a wry smile. "Not Abby and her husband, evidently. Did you read the description of this place? It has no central heat, no electricity except in the modernized kitchen wing, and 'plumbing fixtures that give the visitor an appreciation of the medieval way of life.'"

"Oh, dear."

"You'd better give Abby a call and make sure she knows what she's getting into."

Tiffany's coppery earrings jangled as she nodded. "I will. And as soon as I finalize these arrangements, I'm going to start working the honeymoon package my bridge partner's niece wants me to put together for her. She's getting married a week before Christmas."

Lucy hid a smile as a fervent gleam came into Tiffany's pale blue eyes. After the disasters that had plagued their Halloween and Thanksgiving honeymoon packages, she could only hope the Christmas bride had a safe, relatively uneventful honeymoon.

* * * * *

REQUEST YOUR FREE BOOKS!

2 FREE NOVELS PLUS 2 FREE GIFTS!

HARLEQUIN®

Blaze™

Red-hot reads!

HARLEQUIN®

A Romance

FOR EVERY MOOD™

Experience the variety
of romances that
Harlequin has to offer...

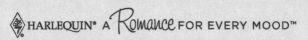

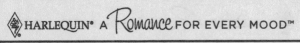